Praise for Alex Clare

, the police procedural into new realms, Alex Clare has created
emporary and relevant heroine in Robyn Bailley.'

— Alice Clark-Platts

c crime fiction with a compelling, complex and brilliantly con-
central character. Robyn Bailley is a wonderful creation and
lare is an exciting new talent.'

— Sheila Bugler

'lare has delivered a crime novel that is a match for those by
tablished authors in the genre.'

— Joy Isabella, Joyisabella.com

Gone by Alex Clare is a thrilling post-modern novel in which the
on of a trans woman detective questions the conception of the
ive novel ... I, for one, was very happy to meet Robyn.'

— Elena Adler, booksandreviews.wordpress.com

ı are a fan of crime fiction and you love an original protagonist,
d highly recommend.'

— The Book Review Café

Also by Alex Clare

He's Gone

She's Fallen

Alex Clare

IMPRESS BOOKS

First published 2018
by Impress Books Ltd
Innovation Centre, Rennes Drive, University of Exeter Campus, Exeter EX4 4RN

British Library Cataloguing in Publication Data

A catalogue record for this book is available from the British Library

ISBN 13: 978–1–911293–12–5 (pbk)
ISBN 13: 978–1–911293–13–2 (ebk)

Typeset in Garamond
by Swales and Willis Ltd, Ex

Printed and bound in Engla
by imprintdigital.net

SATURDAY 17 SEPTEMBER

1

Unable to suppress a giggle, Jade covered the phone with her hand.

Sophie looked up from her *Meresbourne Gazette*.

Composing herself, Jade held the receiver back to her ear. 'Well, I'm very sorry, sir. I'm not really sure what –' Her eyes widened at the reaction. 'Let me see what we can do, sir.' She put the phone down. 'Jeez. Lighten up.'

'What was he getting so upset about?' Sophie didn't bother to lower her voice. With the lobby full of music coming from the ballroom, they could talk behind the reception desk without worrying about guests overhearing.

'That was 106. Have you seen them, a pair of oldsters?'

'Oh yes, I spoke to them earlier. They weren't very happy there was a wedding today and said something about their breakfast being disturbed?'

'When they arrived yesterday, they moaned at the long-life milk on the tea tray.' Jade rolled her eyes. 'Now they're complaining about banging from the room next door.'

'Banging?' Sophie's plucked eyebrows shot up.

'Yeah. Apparently the wall's shaking.' Jade smirked, showing a yellow wad of chewing gum. 'And in a family room as well!'

Sophie cocked her head. 'Well, how do you think you get a family in the first place?'

They both sniggered.

'I suppose I'd better try calling them.' Jade's pudgy fingers paused over the keypad. 'Dear guests, please shag more quietly.' After a few seconds, she put the phone down. 'They must have taken it off the hook, it's not even ringing.'

'Someone will have to go up.' Sophie turned a page of the newspaper.

'Well I'm not going. Ah, there's Keith. Keith!'

There was no response from the stooped man on the other side of the lobby. Sophie smoothed out the crossword page and reached for a pen. 'Don't shout across the lobby like that, go over.'

After making a face behind Sophie's back, Jade left the desk. 'Keith.' The man turned towards her, cupping a hand behind his ear. '108 are being noisy. They're part of the wedding booking.'

'And you want me to go up?'

Jade's forehead creased as she spoke, the words slow, as if speaking to a child. 'Yeah, we've had a complaint.'

'Oh very well.' Keith turned for the stairs then paused. 'In that case you will have to tell the DJ not to leave his boxes blocking the fire escape.' He began trudging up the staircase to the first floor, conscious of eyes watching him, making sure he didn't chicken out.

The music from the ballroom speeded up. 'Ooh, I love this song.' From the middle of the lobby, Jade began to shimmy back to the desk, seams straining on her dress.

'They do say weddings make people frisky.' Sophie picked up her pen again. 'What time is it? I'm hoping Lawrence will say I can go now it's calmed down a bit. I'm getting a headache.'

A couple, he with a cigarette already in his mouth, crossed the lobby towards the main entrance.

'There's going to be a bhangra DJ later, can't wait.' Jade slid back behind the desk.

'Watch out!' In the doorway, a man in running gear was untangling himself from the smoker. The jogger was panting, pointing back over his shoulder. 'Sorry, sorry, sorry. Ambulance, call an ambulance.' He stared around his frozen audience. 'Out there, someone on the ground, a woman, she's fallen!'

The changing-room door was pulled open. Detective Inspector Robyn Bailley stood in her underwear holding the dress she'd just tried on.

'Oh, I'm terribly –' The automatic apology broke off. A middle-aged woman stood frozen in front of the cubicle: a blouse dropped from her outstretched arms. Her eyes flicked up and down, across Robyn's bra, where the breast pads had pushed out above the cups and lingering below where there was still a bulge at the crotch. Over the woman's shoulder, a sales assistant's mouth dropped open, eyes wide with shock.

Robyn slammed the door shut. From outside, there was a sudden burst of giggling. She didn't know which shame she wanted to cover first and wasted precious seconds before pulling on her jeans. One foot got stuck in the leg and she overbalanced, banging against the wall of the cubicle, sending empty hangers rattling to the floor. Her blouse had green buttons all down the front: with hindsight, it had been stupid to go shopping for clothes wearing something so fiddly. There was a knock on the door.

'Sir, I'm afraid you'll have to come out of there.'

Robyn reached the last button, realising she had gone wrong somewhere because there was no button-hole left.

More knocks, harder this time. 'Sir, please come out of there.' The words were firm; the voice was young. Robyn gave up on refastening the blouse because it would take too long. She picked up a coat hanger and the discarded dress then stared at herself in the mirror, wondering why on earth she was considering tidying up when she was being thrown out. Gathering her earlier purchases and her handbag, she opened the door, leaving the clothes on the floor. The manager, who couldn't have been more than twenty-five, had her fist raised, about to start another sequence of knocking.

There was a lot Robyn wanted to say but even glaring at the manager was too painful because the skin on her face was taut and hot following her second session of laser hair removal that morning. Holding her head high, Robyn swept through the shop, ignored the stares and walked out into the spitting rain on the High Street. She kept walking at an even pace, feeling eyes following her from the doorway. After a morning of chores, this afternoon was supposed to have been the fun part of Saturday, clothes shopping followed by a manicure. The shopping wasn't even really a treat, it was a necessity. The first outfits for her transition had been bought mail-order and most had to be returned as they didn't fit. For the two months she had been living openly as a woman, she'd had to wear the same two suits to work. As all she wanted to do now was go home, she would have to make them last a bit longer. At least she had managed to buy what she needed for her daughter's planned visit.

Walking through the automatic door of Whitecourt Shopping Centre, a blast of icy air chilled the moisture on her face. She wiped away the mix of rain and tears. The shopping centre looked its worst, the floor a slick of muddy footprints. A banner advertising the Edmund Napier Loveless festival hung slack where a fixing had come loose, the stern face of the feminist author creasing and bulging in the breeze. Walking the central aisle brought back unpleasant memories of her first case as Robyn. After all of the publicity surrounding the disappearance of Ben Chivers, she'd assumed that everyone in Meresbourne and the villages would know what she looked like and understand what she was doing. As she pushed open the heavy door to the car park and began the trudge up the concrete stairs, she wondered if the problem was more that some people would never feel comfortable being around a trans woman. Her doctor certainly wasn't: that morning, he had refused again to refer her to a specialist gender identity clinic. The appointment had been an awkward stutter of questions leaving her feeling fobbed off and wondering whether she would need to find another GP. Robyn wiped her eyes again.

When she stepped out onto the top floor of the car park, the rain was heavier. The juddering of a helicopter sounded close by. Somewhere below, car horns blared. Unlocking her Mondeo, she put the bags into the boot, hearing a siren rise then fall. It was impossible to tell where the police car was heading because the sound bounced off buildings in the gusty wind. Her phone rang.

'Hi, Lorraine.'

'Hello, Guv.' DC Lorraine Mount sounded serious. Wherever she was, it was noisy, with another siren in the background. 'Sorry to disturb your day off. There's something you should know about.'

2

Robyn settled into the driver's seat, closing the door against the damp. 'Go ahead, Lorraine.'

'We've got someone in a coma, apparently fell from a balcony of the Lady Ann Hotel but there are things making me suspicious and, worse, it's Ravi's cousin.'

'Christ.' Letting her head fall back, Robyn stared at the roof of the car for a second. 'OK, I'm just around the corner.'

'Glad you're already in town, Guv. The traffic's backed up to the ring road.'

'Ravi – how is he?' She remembered removing Detective Constable Ravi Sharma from the shift rota for the weekend because he was attending a family wedding.

'Not good.'

'I'll be with you in about ten minutes.'

Hand on the door, Robyn glanced at her make-up in the rear-view mirror: it had become a habit to check every chance she got because people now tended to judge her on her appearance. Grabbing her handbag, she left the car and started back down the stairs to the street exit. Heading left towards the river, she strode past a long line of stationary cars; ahead, the traffic lights on Bridge Street changed in a futile sequence. She turned onto Quayside and saw the Georgian frontage of the Lady Ann hotel shut off by blue and white tape strung between the decorative lampposts. The symmetry of the façade was spoiled by a screened-off area to the left of the entrance. More blue and white tape fluttered on the rail of a balcony on the first floor. Inside the tape line, a cold-looking constable kept up a slow patrol. Robyn struggled for her name.

'Guv. Over here.'

Lorraine had appeared at the hotel's front entrance and beckoned her in. The constable nodded and held the tape high, her attention now on passers-by who had stopped to gawp.

As she walked towards the hotel, Robyn thought how much Lorraine's yellow, turtle-neck sweater suited her. This was the colour of the season, according to the last *Meresbourne Gazette* fashion feature. Robyn had tried on a dress of the same colour earlier and looked jaundiced. Against Lorraine's dark brown skin, the colour glowed a warm gold.

'Hi.' Robyn pulled her thoughts back to the case. 'Looks like everything is under control here. Where's Ravi?'

'Thanks, Guv. It is now.' Lorraine ran her hand through her short hair. 'I got here about fifteen minutes after the ambulance was called and found Ravi having a stand-up row with a woman, one of his aunts, I think.' She dropped her voice. 'My guess is he tried to take control and tell everyone what to do. He's so upset, he can't have been thinking straight. I've called Chloe too and she's on her way.' They climbed the steps to the front entrance, the wind at their backs.

'Good idea. Who's the victim?' Robyn stopped in the lobby where the wall lamps, designed to look like candles, made little headway against the day's gloom. A knot of staff clustered around the reception desk, talking in low voices.

'She's Shazia Johar, a cousin of the bride, like Ravi.' Lorraine waved her hands to the blood-red garlands twined around the pillars in the lobby. 'All looks a bit sinister now, don't you think? So far, most of the guests have been pretty good about staying in the ballroom. I didn't want anyone to leave, in case.' She hesitated, biting her lip. 'Well, in case I'm right about what's wrong.'

'Do you think someone pushed her?'

There was sudden movement on the other side of the lobby as the staff gathered around the reception desk scattered. A tall, Indian man was marching towards them.

'There was certainly someone else in the room at the time – one of the porters. It's more what must have happened beforehand that I want to show you though.'

Before Robyn could ask what she meant, a voice carried across the room. 'I demand to know when we can leave.' The chubby reception-ist pointed him in their direction and the man began striding towards them.

'Right.' Robyn welcomed the need to act, the sense of purpose which could block out other feelings for a while. 'I'll deal with this. Lorraine, get some bodies on standby to do first interviews if we decide to investigate. You need to show me what made you call me.'

'I understand you are police officers. Who is in charge?' The man in the indigo kameez stared at Lorraine for a couple of seconds, then turned his gaze to Robyn. Lorraine took the opportunity to move away.

Robyn stepped forward. 'I am, sir. Detective Inspector Bailley. I know this is a traumatic time. I'm afraid we will need to keep you a lit-tle longer while we establish what happened. If you can be patient?'

'This is my daughter's wedding day. My niece is in a critical condi-tion in hospital and we are being kept in a room like farm animals.' The man emphasised the words with jabs of his finger. 'Nobody is telling us what is going on.'

'I appreciate this has been a horrible shock for you all. We will need time to establish the facts.' Robyn pointed to Lorraine. 'My colleague is calling up support so we can get through this as quickly as possible. Please, sir, will you go back to the ballroom?'

The man scanned Robyn, lip curling so his moustache hid his mouth. Into the silence came Lorraine's voice. 'OK, look, call me back as soon as you get this.'

'When is something going to be done? Because my daughter has a plane to catch.'

'It is happening now, sir.' Trying to project authority to calm the man, a draught of cold air on her stomach reminded Robyn of the gap in her blouse where she had got the buttons wrong. She was glad when her phone rang and she could turn away. 'Excuse me, sir. Hello, Khalid.'

'Robyn, hello.' The media manager's voice was its usual smooth burr. 'Do you have a moment?'

'Go ahead.'

'There's been an incident at the Lady Ann Hotel. I'm sure you're already aware?'

Across the lobby, the bride's father was now talking to a woman in a fuchsia-pink sari. Robyn moved further away, willing them not to come back. 'Yes, I'm there now.'

'There's a lot of speculation on social media already. I wanted to understand what happened.'

'I've only just arrived. Lorraine was first responder. We've got to check some things so I'd rather we didn't say anything if we can get away with it.'

'Sure, well let me know. While I've got you, I need to prepare a brief for the Superintendent. You know there are all these events for the Loveless festival? He's speaking as part of a panel on Monday debating violence against women.'

'Is Fell for or against?' Robyn couldn't tell whether the splutter from the other end was a laugh.

'If you saw who else is on the panel with him, you wouldn't joke.' Khalid coughed. 'Excuse me. Fell's sharing a platform with someone who's previously recommended all boys be given hormones to delay puberty until they're twenty-one. She's some academic and rent-a-gob.'

Robyn shuddered. 'I think you mean Dr Felicity Bergmann. She has interesting things to say about a lot of people.'

'Yeah, her. Isn't it funny how her name's got "man" in it?' Khalid paused. 'OK, just me. So the others on the panel are the Mayor and the local girl who got through to the quarter-final of *Superstar Seeker*.' Khalid paused. 'I can't wait to hear her views on the gender divide.'

'That's not going to be a debate, it's going to be a one-woman show.' Conscious the bride's father was still watching her, Robyn held up her hand to him then watched with relief as the man headed back towards the ballroom. 'Bergmann's only got one setting and attacks everyone. She'll make mincemeat of Fell.'

'I'm trying to make sure he just talks about topics where he's got evidence. The problem is, Bergmann's articulate and gets a lot of publicity.' There was almost a hint of admiration in Khalid's voice. 'She's founded this group called RAW – Real Adult Women – to make sure there's always a female commentator when the media are looking for an opinion.'

Much of the criticism of trans people Robyn had read was from trans-excluding radical feminists like Bergmann. 'The problem is they're single issue and don't like anyone who they don't count as a "real woman".'

'Oh, sure. I've been showing the Superintendent extracts from their website to try to persuade him just to provide a statement. He's insisting we go ahead as we need to present Meresbourne as a "diverse and tolerant town".' Khalid laughed. 'In other news, I've just started writing the entry for the "Division of the Year" competition.'

Robyn smiled. 'Fell's desk wouldn't look the same without that big, silver cup on display, would it?'

The doors to the ballroom opened again. The man in the indigo kameez had one arm around a slim woman in a deep red sari, gold trim glinting even in the dim light. A white man in a tail coat trailed behind, holding up a long train of fabric.

'Khalid, sorry, I've got to go. We've been trying to hold the guests here in case we need to interview them but they're getting restless.'

'Just one other thing: I've been looking up details of relevant cases recently. Compared to the regional averages Fell loves so much, Meresbourne is ahead in attacks on women and below in clear-ups which is exactly where we don't want to be. The panel starts at seven on Monday, so if you can give me a call tomorrow afternoon to give me the latest I'd be grateful – bye.'

Robyn put the phone back in the holster and re-joined Lorraine. 'OK. At the moment, we have no reason to hold people, so you'd better show me what made you suspicious.'

'It's the room, Guv.' Lorraine led the way to the reception desk. 'Right. I need to go up to 108.'

'I'm afraid I will have to see some ID.' The older of the two receptionists stuck her chin out.

'Your manager let me in twenty minutes ago.' Lorraine grimaced at the woman's badge. 'Sophie. Oh for crying out loud, here.' She held out her warrant card.

Sophie scrabbled a plastic card from a rack on one side of the desk and inserted it into a slot on the other. Ignoring Lorraine's outstretched hand, she put the key-card on the counter.

Shaking her head, Lorraine swept up the card and marched across the lobby. 'The good thing about these things compared to regular keys is the hotel should be able to tell you who they were issued to.'

Robyn started up the staircase. 'That could be useful. By the way, where's Graham?' As the team's sergeant, Graham Catt should have been the default call.

Ahead, Lorraine paused at the landing, looking down. Three

13

women, two in saris, one in a garish floral frock, marched towards the reception desk, faces set in angry lines. Lorraine grinned. 'Maybe there's something in this karma lark.' She led the way up the right fork of the staircase. 'I called him first. He isn't answering. Probably stuck in traffic.'

They were now level with the chandelier. Robyn spotted three bulbs out before she stopped counting.

On the first floor, Lorraine stopped dead. 'Someone's been into this room.' A bundle of police tape was lying on the burgundy carpet next to a yellow 'Wet Floor' sign lying on its side.

'Was there no one you could ask to secure the scene?' The rebuke was as mild as Robyn could make it, given Lorraine was already stressed.

'When I got here and found Ravi and, well – I guess I screwed up.' Lorraine bit her lip. 'I'm getting the manager.'

Robyn leant over the rail, watching Lorraine retrace her steps. From here, you could see most of the lobby. There was something there, an impression her instinct told her she needed to catch. She found herself staring at a large painting on the wall above the landing. A red-haired woman in a green dress was leaning so far over a balcony it looked as if she might plunge into the water below. One arm was stretched out towards a sailing ship just visible in the corner of the frame as it disappeared into mist. Set into the heavy, gold frame was a sign in Gothic script: 'Lady Ann.'

A hubbub of angry voices drifted up to her. Two more women were approaching the reception desk, both in pastel coats and dresses. They disappeared out of view and the volume increased. A small man in a grey suit scurried to the stairs, Lorraine following. One of the pastel women followed, demanding to be allowed to leave. 'You'll get a one-star review!' Her voice echoed around the lobby.

Lorraine kept close behind the man to hurry him up until he stood beside Robyn. 'Right, look. Who has been into this room?'

'I can assure you, madam, no one has been in this room since you left it.'

'You can assure me?' Lorraine pointed at the door. 'When I told you this room was off limits, I made sure this tape covered the key-card slot. The only reason to push it aside is to open the door. How many people have access to this room, including your staff?'

'Everyone has been told not to come here and we have been doing our best to keep the guests in the ballroom.' The man stopped his shifting from foot to foot. 'Doing your job, in fact. Now, can we have the room back?'

'In due course.' Robyn was conscious of time passing: she wanted the man to be gone. 'And,' she narrowed her eyes to look at the badge on his lapel, 'Lawrence, you haven't answered my colleague's question and the quicker you do, the quicker we can get on.'

Lawrence's lips narrowed. 'I recognise you now. You're the policem – person who had to hunt for the little boy. Of course. The hotel will be happy to help but this seems to be a tragic, ah, accident.' There was a second of silence.

'How many have access?' There was an edge of impatience in Lorraine's voice.

'Ah yes. I checked and we issued five key-cards. The maids and porters have master keys.'

'Why so many?' Lorraine rested her card on the reader and slipped on blue latex gloves.

'This is one of our largest rooms and it was where the groom, best man and ushers got ready before the wedding.'

'Well you can cancel all those immediately. If anyone else asks for one, I want to know about it.' Turning her back on Lawrence, Lorraine shoved the card into the slot. After a whirr, the latch clicked open. 'Just remind your staff not to use their cards either.' She strode into the room.

Lawrence moved forward. Robyn put out her hand and let the door swing to. 'We'll let you know when you can come in.' She waited until it became clear he was not taking the hint. 'I'm sure you have urgent things to be getting along with?' Only when he had started down the stairs did she push open the door.

Standing in the room's narrow hallway, she let the door shut behind her, testing the atmosphere. In the yellow glow from the wall lamps, the floor-to-ceiling dark wood unit to her right seemed to suck in light. At the end of the room, a grey net curtain flapped inwards: a draught reached her a second later. She took a step forward. A pile of kit bags and a luggage trolley lay under a clothes rail where a single tail coat swung from a hanger. A shirt was on another hanger, trousers and tie resting on one of the bags. She took another step. From her left, heat radiated from the open bathroom door. Every surface was covered with bottles and jars. The tiled floor was covered with towels.

Robyn continued past the bathroom and joined Lorraine in the body of the room. In front of her, two single beds were covered in debris, more grooming products, empty spirits miniatures and plastic wrappers. Slipping on her own gloves, she smoothed one out. 'Drinking I can understand – why would you eat steak pasties before your wedding?' A telephone and everything else that looked as if it belonged on the bedside unit was on the floor. The cushions and covers from the double bed had been pushed to one side, the bottom sheet marked by livid smears. Where the pillows should be, a larger patch glowed bright red.

'This is what I wanted to show you, Guv.' There was a tremor in Lorraine's voice. 'When I came in, the quilt was pulled up but I could smell something, so I checked. Blood. Whose is it and why is there so much of it?'

'I see why you called.' Robyn looked around the untidy room. The things on the floor now suggested violence, not clumsiness.

'One other thing. The reason the porter was in here was because there was a complaint about banging on the wall from the room next

16

door.' The ornate metal bedhead wobbled as Lorraine touched it, then tapped against the wall as she pushed harder. 'I think we can guess what caused the banging.'

In the wall mirror, she saw the curtain billow. Robyn frowned. There was a starred break in the pane. When she moved closer, something crunched under her foot. Broken glass from a smashed mineral water bottle caught the spotlights. 'Was the outer door open when you arrived?'

'Felt like it, Guv, the room was freezing.'

Stepping outside, the wind blew water droplets into Robyn's eyes. She blinked to clear them, taking in a pair of metal chairs and a small table, police tape flapping in the chill wind. 'On a day like today, this isn't a place you'd choose to come out to.'

'Nobody saw her fall.' Lorraine spoke from the doorway. 'Just saw her hit the ground.'

Robyn turned when she heard the sniff.

Lorraine was wiping her eyes. 'Sorry, Guv. Don't know why this one's getting to me.'

'I understand.' Robyn put a hand on Lorraine's arm. 'It's OK. This isn't some closing-time brawl, it's different when it's someone you know or a person you can recognise yourself in. And good work – this would have been easy to miss.'

'Yeah.' Lorraine managed a small smile. 'Thanks, Guv.'

'This is now a formal investigation.' Robyn stepped back into the room and looked around, to fix the image in her memory. 'Two questions: one, did she jump or was she pushed? And then, was there some form of assault, potentially sexual? We'll need some backup.' On her way past the bathroom, her nose cleared by the outside air, Robyn caught a hint of something bitter. Under the smell of products and soap was a tang of sourness or sickness. She took a step into the room. A red light glowed on the towel rail, the dial was turned up to maximum. Robyn laid the back of her hand against the towels on the floor and found them almost dry.

'What are you thinking, Guv?' Lorraine stood in the doorway.

'What time did the wedding start?'

Eyes lifting, Lorraine thought for a second. 'I think it was eleven, why?'

Robyn felt each towel in turn. The one on the closed toilet was damp. 'This was used after the others and, given how warm it is in here, not that long ago.' She opened the toilet seat: the smell of sickness was much stronger, making her tongue retract. 'In a room with five lads, somebody came in here and was sick and then put the toilet seat down. Maybe this is a stereotype but isn't that more likely to be a woman than a man?'

'Look at this.' Lorraine held up the damp towel by one corner, showing red smears across the middle. 'Looks like someone had their fun then must have cleaned themselves up and went back downstairs to re-join the party. Bastard.' She already had her phone in her hand. 'Right. I'll call forensics and Uniform to help with interviewing. We'll need the guest list for the wedding and the register for the hotel and the staff lists.' She took a breath. 'I'll check if they've got CCTV in the corridors – anything else?'

'A good start. And get someone stationed on this door, given this is a crime scene.'

'Yes, Guv.' Lorraine led the way into the corridor.

There was still noise from the lobby. Robyn paused, her hand on the door for support. 'For the interviews, given what, ah, I mean, given some people don't always feel comfortable talking to me and Ravi was a bit, well, what I'm trying to say is maybe it would be best if you took the family ones and I'll do the staff?'

Lorraine opened her mouth then closed it again. 'Sure, Guv.'

'Oh and did you hear back from Graham?'

'I'll call him again.' Lorraine shrugged. 'He hasn't come back to me.'

'Keep trying. We'll need all the help we can get.'

3

As Robyn and Lorraine reached the lobby, the manager appeared from the ballroom, taking elaborate care over shutting both doors. He clapped his hands in the direction of the group of staff again huddled around reception. 'Right. Let's get this area tidied up. We have a full house tomorrow, everything must be ready.' Moving behind the desk, he straightened the monitor. When he looked up at Robyn's approach, there was a second of scrutiny before a professional smile.

'Are you finished, officers? As I'm sure you are aware, the guests are anxious to leave.'

'No, Lawrence, we're not.' Robyn folded her arms. 'More officers are on the way and we are going to do initial interviews with all guests and staff. The room upstairs is to be treated as a crime scene which needs to be inspected by a specialist forensic team, so the area is out of bounds until they have finished.'

'What happened in there?' Lawrence slumped, knocking over a display of *Marvellous Meresbourne* tourist trail leaflets.

'We don't know yet, which is why we have to investigate. We will need somewhere to interview guests and somewhere else to talk to your staff. I want to start with the porter who went into 108.'

The manager cast a worried glance around. His staff were looking at him, waiting for orders. 'Oh yes. Jade, the daily sheet, please.'

The receptionist fumbled under the newspaper and produced a clipboard. Muttering, Lawrence scanned the page, checking his watch. He looked up. 'The Dove Lounge is free for the rest of the day, you can hold interviews in there. And officer, could you be discreet? We don't want guests inconvenienced – we're fully booked tonight and tomorrow, you know.'

Robyn counted to three. 'We'll do what needs to be done, sir. And I presume you have an office? That will do for the staff interviews.'

The office turned out to be a windowless cubbyhole behind reception, the fluorescent lights too bright for the small space. Robyn took the battered swivel chair: Lawrence seemed reluctant to leave, fussing with papers on the desk. There was a knock at the open door. A slight man stood in the doorway, one hand on the frame. Behind him was the solid shape of PC Donna Pound, wearing a short-sleeve uniform shirt despite the cold.

'Afternoon ma'am.' Donna sounded far too cheerful. 'This is Keith Eldon. He's a porter here, the one who entered the room.' The man sank into one of the hard plastic chairs facing the desk, putting his head into his hands.

'Hello, Donna.' The PC's rather knowing smile reminded Robyn she owed Donna for her support during a recent Professional Standards investigation. 'Is Clyde around somewhere?' The pair were frequent shift partners and PC Clyde Boothe's slow courtesy would be ideal for this situation.

'No, ma'am. He's coming in for the late shift. I'm doing a double as I need the money.'

'Don't worry, Keith, everything will be cleared up.' The manager had his hand on the older man's shoulder.

Robyn caught Donna's eye then looked from the manager to the door.

'We could do with you in the Dove Lounge, sir.' Donna held out her arm to direct Lawrence. 'Come along, sir. You can help us keep the guests in order.'

The door swung closed behind them and Robyn inspected the man in the chair. Spare fabric sagged across the shoulders of his uniform jacket. Above the Nehru collar, his pale skin was damp.

'Mr Eldon? I'd like to talk about what you saw earlier.'

The man did not move. His breathing was shallow, a hint of a whistle when he inhaled.

'Mr Eldon, I'm Detective Inspector Bailley. I need you to tell me what you saw upstairs.'

'The poor girl – how is she?' Eldon's watery blue eyes looked up into Robyn's. 'I couldn't bear it if she were dead. So pretty, everything to live for.' A teardrop detached itself from a gobbet of yellow sleep.

'She's been taken to hospital. I have no update, I'm afraid.'

Eldon's chin sank to his chest.

'Tell me everything you did.' Raising her voice to get back his attention made Robyn conscious of how deep her voice sounded in the confined space.

There was another slow blink, the left lid a little behind the right. 'She looked so frightened.' Eldon's voice was little more than a whisper. 'All I did was to check if she was all right. She … she …' His hands found a handkerchief and raised it to his face.

'Why did you go up to the room?'

'We got a complaint.' Eldon sighed. 'Jade on reception said I had to go up.'

'Was anyone on the staircase or in the corridor?'

Eldon shook his head, gazing at his clasped hands.

'Why did you go into the room?'

21

Whether he heard a hint of the impatience in her tone as suspicion, the reaction from Eldon was immediate. He looked up, moving his hands to the desk. 'I wanted to check they hadn't damaged any hotel property.' He swallowed. 'The pair on reception thought it was funny.'

'So you used your staff key-card?'

'I knocked first but no one answered.' His shoulders hunched again.

'What were your impressions when you walked in?'

'There was a funny smell.' Eldon looked up, eyes unfocused. 'I wondered if a dog had been in there. The chair was on the floor – I knew something was wrong.' Tears were clinging to Eldon's lashes. 'Then I saw her. I thought she was drunk, lying curled up on the bed.' He shook his head. 'But then she saw me.'

'What did you do?'

'I didn't know what to do.' He blinked. 'I offered to make her a cup of tea but she –'

'Guv, there you are.' Ravi appeared in the doorway, looming over Eldon. 'You. Did you try to kill Shazia?'

Getting to her feet, Robyn banged her head on the slanting ceiling. Blinking, she took a step forward but the desk was still between her and Ravi.

Ravi's hands clenched into fists. 'I need to interview him!' The silk of his olive kameez was rumpled, dark sweat stains showing under the arms. Eldon shrank back into the chair, the white handkerchief clutched in his hands.

'Ravi, the only thing you should be doing is comforting your family.' Robyn held her hands up, taking awkward steps around the desk, willing his attention towards her. 'Have you heard anything from the hospital?'

A blob of dye on Ravi's forehead was running with his sweat, ragged stripes of bright red above one eye and across his cheek.. 'She might as well be dead.' His voice became wet. 'The air ambulance has taken her to a specialist neurological unit.'

Robyn was close enough to reach out and put her hand on his upper arm. She balanced herself, ready to respond to another flash of anger. The memory of Ravi's horror when she had first appeared at the station as Robyn was still fresh. Now, his open distaste had calmed down – or he was just better at hiding it – but she didn't want to provoke another reaction.

'They said you were in here, Guv. Oh!' Robyn heard acting DC Chloe Talbot's voice but didn't dare look away from Ravi. Before she could speak, Chloe had ducked around Eldon and took Ravi's hands, turning him towards her. She tugged and Ravi almost fell forward into her arms, his height making her step back for balance. Chloe held him as he began to cry.

Robyn breathed out. For Ravi's own sake, she was going to have to make sure he had nothing to do with the case. For the moment, she just needed to get him away from the witness and prevent a complaint. She edged forward to where she could catch Chloe's eye. 'Can you get him out of here? Lorraine's in the Dove Lounge interviewing guests if you need help.' She spread her hands. 'I ... Well, you know.'

Chloe managed a tiny nod. 'C'mon pet.' Her Yorkshire accent sounded stronger than usual. 'Let's get you out of here.' With her left arm around Ravi, she took a small step back, then another, until they were side by side. 'Get some fresh air.' She moved forward until Ravi began moving with her. Keeping her arm around him, she manoeuvred them both through the door. Robyn pushed it shut.

'I'm sorry, Mr Eldon.' Robyn shuffled back behind the desk and sat down. 'Go on with your story.' The man was staring across the room. 'Mr Eldon.' The lined face swung back towards her. 'So you went into the room?'

The man nodded once. 'She ran away.' His mouth opened, then closed. 'Something awful must have happened because she was scared of me – I don't understand how anyone could be scared of me? The balcony door was open. It was the only place she could go.'

His voice was so low, Robyn had to lean forward to hear.

23

'When I got to the balcony, she was standing on one of the chairs.' He blew his nose. 'Then she stepped up onto the rail – I think I shouted something. I don't know if she heard – she wasn't looking at me, just gazing up into the sky.' He closed his eyes, hand to his face. 'Then she took another step.'

'Did you touch her at any time?' Robyn tried to keep her tone gentle. She was not getting any sense of a threat from this man.

'No!' Eldon's eyes snapped open. 'Is that what you think of me? I've been married forty-two years. I wanted to help but I was never within six foot of her.'

'We will need to verify your –' Robyn paused as the door opened.

'Sorry, officer, I need to check details for a booking tomorrow.' The manager slid into the office, eyes flitting over the scene.

The irritation building inside Robyn found an outlet. 'You don't seem to realise this is a criminal investigation and by barging into an interview, I could charge you with obstruction. But, as you are here, I will interview you next.' Robyn tried to classify the look flashing across Lawrence's face: his eyes had widened, mouth forming into a little 'o'. 'That's all the questions for now, Mr Eldon. I'll call a constable to take a DNA sample for elimination purposes and your clothes for analysis.'

Watching the manager hovering over Eldon while she waited for Lorraine to answer her phone, Robyn wondered why he irritated her so much. 'I will also need all your staff personnel files.'

The manager adjusted his tie. 'Of course, of course. I trust you are now convinced of Keith's innocence?'

'Hi, Guv.'

'Hi, Lorraine. Could you send someone to take Eldon's clothes and samples, please?' It didn't look as if Eldon was listening but the manager was hanging on Robyn's every word while he fussed through the huge bunch of keys hanging from his belt. She put the phone down.

'Officer, is this really necessary?' The keys rattled as they slipped out of Lawrence's hand. 'Keith is one of my best employees. He's worked here nearly five years – he was pensioned off from his previous job because of a heart condition, you know, so he doesn't need this level of stress.' Lawrence's voice was rising. 'He's reliable, conscientious and the idea of him hurting that girl is ridiculous. Look at him!' He waved his hand towards the hunched figure in the chair.

'This is in his interest because, by taking samples from his clothes, we will be able to confirm whether we need to arrest him or not.' Robyn had to keep reminding herself Eldon was there. 'You were getting the staff files.'

'Oh, yes.' Lawrence blinked then spread the bunch of keys. 'We choose our staff very carefully, officer. Most have been with us at least a year.' He opened a drawer and began piling files on the corner of the desk.

Robyn skimmed over the covers. 'Yours doesn't seem to be here.'

'You want details about me?' The manager's hands adjusted his tie: it looked like a reflex action.

'Yes, please. We need to look at everyone who had access to the room.'

'But I report directly to the owner.' Lawrence looked as if this settled everything.

The sense of being hemmed in was making Robyn fidget. She was assessing whether the manager's shiftiness was down to guilt or the challenge to his authority. 'Then I will need your full name, date of birth and contact details.'

The clock in the hallway chimed once. The manager stepped back. 'I'm so sorry, officer. I have a call right now with the golden wedding party booked for tomorrow but I shall be back in no more than twenty minutes. I shall send a colleague in.' He turned towards the door.

'You have to answer my questions.' Robyn raised her voice to Lawrence's back. His hopes of leaving were ruined by Donna's solid appearance in the doorway.

'You're in a hurry, sir.' With Donna blocking the exit, the space felt even smaller.

Lawrence turned back. 'Officer, I feel like I am under suspicion.'

'Everyone in this hotel is a suspect and if you continue to be less than co-operative, you will attract more suspicion.' Robyn smiled, enjoying his discomfort. 'Lawrence, we suspect a potential rape in your hotel and will do what is needed to investigate.' A sudden buzz of talk intruded and Robyn remembered the door wasn't shut. She got up and looked over Donna's shoulder, seeing the two receptionists standing right outside. She could only see Jade's back but across Sophie's face was a look of mingled shock and delight as if she had found out a secret.

Taking a deep breath, Robyn turned back to the room. She needed to keep her temper. 'Donna, could you take samples from Mr Eldon and we'll need his clothes.'

'Yes, ma'am. This way, sir.' Donna's brisk tone brooked no argument.

'Hang on. Doesn't he even get a male officer? This is double standards.' Lawrence folded his arms.

'He will be treated appropriately. Now, you said you were busy, so let's get on.' Robyn bent to be near Eldon's ear. 'Mr Eldon, please go with my officer.' From the way the old man started, Robyn wondered if he had dozed off. Donna indicated the door, he stood and allowed himself to be led out. Robyn shut the door, checking the catch. When she turned back, the manager was sitting in his chair, leaning far back in the seat. She bit back her comment and walked around to perch on the corner of the desk, feet almost touching his, looking down onto him. Lawrence shifted in his seat, pushing it back from the desk until it hit the back wall. She guessed he was no more than thirty-five but the thinning hair and deep lines on his forehead belonged to someone older. 'How do you keep track of your staff when they have access to all of the rooms?'

'Why do you keep blaming my staff?' Lawrence banged his hand on the armrest. 'No one had any time to spare because we were all rushed off our feet. Everyone apart from Sophie and Keith were helping in the kitchen or the ballroom because the clients were rather, well, exacting in their requirements. We didn't stop.'

'They kept you busy then?' Robyn leaned back a little, giving him more space. 'It must be really stressful running these big events. Such a weight of expectations. We're lucky – nobody expects the police to provide the happiest day of their lives.'

The manager's shoulders relaxed a little. There was even a hint of a smile as he nodded.

'So this party was very demanding?'

'It's been a nightmare. You know it's a mixed wedding? The groom is white, the bride is Indian. So it all sounded lovely, incorporating the best of the Christian and Hindu traditions. In fact, each side had their own ideas of what they wanted and kept contradicting the other. One of the bride's uncles kept demanding the cost of everything and cancelling bits because he said he could "get it cheaper".' Lawrence mimed the speech marks. 'A whole load of decorations only turned up at ten o'clock this morning because of some dodgy deal he'd done. They didn't believe my chef could cook curry, so we had to install outside caterers in the car park.' He shook his head. 'I don't think we've made a penny on the day and now this.'

Robyn had been nodding throughout, to show she understood. Now Lawrence had started, it looked like it wouldn't be difficult to keep him talking. 'What about the guests?'

'Bang on the stereotypes, both ways.' Lawrence's laugh was without humour. 'The white guests were getting drunk, loud and aggressive. The brown ones didn't drink but were complaining about everything.'

'Who became aggressive?' For the first time, something seemed worth following.

'It started with the groom and the ushers.' The manager rolled his eyes. 'They were the first here and went straight into the bar, insisting we serve drinks. When I refused, one of them climbed over the bar and started pouring pints himself.' He shut his eyes. 'At nine-thirty. When other guests were having their breakfast.'

'Go on.'

'And then the fun really started.' The manager gripped the chair arms. 'When I insisted the man signed for the drinks, he just wrote "Axeman". Next, he played some prank on the groom. He'd replaced the wedding rings with jelly ones.'

'How did the groom take it?'

'Badly. He started having a go at the best man for letting go of the rings. Then there was panic as the bride's ring really was lost because it had fallen out of this idiot's pocket when he'd climbed over the bar. I thought another usher was going to punch him – there were children there!' Lawrence closed his eyes for a second. 'I had to call all my staff to hunt for the ring while these oafs were shouting and swearing at each other. The language was terrible.'

'What about the two families. Did they seem to get along?'

'Oh, God.' The manager began laughing. The sound had a hint of hysteria. 'They had nothing good to say about each other apart from the ushers saying what they fancied doing to the bridesmaids at the top of their voices.' His eyes widened. 'Do you think …?'

'We will consider everything. Did you see who said this?'

'I was dashing past.' Lawrence's eyes lost focus for a second. 'No, I don't know which one said it, they were all clustered at the bar.'

'Is there anything to stop someone walking off the street and going up to a room?'

Lawrence sagged back into the chair. 'Anyone passing through the lobby would be seen by reception and recorded on the CCTV cameras in the corridors which also cover the rear exit to the car park.'

'We will need the footage.'

'Yes, yes, I'll get someone to give you a link to the website. It's all stored somewhere,' he flicked his hand, 'in cyberspace.'

'If you think of anything else, can you let us know?' Robyn stood up, allowing him to leave. 'Could you give me a couple of minutes, then send in the receptionist who was on duty at the time?'

'You must get this resolved quickly, officer. The Lady Ann is the best hotel in Meresbourne.' Lawrence gripped the chair's armrests. 'We have a reputation to maintain.'

4

Alone in the office, Robyn skimmed through the files of the staff on duty. One of the porters was on a final warning for taking food from the kitchen and there was an ongoing investigation of a missing laptop. She was looking through Eldon's file when the door opened and the younger receptionist shuffled in. Brown smears of foundation showed on the collar of her dress where her skin bulged over the neckline. She sank into a chair and began playing with the charms on her bracelet.

'Good afternoon.' Robyn paused: there was no acknowledgement. She shuffled the woman's file to the top and scanned the front page. 'You're Jade and you've worked here part-time for eighteen months.'

The girl's face flicked up towards Robyn for a second, then down again. She had been crying. Robyn gave up on small talk. 'What can you tell me about this afternoon?'

The girl took a shuddering breath. '106 phoned down complaining so I sent Keith up. I didn't know it was Shazia.'

'You know Shazia?' Robyn picked up her pen.

'We're at college together. Tourism and hospitality.' Burying her nose in a tissue, Jade sniffed. 'Is she going to get better? I'm the first aider, I went out there because a passer-by said someone had fallen – I thought they meant tripped over.' The tears were coming again. 'She was lying on the pavement, blood everywhere and all I had was plasters.'

'That must have been horrible, when you realised it was your friend.'

'I held her hand.' One sob, two. 'I didn't know if she could hear me. Just told her to think about the beach bar she wants to run.' A deep, shuddering breath. 'Will Shazia be OK?'

'She's been taken to a specialist unit.' Robyn paused to let this sink in. 'Had you spoken to her today?'

'She messaged me a picture of her outfit but I hadn't seen her yet.' Jade gazed down into her lap. 'When I got here, I ended up being stuck helping in the kitchen because this place isn't managed properly and there aren't enough staff.'

'Can you think of any reason why Shazia might want to harm herself?'

For the first time, Jade looked Robyn in the face. 'No way. She had plans. Couldn't wait 'til college started again, to get her life back. Said it was so unfair she wasn't allowed to get a job in the holidays because it meant she had no money. That's why she was studying tourism so she could go and work abroad somewhere away from her family.'

'Do you know if she had a boyfriend?'

'What's that got to do with anything?' Patches of red blotched across Jade's neck. 'Is this to do with what you said earlier? A girl gets raped, so it's her fault because she sees boys?'

'No, I –'

'Just typical. Shazia is the victim here and you're acting like it's her that's the problem.' Jade stabbed the desk with her finger. 'You didn't see her when they took her away. She looked like a bizarre doll, all beautiful in her green sari and this huge weird head, bandaged up where they were trying to keep her brain in.' Jade buried her face in her hands.

Waiting until the girl quietened, Robyn wondered whether it was worth trying to explain what she'd meant. 'We are taking this very seriously. That's why we have to ask questions, including those that don't seem fair. Can I go on?' She took silence for an assent. 'You said she wanted to get away from her family. Can you tell me what you meant?'

'They're really strict. Wanted to know who she was with, that sort of thing.'

'Did you get any sense of Shazia rebelling against her parents?' Robyn braced herself for another potential outburst.

Jade wiped her eyes, frowning at the make-up on her hand. 'She wasn't oppressed or nothing, like they wanted her to do well at college, be a credit to the family. Just she had to be back by nine o'clock and stuff.'

'Did you see Shazia go upstairs?'

The girl shook her head. 'I'd only just got out to reception. The call was the first thing I did.'

'And what time was that?'

'Dunno.' She was not wearing a watch. 'Probably like half past two, after the music had started anyway.' Jade's head tilted to one side. 'It really seemed like nothing big.'

'So you told Keith Eldon to go up.'

'Well, he was right in front of me.' She took a noisy breath. 'Keith's all right. Quiet except when he's talking about his family.' For the first time, Jade smiled. 'You'd think his grandson played football for England the way he goes on about him.'

'And how long between him going upstairs and when you knew something was wrong?'

'Like minutes? It wasn't long. After he went, the band started playing something what was done on *Superstar Seeker* last week and I said to Sophie, I like this song and it was still playing when the bloke run in from outside.'

'Did you see anyone else going up or downstairs?'

'I wasn't there. You'd better ask Sophie.' The girl bit down hard on her gum.

There seemed to be little point in further questions. 'OK, thank you, Jade.' Robyn shifted the files across. 'Could you send your colleague in, please?'

'Yeah. But you need to find out who done it because otherwise no one'll want to stay at the hotel any more. We learned about this, all about how you build reputation and how easy it is to lose it. Shazia and me had to do a presentation on it for one of the modules.' Tears started again.

'Right. Thank you.' As the door swung closed after Jade, Robyn stood up to stretch. There was a discreet double-tap on the door. Taking advantage of the excuse to move, Robyn stepped forward to let the person in.

Sophie stood outside. Her uniform still had ironed creases. 'Are you ready for me, officer?'

'Yes, please sit down. This won't take long.'

'Take as long as you need, officer. I finished at two but I wanted to stay and see if I could help.' Sophie sat down, keeping her back straight, ankles crossed. 'Oh and you may be interested to know that the majority of guests have left the ballroom.'

'Thank you.' Robyn matched the woman's small smile. 'Now could you think back to earlier this afternoon? You were on the reception desk between two and around two-thirty, I understand?'

'Poor Keith, we are all so worried about him.'

Robyn made a mental note of the passion in the voice. 'Were you busy?'

'The kitchen was struggling. All spare staff had to help, Lawrence asked me to stay on and cover the desk.' Folding her hands in her lap, Sophie blinked a couple of times. 'Let's see. Out front, it was all quite quiet. I booked a taxi to the air force memorial for the retired couple in 106. I remember because while they were at the desk, the clock chimed the hour and the gentleman commented how it reminded him of his grandfather's house. Which is nice, isn't it?' When she smiled, her shoulders lifted and she angled her head, pausing for a second, as if she was expecting someone to take a picture. 'Then the music started and they weren't very happy because they hadn't known about the wedding when they booked. They went up to their room and the next thing, the ballroom doors opened.'

'Go on.'

'Suddenly there were lots of people. Some went outside, for a cigarette, I suppose.' She smiled again with the same simper. 'Others made phone calls or went upstairs. And then the phone rang with a Christmas enquiry, so I had to check dates and prices and that must have been ten minutes when I wasn't looking at anything else.'

'Did you see anyone acting in a strange way at any time?'

'A woman with a big hat seemed to be a bit tipsy.' Sophie shook her head. 'And she wasn't the only one.'

'Anything else?'

'Now, let's think.' The corners of the woman's mouth turned down. 'Just as I put the phone down, this scruffy man turned up and started leaving boxes all over the place.' Sophie's nose wrinkled. 'He was very rude when I told him to move them but I'm not sure he understood much English. Keith was going to speak to him, he's such a dear man.'

Beneath the desk, Robyn clenched and unclenched her hands.

'As I'm sure Jade's told you, someone then came running in from outside and we called an ambulance. It's really not right.' Sophie's lips were pressed together.

'No. That's why we're asking these questions.'

'He shouldn't have married her. This is what they do.'

After a second of trying to work this out, Robyn gave up. 'Who do you mean?'

'The Pakis, of course.' Sophie rolled her eyes. 'They chuck people off balconies if they're gay like you or a woman who doesn't do what she's told.'

Robyn swallowed. After she'd blinked, the woman was still in front of her with her satisfied smile. 'Are you saying you believe the young woman was thrown deliberately from the balcony?'

'Well, what else can it have been?' The woman smoothed a wrinkle in her skirt. 'You said earlier there had been some sort of sex, so the obvious thing is it is one of these honour killings. And the women are just as bad as the men. You hear of mothers killing their own daughters if they've brought disgrace on the family in any way.'

A part of Robyn wanted to be offended but another wondered how far the woman's smug certainty stretched. Compared to the casual phobia of the shop girls earlier, this was a professional at work. Robyn took a deep breath for a final question. 'Do you have any evidence that the bride's family being of Indian origin had an influence in the girl's fall?'

'Haven't you been listening? This is what Pakis do. Unless the girl decided she couldn't face being sewn into a burka and decided to commit suicide?'

'I have no more questions.' Robyn was relieved to see Sophie leave. She had a further flick through a couple of files then sought the fresher air of the lobby. An Indian couple hurried across, dragging a screaming child by the hand.

The manager appeared from somewhere. 'Ah, officer, I wanted a word. You may not know that some of your people arrived to examine room 108 a short while ago. I just wanted to check whether they are going to clear up after themselves. We only have two family rooms and both are booked for tomorrow night.' His hands went to his tie, then dropped again.

A little ashamed of how much she was enjoying his suppressed annoyance, Robyn smiled. 'I'm sure you have an excellent team of cleaners.'

Lawrence tutted. 'Of course. We were supposed to be full tonight and tomorrow, we have lots of guests who are coming for the

Loveless festival, including some very distinguished academics.' He brought his hands together, almost as if he were praying. 'When it's so busy we really cannot afford to have rooms out of use.'

'We will let you know when we are finished.' Robyn opened her handbag, reaching for her notebook. 'You didn't give me your full details. I'll take them now.'

It was hard to tell in the dim light but Robyn thought she saw a momentary flush cross Lawrence's face.

'Very well officer, if we must.'

While Robyn was writing, the sound of a step made her look up. Chloe was standing behind Lawrence, bouncing on the soles of her feet. 'Guv, we've got something.'

Making it clear the manager could not come with them, Robyn followed Chloe who crossed the hall and into the ballroom. 'We ended up in here because that lounge was a bit small and people could at least see things were being done.' On the stage at the far end, a man coiled cables, using one of the two gilt-covered thrones to stack them on. Garlands were piled in a heap in one corner. The hall was almost empty, just one table of white guests who appeared to be working their way through the leftover booze. Lorraine sat at a paper-covered sideboard tapping a message into her phone. Pairs of waiters were moving back and forth through the room clearing the tables to bare wood before lifting off the tops and rolling them away.

'Oy, matey.' One of the remaining guests called out to a waiter. 'Can you get some music on?' There were shrieks of laughter from his companions.

'What have you found?' Robyn leant on the back of a chair.

Lorraine looked up. 'We've got details for all of the guests but one of the ushers is missing. Nobody knows where he is. There were three of them and one has vanished.'

'Interesting. I've just been hearing about the ushers causing problems in the morning. Do you know which one?'

'Name of Newman, Guv, Jake Newman.'

'When was he last seen?'

'We haven't been able to pin that down yet. We know he was here around two o'clock because all of the ushers and bridesmaids took part in some big set-piece first dance with the bride and groom. Everything relaxed a bit then because the formal part of the wedding was over. We haven't got a confirmed sighting after about ten past two but it seems a reasonable guess it's his suit in room 108.' Lorraine closed her notebook.

'Why would he take off his clothes?' Chloe's eyes opened wide. 'Oh.'

'But if his suit is in the room, what's he wearing now?' Robyn gripped the chair back. 'Have we got people looking for him?'

'Uniform are doing a full search of the hotel, Guv. We've tried his mobile – it's switched off.'

'Hi.' Donna stuck her head around the door. 'We've finished the search. Newman is definitely not in the building. And, we've got someone who says he arrived in his van this morning and it's not in the car park now.'

'Good work.' Robyn smiled, feeling her skin complain at the movement. 'Chloe, can you get the alert out? Anything else I need to know about?'

'The first interviews with the guests weren't very helpful.' Lorraine began piling up paper. 'They all say similar things. Shazia was enjoying the party, nothing out of the ordinary. We've established she was there for the first dance but no one seems to have noticed her leaving. Her parents have gone to the hospital so I've spoken to her aunts who said she was a good girl. I spoke to some of the other teenagers and they suggested there were some things she was worried about but typical teenage stuff, nothing that makes you think she would attempt suicide.'

Robyn turned at a bang from the occupied table, where someone had opened a bottle of champagne.

'Why let a tragedy get in the way of a free drink?' Chloe put her phone in her bag. 'The alert is out, Guv.'

'What about the guy who went into the room?' Lorraine stood up, rolling her shoulders. 'God, these chairs are uncomfortable.'

'He wasn't in the room when the sex took place.' Robyn counted off points on her fingers. 'If we believe his story, he was nowhere near Shazia when she went off the balcony. The reports from his colleagues are all the same, he's a peaceful, old man and he doesn't come across as aggressive. The forensics will confirm whether he touched her but I think we can discount him.'

5

Driven out of the ballroom by the staff wanting to finish packing away, Robyn, Lorraine and Chloe sat in the Dove Lounge. The clock on the mantelpiece, an intricate gilt fantasy, struck four.

'Where's Ravi?' Robyn pulled over a coffee table and dumped the papers she'd gathered.

'He's gone.' Chloe shifted in her seat. 'Went with his family about an hour ago. He seemed a bit calmer but his sisters were in such a state, maybe he just looked better by comparison.' She hesitated. 'I'm worried about him, Guv.'

'The best way we protect him is by keeping him away from the investigation.' She let the words hang in the air for a second. 'And we all should treat this like any other case. We can't let emotions cloud our judgement.' Looking first to Lorraine, then Chloe, Robyn checked for any sign of disagreement. 'Right. Have we got everything we need? I've made notes on the staff list.' She pointed at the pile of paper. 'Have we got the hotel's CCTV?'

'Got the password for online access here.' Lorraine held up her notebook.

'Photos?'

'I've got the photographer's details – he's going to put them all online for me on condition I don't sell them to anyone.' Chloe laughed. 'Shows what he thinks of the police.'

'I've got all the band's details.' Lorraine glanced up. 'I know they're good guys but I'll check them just the same.'

'The outside caterers have promised to send me all the details on Monday.' Chloe looked up. 'Is that OK? I had a nasty feeling there may be a couple of records the owner wants to, ah, tidy up first.'

'It could be illegal working. Did you fingerprint them?' Robyn saw Chloe bite her lip.

'No, sorry Guv. I can go now.' Chloe was already on her feet.

'Pretty sure they've gone.' Lorraine shifted in her seat.

'OK, learn for next time. Call them, say you need the details earlier. Visit if you have to.' Robyn waved at the chair for Chloe to sit. 'What about the jogger who saw the fall? Have we spoken to him?'

'No and it could be hard to track him down.' Lorraine's foot was tapping out a fast rhythm. 'He'd gone before I arrived and nobody got his name. He should be on the lobby CCTV and I got a description from the couple he ran into but I'm not sure how much more he can tell us.'

'OK, let's ask Khalid for a media call for witnesses. Still, on the evidence of the porter, she jumped by herself.' The room was cold and Robyn pushed her knees together to keep warm. 'Which one of you spoke to the couple in 106?'

Lorraine and Chloe looked at each other. 'Didn't you?' 'I thought you –?'

'Sorry Guv, I'll go.' Chloe scooted to the door.

A white shape slipped into the room, making a rustling sound as it walked. Lorraine craned over the top of her armchair.

'Good afternoon. I've got those first results you wanted.' Even in a paper suit, Dr Henrietta Brockwell gave the impression she was going to a garden party.

'That's great, Hetty.' Robyn indicated one of the mismatched armchairs, realising this was the first time she and the crime scene lead investigator had worked together since the start of her transition in July.

Twisting, Hetty looked down the back of her suit. 'Hmm, maybe not.' Pulling an upright chair from under the desk, she sat, grimy knees pressed together. 'We've finished upstairs. The hotel staff don't seem very keen on hoovering so we've got a lot of organic material bagged up.' She clicked her teeth.

Robyn stiffened. When Hetty made that noise, something important was coming.

'From the forensic traces, I have drawn the conclusion your victim was raped before she jumped.' There was no emotion or hesitation in Hetty's voice.

'If I understand right, that's two things: one, she was raped and two, we are looking at a suicide attempt rather than attempted murder?' Robyn paused. 'What did you find to make you so sure?'

'The whole pattern of the room suggested violence.' Hetty angled her head: light flashed on the lenses of her glasses. 'As an example, the top of the chair had scratches on it, with flakes of varnish still attached showing they were recent. Potentially, fingernails would have been hard enough to make them, if someone had been gripping the chair and it was torn from their hands. See if you can get the hospital to do a swab of her fingers.' She held up a clear plastic bag containing tiny golden beads on a slip of bright green thread. 'We've also found traces of ripped fabric and things like sequins.'

'Yes.' Lorraine leaned forward to look. 'Her sari was just that colour.'

'There's a lot of material in a sari, all folded and pinned together – I'd say someone got frustrated trying to unwrap her so just ripped at the material.' Hetty's hands mimed the action. 'If you can get the clothes from the hospital, I'm sure you'll find tearing.'

41

Something with squeaky wheels went past in the corridor.

'As to being certain she jumped, we found drops of blood and traces of bare footprints on one of the balcony chairs and in the smut on the rail.' Hetty pushed her glasses up onto her nose. 'The most likely explanation is that she stepped up onto the rail herself.'

'That matches what the porter described.' Robyn felt her phone vibrate with a message. 'He said she ran onto the balcony and when he followed her, she was already standing on the chair.'

'We've also got the sheets bagged up. The marks look like arterial blood but we'll check whose. The test results will be with you by Tuesday morning at the latest.' Hetty sat back.

Lorraine leaned forward. 'Can you tell us anything about the attacker?'

'As I said, plenty of material, the problem is going to be identifying individuals. The team are taking samples from the hotel staff for elimination but I assume you've already checked all their alibis?'

Talking to Dr Brockwell always reminded Robyn of being lectured by a teacher. 'Thanks, Hetty. Anything you can give us will be important, because we are not going to get anything from the victim, at least in the short term.'

'Shazia. She's got a name.' Hetty frowned.

There was another second of silence while Robyn searched for something to say. 'Anyway, long time no see. How was Australia and your new granddaughter?'

'They're both beautiful.' The suit rustled when Hetty laughed. 'Six weeks just wasn't enough – I didn't want to come back to all the grey skies.'

'You had a good trip then?'

'Fabulous thanks, Roger. Spent the first –'

Robyn's sharp intake of breath cut her off. For a few seconds, Hetty stared over her glasses at Robyn, as if seeing her for the first time.

'Robyn, oh I'm sorry.' Her hands came together on her lap. 'Not Roger, Robyn. I'm so sorry.'

After two months of being Robyn, to be called her old name made her fists contract. She was used to seeing 'Mr R Bailley' on junk mail but he was beginning to feel like someone she used to know, gone and not missed. It brought back the mockery of the afternoon, the feeling people thought she was dressing up, just playing at being someone else. Robyn swallowed, determined to keep her voice normal. 'When did you get back?'

'Just two days ago, still got a touch of jet lag, half asleep, don't know what I'm saying.' Hetty was talking too fast. Behind her, Chloe walked in, her phone in her hand.

Glad of the distraction, Robyn stood up. 'Do you two know each other? Chloe Talbot who's acting DC now, Dr Henrietta Brockwell, head crime scene officer.' While the greeting took place, she told herself this was no more than a mistake, they were inevitable, she should be able to deal with silly slips of the tongue. She took a deep breath. 'OK, thanks for the update, Hetty.'

'I'll get those results as soon as possible.' At the door, Hetty stopped, casting a quick look back over her shoulder. 'I'm really sorry.'

It was an effort to wave her goodbye, Robyn's arm felt as if it weighed more than usual. 'What did you get, Chloe?'

'Not much I'm afraid, Guv. They're both rather deaf, so they didn't hear anything before the wall started shaking. I've got their details in case. What did I miss?' There was a hint of redness in Chloe's eyes.

'Dr Brockwell believes it is a case of rape.' Robyn looked between them. 'Have either of you worked on anything like this before?'

'I had to respond to a nasty domestic once.' Chloe sighed. 'We collared the ex-husband with the hammer still in his hand and the wife ended up dropping all charges.'

'I've not had a case where there were this many possible suspects.' Lorraine bit the end of her Biro. 'We need to narrow them down a bit.'

Chloe pulled her notebook out of her bag. 'I've been trying to work out how many people we're talking about.' She put the open book on

43

the table, pointing to a column of jottings. 'The wedding party was nearly two hundred, there were twelve unconnected guests booked into other rooms, the hotel had twenty-six staff working, the catering company and the band were about ten each, not counting anyone who could have walked in off the street.'

'It would help if we can work out the exact timings.' Lorraine pulled the pad closer. 'The first guests left the ballroom at about twenty past two. We don't know exactly what time Eldon went up but the call to the ambulance was at two thirty-nine.' She drew a circle around her notes. 'Nineteen minutes.'

'We can get closer.' Robyn tapped the page. 'The crucial time is between when the first dance finished and the call from 106 because that's when Shazia and her attacker made their way to the room.'

Chloe's phone rang and she stood up to take the call.

'I'm guessing you didn't get anything useful from the staff?' Lorraine flicked a corner of the sheet.

'Unfortunately not.' Robyn sat back. 'Just that someone who knew Shazia said she didn't have any reason to commit –'

'You're kidding!' Chloe's exclamation caused them both to turn. She finished the call and laughed, rocking back on her heels. 'You'll never guess, Guv. Someone up there is in a very good mood today.'

Even though Chloe had only been in the team a few weeks, Robyn thought she was already copying some of Graham's more irritating mannerisms. She wasn't going to encourage her but Lorraine didn't have the patience to wait. 'What, what is it?'

'You know I put the call in earlier to look out for our missing usher?' Chloe paused, milking the moment. 'Well, turns out we know exactly where he is. He's in cell three after being arrested for drink driving.'

'He's already in custody?' The prospect of an easy solution made Robyn almost light-headed.

Chloe nodded. 'Picked up earlier this afternoon. His van went into the back of a car. A patrol was called and they breathalysed him. They'd done all the paperwork and were just about to let him go when they saw the alert.' She sank into an armchair, swinging her legs over the arm.

'Who's in custody?'

Robyn jumped at the voice: Ady Clarke, chief reporter of the *Meresbourne Gazette* was standing in the doorway. 'How long have you been listening?' She saw Ady stiffen. 'Sorry. I didn't see you come in but you shouldn't be in here.' Even though Ady was an old friend, he was still a journalist.

'I sent you a message to say I was here. How's the girl?' Ady stepped further into the room, hand reaching into an inside jacket pocket.

Robyn guessed he had activated a recorder. 'I haven't heard anything except she's gone to a specialist unit.'

'So is the person you have in custody connected?' Ady's blue eyes were eager. 'Come on, I need something, Robyn.' He smiled. 'You know what my editor suggested? She said I should frame the story as a tragic recreation of the "Lady Ann" legend. Bloody woman. She's come from some magazine in the south west, knows nothing about Meresbourne local history.'

'But I thought Lady Ann threw herself off the balcony when her lover left her?' Chloe sat forward in her chair.

Ady took the opportunity to install himself into a chair opposite Chloe. 'You've been looking at the portrait upstairs. The real Lady Ann, who lived here, hence the name, didn't kill herself. Her father was making her marry some merchant who was very rich and very ugly. She said she would only marry in Flanders lace which her fiancé had to fetch himself. As soon as his ship had left the harbour, she ran away, married someone else, had eight children and lived to seventy-two.' While he was talking, Ady's eyes were scanning the open notebooks. 'Not such a romantic story, I guess.'

'You can have two minutes, Ady.' Robyn bent forward and gathered up the notebooks.

Ady's attention immediately switched away from Chloe. 'Just give me the basics – was it an attack or a suicide attempt?'

'I can't say at this stage. We're keeping an open mind.'

'Right.' Ady raised an eyebrow. 'Any connection with the attacks on women recently?'

Robyn knew Ady was a good journalist because he got his facts right: that also made him infuriating. 'Uniform are following up on those. Look, just because there's all the focus on Loveless, our one local celebrity, does everything have to have a female angle? If you want to help out, couldn't you run a safety guide or something? Remind women not to walk home alone?'

'Would you front it?' Because they had been at school together, Ady often asked things others wouldn't.

Robyn glared at him. 'Ask Fell. He likes getting his picture in the paper. We need to get on.'

'Who's in custody?'

'Ady, I'm sorry, it's too early to say. I'll let you know when we can.' She stood up, nodding to Chloe and Lorraine. 'Come on, we need to get back to the station.'

Chloe's phone buzzed. When she looked at it, her face tightened. 'Sorry, Guv. It's Ravi. I'd like to see if he's OK.'

Robyn nodded, seeing Ady move closer to Chloe, sensing further revelations.

'I think we've done all we can here anyway. Look, thanks for today, good work.' Robyn began shepherding them to the door. 'Goodbye, Ady.'

In the lobby, Chloe headed for the car park. Lorraine muttered something which could have been 'Look after him.'

'Right, back to the station.' With a jolt, Robyn remembered how she had got there. 'Lorraine, I'm going to be a few minutes behind – my car's in the shopping centre car park.' She crossed to the reception desk. Lawrence's face creased as she approached. 'We are leaving now and the room can be cleaned.' For the first time, his smile was genuine. She checked behind her: Ady wasn't in sight. 'You need to know there is a journalist around asking questions – I'd advise your staff not to talk to him.'

The desk phone rang and Lawrence's hand reached out though his eyes were fixed on them. 'You'll get those sheets back soon, won't you?'

'Are you really so upset about a few old bedsheets?' Lorraine put the key-card back on the desk. 'How nice to have such easily solved problems.'

'You don't understand.' As Jade stepped in to answer the phone, Lawrence drew himself up. 'We are an ambassador for the town. Our sheets are the finest Egyptian cotton and are toned to the rooms. These can't just be bought on the High Street.'

Lorraine laughed. 'An ambassador?' She cast a glance at Sophie. 'I think some of your staff must have missed the diplomacy course.'

6

When he was brought into the interview room, Jake Newman didn't wait to sit down before starting talking. 'Oh man, not more – who are you? The woman at the desk said I'm being held for something to do with the Lady Ann but she won't even tell me what.'

They sat down. Lorraine went through the caution and started the recordings. 'Mr Newman, do you know why you're here?'

The man leaned back, putting his hands on his head. 'Didn't I just say? Look, I know why I got pulled in. I've explained all this.' His hands came down to the table. 'I don't know why you're keeping me here and the only thing taking place at the hotel was a wedding.'

'Explain it again to me and DI Bailley. Why did you leave the hotel?' Lorraine crossed her legs.

The man sighed. 'Someone called, an emergency job, water spraying everywhere. I've got a baby, so can't afford to turn down work. I changed out of my suit and went.'

'You're a plumber?'

'No, I'm a hairdresser. Course I'm a bloody plumber.' Newman pulled out the front of his blue t-shirt, showing the logo of a heating company.

Robyn sat back, letting Lorraine continue. She approved of the technique, irritating him enough so it would be hard to maintain a lie.

'Now, now, Mr Newman, we have to be sure. What time did you leave the wedding?'

'Not long after two when I didn't have anything else to do.'

'To do – what do you mean?'

Newman frowned. 'I told all this to the first guy?' He rolled his eyes. 'OK, OK. I was an usher for my mate, Lulu. It was me made sure he was ready on time and took his speech and everything 'cos the others are hopeless at organising and his brother, supposed to be the best man, was a waste of space. At the hotel, we had to put some decorations up and then welcome everyone and see guests to their seats. The last thing was to partner the bridesmaids in the first dance. Once the formal bit was over, we was all planning to get drunk, so it didn't matter if I slipped off.'

'Did you tell anyone you were going?'

'Nah. I figured I'd not be long.'

'Was there anyone else in the room when you got changed?'

'Nope. All the lads were in the party.'

'So you got in your van?' Lorraine raised one eyebrow.

The man shook his head. 'Yeah, yeah, I know it was daft. Like I said, I need the money and I was really careful.'

'The name of your client?'

'Bloke I know called Jason. He's fitting out the new site for Pickley Plastics – I gave the other guy all the details.'

'Tell me what you did after you left the hotel.'

'I didn't have to go far, it was the industrial estate just past the football stadium. Blokes working in one of the units went through a pipe. Simple fix, so I wasn't there long.' Newman folded his arms. 'Why are we going through this again?'

'Because I want to.' Lorraine inclined her head. 'What time did you leave their premises?'

'Dunno exactly. The match was on the radio while I was driving back. I heard the own goal.' He grimaced. 'I shouted at the radio and it was then I bumped into that bloke's car.'

'And were found to be over the limit.'

'Yeah, yeah. So I got brought here.' Newman was staring at Lorraine. 'You lot was just about to let me out and then, bang, I'm back in a cell. Now unless you haven't been listening, I was nowhere near the hotel since just after two o'clock, so if you're interested in something there, I'm not the one you should be talking to.'

Lorraine glanced across. Robyn inclined her head to the door.

'Interview terminated at seventeen twenty-four. Just think about what you did next.'

Robyn stood up. Lorraine held the look with Newman for a second more, then followed.

'Oh come on, what are you playing at? When can I go back to the wedding?' His shout followed them into the corridor, over the sounds of the ring road coming in through the open windows.

'So, Guv, do we tell him Shazia was raped and watch his reaction, or keep pushing him?'

'If he went when he said he did.' Her voice sounded wrong, too deep and she had to cough. 'It looks like he was nowhere near the hotel.'

'Damn, I thought we had this sorted.' Lorraine shut her eyes for a second. 'Shall we put it to him and see how he reacts?'

Robyn nodded. 'He might give us some insights into who could have done it.' The earlier sense of an easy solution had gone.

When they re-entered the room, Newman was slumped forward on the table, head pillowed on his arms.

'Mr Newman? Mr Newman, we have some more questions for you.' Lorraine slapped her pad on to the table.

Newman shifted, blinked, then pushed himself up from the table, yawning. 'Sorry, the baby's not sleeping well at the moment.'

Robyn nodded to Lorraine to start. 'Mr Newman, what were you doing at around two-thirty this afternoon?'

Newman's eyes narrowed. 'Are you kidding? We just went through this. I was driving to the industrial park. Go and talk to the guys. They might be still there now, they were talking about pulling an all-nighter to get things finished for Monday.'

'Do you know Shazia Johar?'

'Shania? Isn't she a singer?'

'Shazia. Shazia Johar. She's one of the bride's cousins.'

He shook his head. 'All we was doing was saying "bride or groom?" which wasn't difficult anyway, given one lot was brown and one white. Vasanti's got about a million relatives – I don't think I know any of their names.' He scratched his chin. 'Apart from Daffy, obviously.'

Lorraine raised her eyebrow. 'Not that obvious – who's he?'

'Daksh, Vasanti's brother. He's on our team. That's how they met, after one of our football matches. He was supposed to be an usher too until Lulu realised it would spoil his plans for a final steak feast.' Newman looked between them. 'Because her family don't eat beef, do they? So that was like the most rebellious thing he could do before the wedding –'

'We're asking these questions because at around two-thirty this afternoon, Shazia was raped in your hotel room.' The casual banter was getting under Robyn's skin: her dry throat made the tone sound harsher than she had meant.

Newman's mouth slowly opened. On the table in front of him, his hands clenched into fists. 'What?'

'I repeat, a girl was raped in room 108 and you admit being in there at a similar time.' Robyn leant forward. 'Did you do it?'

Newman sat bolt upright in his chair. 'No way. Why would I do something like that? I've got a girlfriend, we've got a baby.' He was

51

breathing fast, short snorts of air. 'Anyway, I was away before half-past two. I wasn't even there.'

'We'll find out if you're lying.' Lorraine's tone was conversational. 'What did you do with your key-card when you left the hotel?'

Face flushed, Newman looked between them, slumping back down in his chair. 'I took it with me.' He dug into his pockets 'It must be still in the van. It was only a plastic card and the others had their own.'

'Who are the others?' Lorraine sounded brisk.

'Lulu, Axe and Lassie. Oh and Julian, Lulu's brother.'

'Can you give us their full names, please?'

'Louis Gage, Justin Trudwick and Colin Bartholomew.' He seemed to realise something more was expected of him. 'We all play football – it's just a team thing.'

'OK, Louis to Lulu I can just about get but how did you get from Justin to,' Lorraine paused, 'which is which anyway?'

Newman shrugged. 'Justin is Axe or Axeman because he looks like a bloody Viking and he brings down a lot of people. He plays centre back.'

'So Colin is Lassie. Really?' Lorraine chuckled. 'You mean you macho football types are happy to be called after a fluffy dog? Come on.'

'It's the football team. We just call each other stuff.' Newman hunched his shoulders together, closing in on himself. 'Like it means anything.' His hand brushed his eyes. 'How is she? Is she OK?'

Lorraine paused. 'She jumped from a first-floor balcony and is in hospital.'

Newman's mouth opened. He looked between them as if waiting for one to crack and admit it was a joke. 'No way, no bloody way.' He ran his hands through his hair. 'What bastard did this?'

'Anything you can tell us about where you all were before you left would be helpful.' Lorraine gave him a small smile.

'Well, Lulu was up on the stage, of course. He and Vasanti had to sit on these decorated thrones for everyone to come and pay homage. Some part of her culture, apparently. I thought he looked a right twat and I tell you, when I brought them over in the van this morning, the glue wasn't even dry on some bits.' Newman gave a mirthless laugh.

'Can you think of anyone who might have done this?' Robyn narrowed her eyes.

'No!' Newman recoiled. 'It must have been someone who broke in.'

It was the reaction Robyn had been expecting. 'Did the day go as planned up to the dance?'

Newman's shoulders relaxed. 'Yeah, pretty much. Not been to a wedding so big before, so some stuff was bound to go wrong, wasn't it?'

'Like an usher losing the rings?'

Newman folded his arms, sitting back in his chair. 'Axe was just pissing around. Even Lulu laughed about it. Well, after he'd had a drink.'

'Not at the time, though.' Robyn tapped her pen on the table. 'And I understand you talked about what you'd like to do to the bridesmaids too.'

'Hang on.' Newman had gone pale. 'Like, maybe you, being like, well what you're like and don't know but men talk about stuff like that. We talk about women.' He turned to Lorraine. 'Especially the good-looking ones. You must know, it's just talk. I live with my girlfriend, Jess.'

'And I bet Jess will be delighted you're talking about other women.' There was a hint of a sneer in Lorraine's voice. 'So who said they'd like to do a bridesmaid then?'

'I can't remember.' Newman buried his head in his hands. 'I really can't. It was early, we'd had a couple to drink, I think we all said something.' He lifted his face, chin resting on his hands. 'It didn't mean anything.'

Robyn caught Lorraine's eye and looked towards the door.

53

'Right, we're letting you go.' Lorraine shuffled her papers together and stood up.

'Thank Christ. What about my van?'

Lorraine paused by the door. 'You were in the clear on the second reading so you can drive. There was no question about the reading before, so the points will go on your licence.' She held the door open.

Newman looked up at her for a second before standing.

Robyn waited until he passed her. 'What's your nickname?'

Newman swung his head towards her. 'You what?'

'You've told us the lads all went by nicknames – I want to know what yours was.'

Newman barked a laugh. 'Paul.' He paused, holding his palms out as if waiting for a response. When there was none, he shook his head. 'Paul Newman. Christ, you thick or what?' He walked between them into the corridor, shrugging his arms into his blue jacket. 'Where do I get my stuff back from?'

'Just wait there, someone will be with you shortly.' The custody sergeant pointed to a bench. Newman looked at the couple of teenagers sprawled across it, one pressing a thick dressing to his arm and remained standing.

Robyn and Lorraine retreated back into the interview room. Lorraine stretched out, up on her toes, the tips of her fingers touching the low ceiling. 'Now what, Guv?'

'Now we start again with the basics, like who let Shazia into the room? If we accept the evidence to date, we're looking at a sexual assault leading to an attempted suicide.' Robyn straightened. 'Right, I'm going upstairs to go through the family statements you collected. For the rest, we'd be better tackling everything else when we're fresh tomorrow.'

'I'll need to leave by one, Guv, so I'll be there first thing. My band's playing at the Markham air memorial festival tomorrow – it's a whole weekend of 1940s events with a jazz dance in the afternoon.' Lorraine gave a quick smile. 'See you.'

In the corridor, Robyn swung her handbag to her shoulder and headed for the lift. The teenagers were now flipping a plastic bottle. There was no sign of Newman.

'DI Bailley?'

The custody sergeant was waving from behind the desk. With the telephone tucked under one ear, she scrabbled through the paperwork in front of her until she found a Post-it. 'Hang on a sec.' She turned the receiver into her shoulder. 'Message for you. Came in about fifteen minutes ago.' She handed over a scrap of paper and turned back to her call.

'Thanks, Martha.' The writing was almost illegible. It took Robyn a few seconds to work out the scrawled 'Kall ID' meant the message was from Khalid. The only other legible word was 'urgent'. After squinting at the rest, she gave up and decided just to call him direct. Her mobile didn't work well down here in the basement: she punched the number from her phone into another desk phone.

'Hi, Kh –'

'Robyn. Did you get my message?'

'Just now. I couldn't read it, so I thought I'd call you.'

'Is the rape suspect still with you?'

'No, we've just let him go, why?' Robyn switched the phone to her other ear.

'Bugger. Where is he? Is he still in the building?'

She'd never heard Khalid swear before. 'I'm not sure – hang on.'

The sergeant was still on the phone. Robyn reached past her and checked the clipboard. 'He's gone. What's up?'

'I guess you haven't seen outside. There are protestors out there. They've picked up there was a rape and somehow they know you had a suspect in custody.'

'Christ. Ady turned up at the hotel and he overheard us talking. Is there an article in the *Evening Gazette*?'

'All of this stuff is through social media now.' Khalid paused. 'They

55

came and unfurled some banners about half an hour ago. Something has got them angry, can't you hear the chanting?'

'Not down here. Isn't anybody out there keeping them in order?'

'No, it wasn't this angry when they first got here. Wait.'

'What is it?'

'Is your man tall with fair hair? He's out there now – the crowd has just seen him. They're closing in.'

7

'That sounds like him.' Robyn moved back towards the desk, where a bank of screens showed the views from the CCTV cameras around the police station.

'He's just walked out of the front door. Why did you let him out?'

'Because he hasn't done anything.' Martha was still on the phone. Robyn waved a hand in front of her face. 'Can you switch any of these to the cameras at the front entrance?'

Khalid shouted something. The only word she understood was 'surrounded'.

The sergeant frowned then reached for a remote control and got a menu up on the screen. The picture changed. It took a second for Robyn to make sense of the scene: the square in front of the police station's main entrance was a mass of bodies.

'What did you say, Khalid?'

'They're all around him.'

'Where are the uniform team? Has anyone told DI Pond what's going on?' Martha gazed at the screen, her phone call forgotten.

The back of Newman's head was just visible at the bottom of the screen. In front of him was a massed rank of people, some holding banners. The screen automatically switched to the next location. The sergeant began stabbing at the remote.

'What's happening, Khalid?'

'They're clustering around him. I can't see him anymore. Someone's going in – one of ours. He's trying to get through, it's Clyde, I think it's Clyde.'

The pictures scrolled through the car-park, the back gate and the fire exit before there was a glimpse of the front entrance and the picture moved straight on to the car-park.

'Get it back, get it back.' Robyn pounded the counter.

'He's down, Clyde's down!' Khalid's voice was close to hysteria.

Dropping the phone, Robyn ran for the back entrance. Racing around the edge of the car park, she could hear nothing over her own footfalls. The pedestrian gate took precious seconds to open and she could hear a rumbling. Rounding the final corner to the front square, she ran into an angry mass of sound. There were a lot of people, their backs to her. She aimed for where the chanting was loudest, protest signs jerking up and down to the angry rhythm. She slowed, dodging though clumps of people. Approaching the denser crowd, her foot struck something. Momentum pitched her forward, slamming into the people in front. The bodies absorbed the impact, sending her sprawling. She landed on the paving stones, rolling to a stop against someone's feet. Through a forest of legs, Robyn caught a glimpse of bright blue and Clyde's dark face before he brought his arms up to shield his head. Bodies closed around him, blocking her view. Over the noise, Robyn heard a high, angry voice leading the chant, speeding it up. She staggered upright, seeking a way to get through. The movement of the crowd changed, jerky, irregular: they were kicking the bodies on the floor. Without thinking, Robyn took a step back. She sprinted for the centre of the cluster, dropping her shoulder. She barged between two, barrelling into others who reeled back. She could see Clyde, who'd put his body over Newman's. A woman had her leg back, ready to strike.

'POLICE. Stop this.' The nearest woman ducked away covering her ear. Robyn used the second of surprise to step forward, to stand over Clyde. She balanced on the balls of her feet, ready for an attack, keeping her stance wide. From somewhere, a rhythmic pulse had started. She was surrounded. There was a tang of iron and sweat in the air. She could only take short breaths.

A high-pitched scream drove out all other sounds. Ears numb, Robyn whirled around. A skeletal woman had her protest sign above her head and brought it down like an axe, aiming for Newman who was trying to get to his feet.

Robyn lunged, grabbing for the handle. She got her left hand around it, the wood rough on her palm as the shaft slid until she could get a grip. Her weight pulled the swing short; the sign smashed into the ground inches from Newman's face, the end broken into a mass of sharp splinters. The banging was closer.

The woman twisted, trying to stab with the shaft. Robyn caught the end. Their bodies were locked together. She could hear panting, not sure whose it was.

'Police brutality. I'm being violated.' A sudden slackening of pressure pitched Robyn forward. As she regained her balance, the woman was on her, pummelling at her chest. Robyn kept her hands locked around the shaft, telling herself she must not let go. An elbow slammed into Robyn's ribs. The pounding in her ears was louder. The temptation was to lash out with the shaft but the blows slackened, stopped. She risked a shaky glance around. She was surrounded by colleagues in riot gear; she realised the banging had been them beating a warning on their shields. The woman had her arms pinned behind her back, a pale blob against the circle of black-clad figures. Robyn breathed out, shutting her eyes. The shaft clattered to the floor. Something warm hit her face and began to dribble.

Laughing, the woman allowed herself to be pulled back. 'Oh sorry, copper. Better wash your face.'

Skin crawling, Robyn wiped her face on her sleeve, seeing smears of foundation stain the pale green material. A dizzy moment made her bend forward, needing to suck in lungfuls of air, resting her hands on her knees to keep herself stable. Agony shot up her arms. She looked from one hand to the other, blinking to try and clear her eyes. Her palms were a mess of bloody gouges where the rough wood had shredded the skin.

'You bastard.' A woman with flyaway chestnut hair was struggling in the arms of a constable. She got one arm free and swept the strands away from her face. The policeman pulled her arm back and tried to turn her towards the police station.

'Are you ignoring me?' The woman wrenched herself clear and lurched towards Robyn.

Focusing, Robyn tried to get her body to face the new threat. The woman's face was familiar though the hair was wrong, a different colour. 'Julie?' The last face-to-face meeting with Roger's ex-wife had been nearly three years ago when picking their daughter Becky up for her grandfather's funeral.

'You bastard, you bastard.' The PC had got his arms around Julie again. It wasn't clear who she was screaming at and he hesitated, looking at Robyn. His visor was open and she recognised Jeremy, who would love to hear some gossip about her after being turned down for the fast-track CID programme.

Julie had stopped struggling and stood, stiff. 'So you force me to submit – what are you going to do to me?'

Robyn studied her face. Even without the incandescent anger, Julie's face had aged. The depth of the lines around her mouth made it look as if she spent a lot of time with pursed lips.

'Well, come on then.' Julie stuck out her jaw.

Robyn hated how she could see Becky in the face in front of her. 'Take her away.'

Julie began struggling again: Jeremy hadn't put handcuffs on her. 'How can you say you're a woman?' Her voice was rising, becoming shrill. 'You can never be a woman. You don't know what it's like to bleed, to have a child growing inside you.' She wasn't looking at Robyn, staring past her, into space: Robyn followed her gaze and saw a hand-held TV camera, red light burning. 'You are nothing, Roger. You were a joke as a man so now you're trying to be a woman – why, because you think it's easier? You want to find some rich man to keep and pamper you? You make me sick.'

She tossed her hair on the last words. A clump hit Jeremy in the face: he had to spit. The shock seemed to galvanise him. 'Move.' His push was perhaps harder than it needed to be and Julie stumbled forward, almost out of Jeremy's grasp. Another officer ran across, grabbing her free arm and twisting it into handcuffs. Julie lifted her head, now staring at Robyn. 'How can you claim to be a woman when you have no compassion?'

Robyn watched her go and let the pent-up breath out in a long sigh. She had to shut her eyes for a second as her head was beginning to swim. From the first time she'd seen the posters around town for the Loveless celebration, there had been an uneasy anticipation that Julie, a lecturer in Women's Studies, would be coming to Meresbourne. She began moving, one foot in front of the other, towards the police station.

'DI Bailley? DI Bailley!'

A man in a suit so tight she could see the shape of coins in his pockets appeared in front of her. 'Hi, I'm Danny from South East media. Can you give me your views on this disturbance?'

'I'm sorry, Danny. This is not a good time.' Robyn tried to compose her face into an appropriate mix of authority and concern, conscious of the ruined make-up and blood. 'Anything has to come from Khalid.' All she wanted was to get back to the station.

'The lady seemed to have some very strong views about you.' Danny held the microphone closer. 'I was hoping for your personal comment on what she just said.'

'I don't have any comment to make.' Beneath the sharp pains from her hands, she was becoming aware of aches from other places: each breath she took was painful.

'Oh come on, those words must have hurt your feelings. How do you feel about this sort of criticism?'

Over Danny's shoulder, Robyn could see a small group clustered around a figure on the ground. Otherwise, the square had been cleared, debris and discarded banners were being swept into a pile. With a sudden shock, Robyn realised she hadn't seen Newman since she had glimpsed him on the ground. 'Danny, I'm sorry, I cannot talk to you now. There are things we need to do. Goodbye.' She turned away, knowing the camera would still be filming and began limping towards the station.

Martha hurried towards her with a first aid box. 'Right, let's have a look at you.'

'Don't worry about me, how's Clyde?'

'Not good.' The sergeant looked to where Clyde lay on his side in the recovery position. It wasn't clear whether he was conscious.

Beside him, Donna was checking his pulse, her helmet and baton discarded on the ground. 'Come on, man. Stop pretending. You're not getting out of a late shift with me so easily.'

'Is he OK?' Robyn dropped down next to her, slipping against Donna's shoulder as her leg refused to hold her up. She saw Donna's eyes widen and tried to speak, to take the attention away. 'Clyde may have internal injuries – they were kicking him, we need an ambulance.'

'They're on their way.' Martha checked her watch. 'Don't know what's keeping them.'

With a moan, Clyde's eyelids flickered.

'Hey there.' Donna bent closer. 'How're you doing?'

'I'm all right.' One hand flat on the ground, Clyde tried to push himself up. 'Just knocked heads with someone in the crush.'

'And what do you think you're doing?' Just the touch of Donna's hand on his shoulder was enough to stop the movement.

'You're going to lie there quietly until someone comes along and checks you out.' Martha dropped her voice. 'I didn't realise he'd been hit on the head as well. I'll chase up the ambulance.' She stood up. 'Oy!'

Turning, Robyn looked straight into the cameraman's lens.

'DI Bailley, how seriously is the officer hurt?'

The adrenalin flooding her system drove Robyn forward: she ground the palm of one hand into the lens, ignoring the pain. Blood smeared across the glass and she heard the cameraman swear.

'DI Bailley.' As the cameraman squinted at the lens, Danny spread his hands. 'This is a legitimate news story.'

'Hi.' One of the officers sweeping away debris looked around, which saved Robyn having to remember his name. 'Please escort these gentlemen away from the area to allow treatment to take place.' When they were twenty yards away she turned back to Clyde.

Clyde blinked, trying to turn his head. 'Who's up there?'

'You should stop talking and keep quiet.' Donna squeezed his hand. 'You're not normally this chatty on patrol.' Her tone was light but the corners of her mouth turned down

Robyn sank back into a crouch. 'It's me, Clyde, Robyn Bailley. You're braver than me, arguing with Donna – I wouldn't dare.'

There was something between a laugh and a cough, which turned into a grimace of pain. Robyn exchanged a look with Donna: Clyde's saliva was a foamy pink.

'Seems like the last thing …' He took a ragged breath. 'I remember …' His chest seemed to be moving without air. 'Was you coming in, ma'am …' Another rattle in his throat. 'Like a bull in a china shop to get me out.'

'Don't strain yourself.' They all looked up as the sound of a siren cut across Robyn's reply. They were strobed with blue light before the wail shut off.

'About time. Now you go and have a nice lie down and I'll do my late shift all on my own. I'll save you some villains.' Donna bit her lip.

Clyde's response was a twitch of his lips: it might have been an attempt at a smile. Feet sounded over the stones.

'Now I hear some tossers beat you up. We'll get you sorted out, mate.' The paramedic opened his bag.

Robyn stood up, desperate to escape to the quiet of the CID room. Her body was a mass of dull aches.

An approaching clatter was the other paramedic wheeling a stretcher. Another ambulance pulled in. Robyn watched two more paramedics look around, feeling an odd detachment from the scene.

'Evening. We've got some minor injuries in the custody suite.' Martha pointed to the path to the back entrance and the new paramedics turned towards the station. 'And they should be starting with you, ma'am.' Martha narrowed her eyes. 'I shall expect to see you inside.'

'In a moment.' The stretcher was being wheeled towards the ambulance, Donna still holding Clyde's hand.

Robyn tried to smile, to sound less worried than she felt. 'He'll be fine, Donna. This is just a precaution.' The back doors were closed and the ambulance moved away, lights flashing. Donna's face had crumpled in on itself, tears running down her cheeks. 'Come on. You could use a cup of tea.'

After a huge sniff, Donna nodded. She took a first step in the direction of the station. Robyn bent to retrieve her helmet, then gasped as a stabbing pain jabbed across her chest.

Donna looked around, tissue still around her nose. Her eyes widened as if seeing Robyn for the first time. 'Christ, look the state of you. You saved Clyde and got hurt too. You need to get yourself checked out.' The quaver had gone from her voice. 'You're coming with me to see those paramedics.'

'Donna, I'm …' Thinking about what she had done was making her sick and Robyn wanted nothing more than to be alone.

'Now, ma'am.' Donna drew herself up. 'Seeing as it's me, I don't think you've got any choice.'

8

'Take your shirt off.'

Robyn and a paramedic with an elaborate goatee were sitting in an interview room, which had been turned into a makeshift treatment room.

'What? Ah, no, not here.'

The paramedic looked up from his bag. 'What's wrong? I need to clean your arms to put the dressings on your hands and you're saying you're getting chest pains. Your chest is under your shirt.'

Outside, something banged against a radiator, a sudden noise causing Robyn to jump. The sharp pain made her wince.

'Right, so something's wrong, let's get a look at it.' The paramedic took hold of the collar of the blouse and pulled it back. He froze, staring at the bra strap. 'Oh Christ, you're …' He let go of the material and starting paying lot of attention to the inside of his bag.

Robyn pulled her top back into place. 'Look, I'm fine, I think I've just pulled a muscle.' She willed him to look up. 'Let's make this quick because there'll be loads of paperwork coming out of this. Can you just dress my hands and I'll be off, OK?'

'OK.' His eyes met hers for a moment, then he took her right hand and turned it over. With a pair of tweezers, he began to remove the splinters. Trying to take her mind off what he was doing, Robyn focused on the back of his hand. Through the thin gloves, the dark hairs showed as bumps. The man seemed not to notice the scrutiny and kept up a gentle stream of small talk to take her mind off the pain but Robyn was brooding that hair was starting to show again in the same place on her hands. The wax had been six weeks ago: this process would be a constant until she could be prescribed the necessary hormones.

When her hands were dressed, Robyn left the paramedic zipping up his bag and escaped up the stairs. After a flight she slowed: breathing too hard hurt. At the ground floor, she pressed the button for the lift with her elbow just as the doors came together. When the doors reopened, she saw Fell already inside, his dinner suit jacket undone, bow tie drooping.

Robyn stepped in beside him. 'Evening, sir.'

Fell kept his eyes fixed forward until the doors opened on the second floor. 'My office, Bailley. Ten minutes.'

In the empty CID office, Robyn slumped behind her desk, trying to find a position where something didn't hurt. It was cold and she tried to put her jacket on, struggling as her arms didn't want to bend in the usual directions. She wasn't even sure why she'd come up other than she wanted to clear her head of work problems in the office rather than taking them home. The image of Clyde's scared face kept running through her mind. Waiting for the lift to the fifth floor, she reasoned running into Fell was probably a good thing: she would have to face him sooner or later, so at least sooner got things over with. Her phone beeped with a message: getting it out of the holster was a struggle with her hands made clumsy by the bandages. The sight of Becky's name on the screen made her smile, hoping it might be a confirmation of when she expected to arrive. The doors opened at the top floor.

Dad, wtf? Richard says you arrested mum and she's in a cell. You get her out right now. Not coming to see you unless you let her go. Becky.

Her feet carried her to Fell's office. Without Tracey's perfume to mask other smells, the air was thick with old sweat. DI Matthew Pond sat in one chair, fingers tightly knotted in his lap. Khalid leaned against the far wall, his eyes locked to his tablet, his elbow brushing against Fell's dinner jacket, making it swing on its wooden hanger. Fell seemed to be ignoring both of them. His office had more paper in it than usual and he was picking up sheets, scanning a few lines then discarding them without any apparent system. Robyn slipped into the vacant chair, hoping whatever Fell was about to say was short so she could call Becky.

'This evening I was called out of the Mayor's dinner to tell me I have an officer in hospital with a punctured lung, a man assaulted on his release from custody and a lot of people asking questions about why I cannot prevent a riot outside my own police station.' Fell's Adam's apple bobbed as he turned to Matthew. 'And all this has happened while we have a town full of guests come to celebrate the best of Meresbourne. I would like an explanation of what caused this situation.'

'We underestimated the level of violence the demonstrators would show.' Matthew swallowed. 'They were all women. It appears a peaceful demonstration was hijacked by a minority from an extreme organisation whose intention was to cause trouble. Once we saw what they were capable of, we responded with measured force.'

'This "we" who underestimated.' Fell's nostrils flared. 'Who were they exactly?'

Robyn felt Matthew's nerves. She started to get to her feet. 'Shall I come back later, sir?'

'Stay there, Bailley. We will get to your performance in a moment.'
Robyn subsided.

'The media seems to have lost interest already.' Khalid looked up, a blue tinge on his face from the screen. 'I've been monitoring mentions. We've had a bit of coverage across the regionals though the nationals haven't picked it up.' There was a hopeful note in his voice.

'It was my decision.' Matthew spoke to the floor. 'I got it wrong.'

'We have six women in custody. What charges do you intend to bring?'

'They will all be charged with public order offences.' He shifted in his seat. 'It's more difficult with the assault on Clyde. We don't know which ones actually caused the injuries because the crush was too great to see exactly –'

'Pond, I expect charges to be brought tonight and, if possible, to keep these people off the streets while Meresbourne is hosting this celebration of all things feminist. I am not risking another humiliation.'

'Yes, sir. We will be watching the CCTV and interviewing this evening.' Matthew blinked. 'If we can only charge them with a public order offence, it is likely they will be released on bail, sir.'

'Which would be disappointing.' Fell picked up another piece of paper. 'And all the more reason to make sure their future events are properly risk assessed. Were you aware of this "slut walk" running tonight?'

'Yes, sir.' Standing up, Matthew crossed to a large-scale map on the back wall. 'The plans changed to start from Quayside with a ceremony outside the Lady Ann Hotel at midnight, then a walk through the Docks, finishing outside the Town Hall.' He traced the route before turning back. 'It's tight but I've got cover for it.'

'And why are they doing this?' The direction of Fell's gaze swung towards Robyn, fixing just over her right ear. 'Bailley?'

Robyn cleared her throat. 'I'm afraid I wasn't aware of this, sir.'

Fell's eyes rolled. 'Disappointing. I thought you of all people would be up to date with campaigns for women's rights.'

Out of the corner of her eye, Robyn saw Khalid shake his head.

'This slut walk is supposed to make the point women can go about the streets at night, dressed as they wish, without it being taken as an invitation for sex. I should imagine this one will be well-attended given recent events.' Fell steepled his fingers. 'From the statistics Khalid collected, we have a number of unsolved attacks on women. Could there be a link with the incident at the Lady Ann?'

'Nothing immediately suggests so, sir.' Robyn hated the sound of her voice: she came across as weak and uncertain. 'It's a very different pattern to a street attack.'

'I suggest the street attacks need more focus. Our performance is poor.' Fell gave up with the paper he was holding and put it down. 'Now tell me why you released a suspect into danger and why you acted without backup, potentially endangering that suspect and a fellow officer?'

'The *Gazette* are calling DI Bailley a hero.' Khalid turned around his tablet.

'So now we are supposed to believe everything the *Gazette* says?' Fell had not looked around. 'I do not think that is an advisable course of action.'

Robyn took a deep breath. 'I released the suspect because there was no reason to continue holding him. I didn't know about the demonstration. In terms of what I did, I thought …' She had to swallow. 'It was the quickest way to get Clyde out.'

'You thought? You were without equipment or back-up. I would say you acted entirely without thinking.'

She could argue but if it shortened the time she had to spend in the foetid room, it was worth it. 'Yes, sir.'

There was a slight drop in Fell's eyebrows. 'I am disappointed in both of you. Pond, we have approximately two hundred and fifty academics, writers and social commentators in our town this week. You will identify who is causing trouble and regain control of this situation. When this festival is over, you will speak to the central team in Maidstone and get them to run refresher training on crowd control. Bailley, the longer this Lady Ann case goes unsolved, the more trouble we will have. I want regular updates. And by phone. I can't find anything with Tracey not here.'

They stood up to leave.

'Oh, and Guler. I am extremely doubtful this story will stay quiet, given how vocal some of these extremist groups are. I suggest you need to expand your media sources.'

The three of them filed in silence through the outer office. Khalid shut the door behind them, checking it was closed before speaking. 'He's in a vile mood.'

Matthew grunted.

'I think we've got our proof it's really Tracey who runs the show.'

Robyn appreciated Khalid's attempt to lighten the mood. 'Maybe you should put Tracey up instead of Fell at the press conferences – she'd tell people what's –'

Matthew cut her off with an angry gesture. One of his uniform team had appeared from the lift. 'Ah, sir, can you come? We've got problems in the custody suite and one woman is screaming blue murder because she says the cell smells of men.'

Matthew stopped, Robyn bumping into his back. 'Sorry.' She dropped her voice. 'You OK?' His jaw was set like someone trying not to be sick.

'Fine. I'll call you when we're ready to interview.' Matthew strode forward, passing the PC and disappearing down the stairs, the constable scurrying after him.

'What about you?' Khalid had paused outside his office. 'You should go home.'

The corridor felt very hot, or maybe it was her. 'Do you think Fell's right about things being stirred up on social media?'

Khalid nodded. 'Almost certainly. I've been researching this area, just in case. There are some groups at the extreme end of feminism which have almost as many problems with mainstream feminism as with men. They work almost exclusively online.'

'Was there anything about me?' She realised she was gritting her teeth.

'Ah, yeah, I was going to talk to you about that.' Khalid stepped into his office and perched on the edge of his desk. 'Was one of the women really your wife? Sorry, ex-wife.'

Robyn leant against the door frame, trying to look relaxed. 'We've been divorced seventeen years. Apart from conversations about our daughter, we've hardly spoken in that time. Until recently – she rang me specially to make it clear she didn't approve of what I'm doing.'

'Thoughtful.' Khalid's eyebrows went up. 'I was at uni with one of the senior editors at South East Media – I spoke to her earlier and asked whether she can stop them broadcasting that woman's rant against you. She can't promise anything of course because it's a good story.' He picked up a fountain pen from a tray and began twisting the cap. 'One option is for you to go out with something from your point of view to counter it or keep quiet and hope it goes away?'

The prospect of everyone looking at her was daunting. Online, she'd found out there was no point in trying to justify her existence to certain people, so more publicity might mean more hatred. 'Ady talked about something similar a while ago. Said the *Gazette* could "tell my story", be sympathetic and all sorts of stuff.' She had managed to keep her tone light. 'I put him off because we were hunting for a missing boy.'

'And now?'

'Now, I don't want to do it because I really don't fancy having my life in the paper for everyone to comment about.' Robyn flexed her shoulders, feeling some of the tension release.

'Can I ask you a personal question?' He paused though not long enough for Robyn to object. 'If the divorce was so long ago, why does your ex still hate you so much?'

Robyn laughed, enjoying the surprise on Khalid's face. 'It's because I'm trans.' It was getting easier to say. 'Julie belongs to the branch of feminism that believes trans women are actively a threat to women.' She tried to keep her tone light. 'She believes people like me are just dressing up as women in order to go and act like a pervert in public toilets.'

'I can't see you doing that.' Khalid glanced over his tablet's screen and their eyes met for a second. 'Oh, by the way, was the suspect hurt?'

'I don't know.' Saying the words out loud made her ignorance more shocking. 'I saw him on the ground, then he was gone. I'll check on him.'

'Good idea. He might complain we abandoned him and try and get some sympathy on TV.'

'I don't think he'll be glad to see any more police today.' Robyn shook her head. 'And all of Matthew's resources will be deployed tonight. The earliest we could go would be in the morning.'

'Oh, of course, the slut walk.' Khalid shut his eyes for a second. 'And you. Are you sure you're OK?'

'Fine.' The last thing she wanted was someone making a fuss. 'Thanks.' She turned for the door.

'Call me tomorrow with an update for Fell's panel appearance.' Khalid's voice followed her into the corridor.

She gave up the idea of walking down the three flights of stairs to the incident room. While waiting for the lift, images of the riot ran through her mind but now there was a detached commentator pointing out other things she could have done. She hadn't thought beyond drawing the mob's attention away from the men on the floor. It hadn't occurred to her before that by charging in she might have caused Clyde's injuries. Now the idea was planted, it seemed very possible. With a heavy lump of guilt lodged in her stomach, she resolved to contact Newman as soon as possible because there was nothing she could do at the moment to help Clyde.

A savoury smell filled the incident room. Lorraine was forking noodles from a yellow tub. A chocolate bar and can of drink sat on the desk in front of her. Robyn felt her mouth begin to water.

'Blimey, Guv.' One noodle hung down Lorraine's chin until she poked it into her mouth with a finger. 'Who'd have thought it would kick off like that? I'd packed up, then got a message from the photographer that all the photos were now on the website. I came back up thinking I'd have a quick look when I heard noise outside and I saw the fight start. By the time I got down there, it was all over.' She took another forkful. 'Are you OK?'

'I'm fine. We need to find Newman, check he wasn't hurt.'

Lorraine swallowed, looking down at the bandages on Robyn's hands. 'Shall I type?' Putting down the tub, she entered something into the computer, then swivelled her screen. 'Here are his details. You're not planning on going out there like that are you? And what about Clyde?' She shook her head. 'Those mad bitches downstairs are going to be charged, right?'

Robyn nodded. 'Matthew is sorting that out now. Fell wants them out of the way if possible for the rest of the festival. I'll call Newman and then I was going to watch the CCTV to support Matthew before the interviews.'

'Ah, won't you be a witness, Guv?' Lorraine dropped the noodle pot into the bin. 'You probably shouldn't be on the interview panel. Could I do it? It'll be good practice.'

'Of course.' This meant, at some point, Robyn knew she would have to tell Lorraine who Julie was. 'Good idea, thanks. Can you set up the CCTV and I'll ring Newman.' The phone went straight to voicemail. 'Mr Newman, it's DI Bailley. I wanted to speak to you. Could you please give me a call back?' She gave her number and hung up, frustrated because nothing was resolved.

Lorraine pulled her chair over to sit by Robyn, bringing the chocolate and the drink. She must have caught Robyn's longing look because she broke off a couple of squares and handed them across. Chewing, Robyn searched through the files until she found the daily CCTV. She picked the camera above the front entrance, set the time for an hour before the incident and started the film on fast-forward. The square in front of the police station was an empty space, people moving in a series of jerks to and from the entrance. After the timer showed half an hour had passed, in one corner there was a clump of people. After another ten, the group shifted from the corner of the screen to the centre and stood in an untidy line, some holding signs, the centre group spreading out a banner. 'About twenty of them. Is that all? It looked like more.'

'Hang on, what's this?' Lorraine stretched for the remote and returned the film to normal speed. New arrivals, with their own banners, had joined the original protestors. The enlarged group moved forward, surrounding the main doors. She paused the film. 'Do you recognise any of them?'

The faces were grainy. Robyn had to get close to the screen. One shape stood a little in front of the central group. 'There. That looks like the one I had the tussle with.' A figure appeared from the station and started towards the group, before pausing.

Lorraine leaned closer to the screen. 'Newman has seen them. They haven't recognised him yet.' Someone in uniform had walked out and stood talking to the group. 'That must be Clyde, not that you'd recognise him unless you knew – we need better cameras.'

Robyn was gazing at the line. She had worked out which one was Julie. On the fuzzy film, she was the one pointing at Newman, her mouth a black hole: she must have been shouting. He was surrounded though what she could see from this angle was that a lot of the protestors hung back, not taking part in the surge. She paused the film. The sick feeling in her stomach now was nothing to do with hunger: she knew what she was going to see.

Lorraine looked round. 'You OK, Guv?'

'Look, ah, I think I'll get a cup of tea before watching this bit.'

'Why don't you go home?' Lorraine waved at the clock. 'It's late and you look done in.'

Robyn shook her head. 'No, this needs to get done. You want anything?'

There was a subdued air in the station, no voices in the corridors and none of the usual chatter. In the canteen, people had pulled

74

together chairs to sit in a rough circle. On the way to the counter, Robyn's shoes squeaked on the lino.

On the far side of the group, Donna sat with tissues discarded around her. 'DI Bailley.' There was a raw note in her voice making it sound as if she'd been crying again. Everyone was now staring at Robyn. It was hard to tell what they thought.

'Did you all see what DI Bailley did?' Donna began to clap. A few joined in, then everyone was doing it. In the low-ceilinged room, the noise sounded too loud.

Robyn felt her cheeks colouring. As a reflex, she held up her hands, then dropped them, thinking it must look as if she was showing off her injuries. 'Thank you. Thanks.' She kept moving, thinking the quicker she could get her tea, the quicker she could get out of there. 'Is everyone else all right? I hope no one else was hurt?' Two along from Donna, Jeremy had already stopped clapping and had folded his arms. The applause took too long to die, Donna continuing alone for a few seconds. 'Well, ah, well. Thanks.' She had made it to the counter and grabbed the nearest roll without seeing what was in it. At the till, she added a tea and a couple of bars of chocolate. For one day, the diet could wait.

Conscious of eyes still watching her, she nodded to Donna as she left and was grateful to find the lift waiting. She inspected the roll: it was cheese and pickle which wasn't her favourite but she was hungry enough to eat anything and the cling film was off before the lift doors closed.

The incident room was empty. The screen was paused on the moment just after Newman had been spotted. Lorraine had zoomed in and Julie's face filled the screen. She turned away from it and added an extra sugar to her tea. By the time Lorraine returned, the food had gone and Robyn felt more settled. She was even considering whether she could copy the CCTV footage and send it to Becky, to let her see what her mother had done. The thought was followed by more practical questions: she couldn't ask one of the team to do such a personal

75

thing for her and she wasn't sure how to do it, assuming it was even legal.

The door banged open. 'Ah, Guv, you're back.' Lorraine hesitated as if waiting for a reaction. 'There wasn't much more so I watched it all rather than wait for you.'

'Good work.' Robyn tried to keep the relief from her face. 'What did you get?'

'There are definitely two lots of protestors and everything kicks off when the second ones arrive. Although there are a lot of people around, the number of people actually involved in the ruck is pretty small. I printed off a couple of bits.' Lorraine pulled over some photos. 'On the right, these are the original protestors. Their banners call for justice for rape victims and the big one is professionally printed with a RAW logo. The new lot has homemade signs which are much more aggressive, like *Rape is Murder.*'

'Can you see who hurt Clyde?'

'I checked but no.' Lorraine shrugged. 'I mean, I really looked. Realistically we can only bring specific charges against two of them. There's the one with the sign; we've got clear shots of her and with your statement, there's no doubt. Then there's this one.' Lorraine pointed at the screen. 'She was the one who first spotted Newman and is standing closest to Clyde – if anyone cracked his ribs, it's her.' She sat back.

The feeling of well-being from the food faded. 'Lorraine …' Her mouth was too dry to continue so she took a sip of tea. 'There's something you should know.'

'Mmm?' Lorraine was searching her handbag.

'She …' Robyn pointed at the screen. 'That woman is my ex-wife.'

Lorraine froze, a packet of mints in her hand, her mouth open. She looked back at the screen, studying the face again. 'Of course you were – I didn't realise you – I'd forgotten you were …' She began playing with her handbag strap. 'Awkward.'

'It's been a long time.' Robyn tried to shrug, to show how relaxed she was until her chest hurt too much. 'Her name is Julie Carmichael and she's Professor of Women's Studies at Avonbridge University – the old Bristol Avon Tech.' Robyn didn't know why she now had a need to say this. 'She's always been an activist, into groups like Real Adult Women but never the violent type. She took Becky on a protest march when she was still in her pram.' The part of Robyn listening to herself was cringing because she must have given the impression she wanted Julie released. 'It doesn't change anything. If Julie's guilty, she's guilty. I just don't think it's appropriate for me to interview her.'

'No – obviously.' Mints spilled onto the desk. 'Bugger. What a day.' Lorraine popped one in her mouth and offered the tube to Robyn. 'How long were you married for?'

'No, thanks.' Now the fact was out, it was easier. 'Only three years.' Robyn took a deep breath. 'Not long after we had Becky, we moved down to Bristol and Julie started having an affair with the estate agent who sold us our new house.'

There was a second of silence then Lorraine laughed. 'If I can go out on a limb, Guv, I think you're better off without her.' A beep made her glance at her phone. 'Hope your daughter takes after you.'

The beginning of a smile drained from Robyn's face. She hadn't yet responded to Becky's text. 'Yeah. There's something else. What about me?' It was better to know.

Frowning, Lorraine's lips scrunched together. 'What do you mean?'

'Clyde's injury – did I cause it? Was it me charging in?' A splash of heat seared her finger: she was crushing the paper cup in her hand, tea slopping over the top.

'What? No!' She met Robyn's eyes. 'No, no, no. You can stop worrying.' Lorraine's look softened, head cocked to one side, then she stood up and came to stand beside Robyn's chair. She reached out, hesitated, then rested her hand on Robyn's shoulder. 'I saw the moment Clyde went down. It was at least a minute before you arrived. The mob had already started on him. And where you came in was off to the side, nowhere near him. It wasn't your fault and if you want more proof I'll show you the film.'

Her hand seemed hot through Robyn's blouse. Robyn shut her eyes. She wanted what Lorraine was saying to be true, even though she knew she had run straight towards Clyde.

Lorraine's hand lifted. There was the sound of shuffling, paper or files. 'Righto. I'd better get ready for these interviews then. Go home, Guv.' The door swung closed, a click from the latch. Robyn opened her eyes. There were splashes of tea on the desk where her hands had been shaking.

9

She hadn't stirred the tea properly and the last mouthful was sickly sweet. When Robyn went back to her desk, her phone showed a new message. She hoped it would be from Becky: it was from Khalid.

SE Media running story, sorry.

For a second she stared at the phone. Her life would be exposed again. After a few seconds of panic, she let out the breath in a long sigh. This was after all what she had considered doing herself, albeit only to Becky. The situation would be in the open and people who didn't share Julie's views would make up their own minds. With more confidence, she reread Becky's text. The angry words were a reminder Becky had inherited her mother's temper: there would be no point in calling while she was still steamed up. Her hands were awkward in the bandages and the text took a long time to type.

Becky, I didn't ask for your mother to be arrested. She may have hurt somebody, so there was no choice. SE Media have some film of what happened. It would be good to talk about this. Love, Dad.

She read the message and added. *Please come down, I really want to see you*. She wavered over whether this was too sentimental, then added. *It's been such a long time*. She pressed send before she could change her mind.

Her plan had been to read through the statements from Shazia's family and friends but she was too restless to settle. After a couple of minutes, she stepped out to the lift and pressed the button for the basement. Once she was through the security door, she took a breath of warm air: the interview corridor had to be the warmest place in the police station. Behind the desk, Martha gave her a rare smile.

'Can you tell me where Lorraine is?' Robyn was already sweating.

'Interview room three. She's talking tactics with the Inspector.'

'Matthew's taking the interview himself?' Robyn saw Martha's attention flick over her shoulder. A skinny man had appeared from the lift, tight trousers finishing an inch above his ankles.

'Can I help you?'

'Evening. Duty lawyer for …' The man checked his file. 'Jocasta Caldicott.'

'The prisoner requested a female lawyer.' Martha checked the file in front of her. 'I can't even send you in to see any of the others – they all did.'

'I know but it's me or nobody.' The man pushed a pair of horn-rim spectacles back onto his nose. 'Ruth was supposed to be on call tonight and she needed to swap because her baby was sick or something.'

There was a pause. The man pulled the strap of his satchel over his head. 'Well, I'm all she's got.'

'Cell four, follow me.' Martha pushed up the desk's flap.

They were back within a minute. 'She wouldn't talk to me alone.' The lawyer didn't sound upset. 'OK, let's get it over with.'

When the woman was brought down, Robyn watched her pick up her bare feet between each step as if she were some sort of bird. The big boots she'd been wearing must have been taken away for analysis. Tiny between the two uniformed officers, she sniffed the air in the interview room suspiciously, snapping her head left and right. The bib of her dungarees was falling forward; from her position in the corridor, Robyn could see the woman's bare chest. Under the angular clavicles, the skin was as flat as hers. The chair next to her lawyer was rejected and the woman squatted on the floor, feet crossed. At a sign from Matthew, the officers picked her up and placed her on the chair. The second they let go of her, she dropped to the floor again, this time with her back to the wall, arms wrapped around her knees.

'Are you quite comfortable down there, Ms Caldicott?' Lorraine sounded as if she was trying not to laugh.

'You can't do this. You've got to respect my beliefs. I might be a Muslim. You couldn't bring a man in then, could you?'

'Are you a Muslim?' Matthew sounded as though he was speaking through gritted teeth.

'I follow the spirit of the earth.' Caldicott's voice was a childish sing-song.

'We'll begin then.' Lorraine pressed the button to record and went through the caution. 'You are here because about ninety minutes ago, you tried to assault a man with a wooden stake. You then attacked a police officer. Can you tell me why you did these things?' There was a pause. 'OK, let's try an easier one. Were you part of demonstration outside this station earlier?'

The woman had buried her head between her knees. 'For the tape, the defendant said "no comment".' Lorraine picked up a pen. 'We'll try and find something you can comment on. Are you a member of any organisations? Like The Sisters of Rage, for example?'

This time Robyn heard the 'no comment'.

'Perhaps you could explain why you had one of their badges on your top when you were arrested?' Lorraine waited only a second before continuing. 'I'd also be interested if you agree with their view that rapists should be castrated?'

'Why are you asking the question?' The lawyer looked up from his case sheet.

'It is our belief Ms Caldicott attacked the man because he was suspected of rape. I want to find out your client's views on the subject.'

The lawyer glanced down. 'Yeah, OK then.'

'Ms Caldicott, what are your views on rape?'

Robyn guessed Lorraine had made the question crass to provoke a response. The woman yawned, jaw fully open, making no attempt to cover her mouth. 'Women are oppressed. Those attacked have a right to defend themselves.'

Lorraine looked down at her. 'Your defence is you believed you were being attacked?'

There was no response. Lorraine frowned. 'If you only say "no comment", Miss Caldicott, then you don't have a defence. I'll try again. Do you have an answer to the charge of assault?' Her fingers were tapping on the table.

The lawyer looked down. His face when he turned back to Lorraine was a mixture of bemusement and exasperation.

'Could you give us a moment? I'd like to talk things through with my client.'

Lorraine stood up. 'Of course.' She began to gather her things.

Matthew rose to his feet. 'While you talk to her, you might want to discuss this.' He placed on the table a CCTV still of the moment the woman had raised the sign above Newman's prone body. 'Five minutes be enough?'

Lorraine closed the door behind her. 'Oh, hello Guv, were you watching? How did I do?'

Robyn smiled. 'When a client plays dumb it's always going to be frustrating.' She nodded to Matthew as he passed, getting a brief acknowledgement. 'You could get her lawyer on your side a bit more – show you share his frustration, get him to realise it's hopeless.'

'Righto, Guv.' She turned to watch the lawyer, now holding the photo down in front of the woman's face. 'Even though the photo was fuzzy, he'd have a job arguing it wasn't her when we've got your statement as well.'

The lawyer left the room, slinging his bag strap over his head. 'She's sacked me.' He did not look very upset about it. 'Apparently, she has someone who will take care of things.' He was mimicking a posh accent. 'Are you intending to charge her tonight?' He squiggled a finger across his mobile.

'Yes, we were planning to.' Lorraine smiled at him, all teeth. Robyn thought she'd taken her advice a little too much. 'Can you stay while we –?'

'Sorry, she made her wishes very clear. She's someone else's problem. Bye.' He turned for the lift, phone already to his ear. 'Hi sweetie, good news … hello?'

Robyn glanced into the room, then felt a flash of panic as it appeared to be empty. Pressing her face against the glass, she could now see Caldicott, lying in a foetal position on her side, under the table.

'Even though she's not co-operating, we should check if she needs help.' Robyn's breath steamed up the window.

'What makes you think she needs help? I had a look at her record. Her family home is an Elizabethan manor in the west country worth a couple of million quid. She's got the family solicitor on speed-dial and plenty of money to bail her out. I'm sure she makes her parents proud.' Lorraine dropped her voice. 'Expelled from a posh school for vandalism, this will be her third assault conviction. You can imagine one day she could get carried away and kill someone.'

'Right, let's get this done.' Matthew had returned, his cheeks flushed pink.

Caldicott refused to move from under the table, so the charges were repeated, to ensure she'd heard. When the officers came to take her back to her cell, it required two to physically lift her out.

'Ah, Guv? What about the other one?' There was a pause. 'She's in cell six.'

'We go on the evidence. Does the CCTV give a clear shot of Carmichael assaulting Clyde or Newman?'

Lorraine's lips were pressed together. She blinked. 'No. What we can see is that she identifies Newman and is the closest person to Clyde once the crowd closes in.'

'Clyde mentioned he bashed heads with someone. Unlike the incident with Newman, there is the possibility his injuries were not caused deliberately.' Robyn breathed in, out. 'I'm no fan of my ex-wife or her lunatic-fringe friends but we can't create offences where they may not exist. Fell wants this closed tonight. We'll charge Caldicott with assault and the rest with affray and threatening behaviour. They'll all get bail: it's the best we can do.' She paused. 'Matthew, do you agree?'

'I've missed something here – ex-wife?' Matthew's jaw clenched. 'OK, not tonight. I agree, if we can't see the crime, we can't use it. Could you finish off please, Lorraine.'

Lorraine looked between them. 'Yes, sir.' She turned away.

10

After everything had been entered onto the computer system, Robyn walked out into the sodden evening. Unable to keep a grip on the steering wheel, she kept her speed low as she drove home, thinking about nothing. It was only when she was settled on the sofa she remembered the morning's shopping which was still in the boot of the car. The experience seemed a very long time ago.

Her mobile rang. She took a deep breath before answering. 'Chloe, how are you?'

'I'm OK, Guv.' Chloe's voice sounded brittle. 'There's something you should know.'

Robyn sat up, forcing her mind back to the afternoon. 'Tell me.'

'You remember I got a message from Ravi? Well, he was in a bad way. He was certain there was someone else involved in Shazia's accident because he said she would never want to kill herself. He felt he had to do something. I tried to persuade him to leave it to you but –'

'What did he do?' It was one thing for Ravi to risk his career;

she didn't want Chloe's to be implicated too because of a sense of loyalty.

'He decided to go to the hospital in London and talk to Shazia's doctors, make sure they treated the fall as a crime and collected evidence. I thought it was best to go along, to keep an eye on him.' The words came out in a rush. 'When we got there, Shazia was already in surgery. We met one of the nurses afterwards. She'd taken samples and she also said Shazia had marks she didn't think were consistent with a fall. It looks like Dr Brockwell was right and she was raped.'

'Does Ravi know this?'

'Yes. You can imagine what that did to him.'

'Where is he and where are the samples?'

'I finally got him to go home. I've got the samples here and I'll drop them in tomorrow.'

'And how is Ravi?'

'How do you think?' It sounded like Chloe was at the end of her patience. 'Sorry, Guv, he's in an awful bind. There's a lot of stigma about suicide so if Shazia jumped, people may condemn her for trying to kill herself but if he tells them she was raped, that makes it worse. And he feels he's got to catch the bastard that did this to prove to his family being a copper is worthwhile because they all wanted him to be a doctor or something.' She took a ragged breath. 'You see, Guv?'

'He shouldn't be telling anyone anything because he's not working this case.' Kneading the cushion with her free hand, Robyn tried to think of better words. 'Chloe, I said you need to tell me everything and I meant it. For a start, what made Ravi think something was up? Did he go into the hotel room?' She let the silence lengthen.

'Yeah.' Chloe sounded close to tears. 'He just wanted to help.'

'He's just added another set of DNA to the crime scene.'

'He definitely didn't touch anything.' The words came too quickly.

'What did he do?' Robyn let her head roll back against the sofa. 'Come on.'

'Well, it all sounded really confusing, Guv. Ravi was dancing and the first thing he knew was when the band stopped playing. His uncle made an announcement to say there had been an accident and everything was cancelled. Ravi went to see if he could help and found out Shazia was hurt. From the amount he talks about her, they're pretty close.' Chloe paused for breath. 'He said he went into the room but then got so upset he came straight back down.'

'He has got to accept he must stay away.' She waited for an answer, gripping the cushion, until the silence became oppressive. 'How did the operation go?'

'She's still alive.' Chloe sighed. 'Everything they've done so far is just to stabilise her. Now they have to wait and see what damage was done. She's in an induced coma to give the swelling on the brain time to go down – that could be days or weeks. Or never.'

'I know it's hard and I'm glad you were there for Ravi.' There was something at the back of Robyn's mind, staying out of her focus. 'This has been a shock for all of us. The best thing we can do for Shazia is find out what happened and to do that, Ravi must keep out of the investigation. I'll need your help with that.'

'Yes, Guv.' Chloe's words were no more than a whisper. 'Please don't be too hard on him.'

Robyn scavenged through the fridge for a scratch supper and carried it through into the lounge. The ten o'clock news finished and the coverage shifted to the regions. To her relief, the first item was about the royal opening of a charity's new office in Maidstone. She took a bite of dry cheese. The picture changed back to the newsreader.

The start of a week of events to mark the one hundred and fiftieth birthday of the feminist author Faith Gregory, better known as Edmund Napier Loveless, was marred by violence today. Outside Meresbourne police station, protesters clashed with police causing an officer to be taken to hospital where his condition is described as stable. And now we go live to Meresbourne and our reporter, Amanda Clapton.

The screen split to include a woman standing outside the Lady Ann hotel under an umbrella, a bulky scarf around her neck. Next to her, a pile of bouquets and flowers was visible in the spotlight.

What's the latest you can tell us Amanda?

Well Jenny, I now understand the cause of the disturbance can be traced back here, to the Lady Ann Hotel. This afternoon, a guest at a wedding made an apparent suicide attempt and a source at the hotel told me the police are linking this to an allegation of sexual assault. Trouble started at the police station when protestors learned that a suspect for that assault had been released without charge. Around thirty demonstrators were involved and there were a number of arrests.

Robyn resisted an urge to shout at the television. She wondered who had been talking.

So have the police charged anyone with the assault?

Not so far, Jenny, back to you. The newsreader turned to face to the camera. *Protests are continuing this evening with a march through Meresbourne, called a slut walk. There will be a vigil outside the Lady Ann Hotel at midnight.*

Behind the newsreader, the display changed to the stern face of Edmund Napier Loveless. *Many years after Loveless wrote 'a woman is petted when a kitten, then drowned when she shows her claws' her words are still relevant today. And now over to Stephen for the region's weather.*

Thank you, Jenny. Well, it looks like autumn is really here because it's going to be a cold, wet night across most of Kent, continuing into Sunday. I want to say 'wrap up warm' to those people taking part in the march tonight but maybe that's not quite in the spirit of things.

Robyn muted the television to shut up the inane chuckling. The joy of home-delivery shopping meant she had been able to buy a bottle of single malt even though none of her identification paperwork yet matched her new name. It was very tempting to have a slug to blur the events of the day although that could be the start of a slippery slope. She told herself she could have one next time she had something to celebrate, filled the kettle for her morning tea and went to bed.

She wasn't sure how long the phone had been ringing before she woke up sufficiently to recognise what the sound was. The phone screen said it was twenty past two.

'Lorraine.' Robyn felt a strap of her nightdress slip from her shoulder.

'Guv, we've got a body.'

In the first muzzy moments after sleep, the urgent voice in Robyn's ear could have been in the room with her. She pulled the duvet close, wanting to cover herself. 'Any ID?'

'Yeah, that's why you need to see it. Ah, here's Kelly now to check him over. I'm on the Docks estate, I'll text you the address. Could you come down? Thanks.' She put the phone down.

Now wide awake, Robyn shivered, wondering whose death was important enough to make Lorraine call her. The second more irreverent thought was whether the Australian pathologist, Dr Kelly Shepherd, would still be wearing his usual shorts.

She decided to take the shorter route through the centre of town, wipers on against the drizzle. As part of the council's cost-cutting, street lights now were turned off at midnight and the low mist added menace to the familiar roads. Robyn was sticking to the speed limit and found herself being tail-gated by a minibus, its high headlights dazzling in her mirror. She turned off Bridge Street onto Quayside. Here, a levy on the riverside clubs' late licenses paid for the lights to stay on all night after a councillor's son had been the latest reveller to fall into the Gadd while staggering home from a night out. To her annoyance, the minibus followed her. When Robyn slowed down because of the pedestrians walking in and out of the pools of light, the minibus jinked past her – she was not surprised to see it was a taxi.

None of the people coming towards her looked to be having a good night out. Two men carried another man between them, his legs dragging on the cobbles. Someone was being sick into the river. A typical Saturday night in Meresbourne. Face screwed up, one girl seemed to be walking on tiptoe: her feet were bare, a pair of high shoes clutched in one hand.

About fifty yards ahead, the taxi had stopped outside the Quiksilva nightclub, clouds rising from its exhaust. Beyond, the road appeared to be full of people: Robyn stopped the car. Everyone she could see was wearing a short skirt, some holding banners, the words illegible in the rain and darkness. One walked through the lights with just a bra on her top half: the temperature gauge in the car showed six degrees. Robyn was glad to be ignored, the crowd were focusing on the club. A banner flapped straight in the wind and she could read … *xy Stripping Sat* …

The windscreen was steaming up and rubbing just spread the smears so Robyn got out and stood, leaning on the door, listening to snatches of chanting from the women clustered around the steps leading up to the club's main entrance. Movement caught her eye: a knot of people had appeared from the side of the building. A few shouts, then she heard screams, sounding like rage not pain. From the top of the steps, a man was soaking the crowd with a jet from a high-pressure washer. At the same time, men in dark coats hustled a group of young women towards the taxi. The chanting rose in volume from those out of range of the hose. One of the men heaved open the taxi's side door, the rest stood guard as the young women scrambled inside. The door was banged shut and the taxi tried to reverse. The jet of water was directed onto its windscreen, the spray shooting in all directions, soaking anyone who tried to get close. Now moving, the taxi sounded its horn. When it reversed past her, Robyn got a glimpse of scared, pale faces in the back. There was no sign of any of Matthew's uniform team but the protestors seemed to have lost their unity. Some banged on the club's door; others began straggling towards the town centre. Robyn ducked back into her car, locking the door. She waited until the way ahead was clear and eased the car forward.

Approaching the ugly tower blocks of the docks estate, blue lights bouncing off Flotilla block showed her where to go. In the car park, screens had been set up around a vehicle whose roof rack was just visible. Robyn parked close to a car with three girls draped over the bonnet. They were dressed for a club and seemed oblivious to the damp; when a technician appeared, they whooped. When he raised his hand to them, he was rewarded with cheers.

Lorraine shuffled out through a gap in the screens, pulling her anorak's hood up.

'Evening, Guv, thanks for coming.'

'After earlier, I thought we'd used up our quota of bad news for the day.' Robyn put up her umbrella. 'What now?' As she walked forward, her foot lost traction with the ground and skidded forward: only by windmilling her arms was she able to stay upright. There was laughter from the girls, bringing back an unpleasant echo of the shop assistants.

'You all right, Guv?' Lorraine stopped. 'These damp leaves are a menace.'

Rain dripped from the tarpaulins. Peering through the gap as she forced on gloves, Robyn could see a decal of a hand holding a spanner. 'JN Plumbing and Heating, that's a coincidence. The guy we interviewed this afternoon was a plumber. Newman – was it John Newman?'

'Jake Newman, Guv and it's him.'

'What?' Robyn put a hand on the grimy van to steady herself. 'He's dead? How?' She was calculating timings, wondering what state Newman had been in when he escaped the riot. She should have followed him, found him, not just tried to call. The likelihood was a death so soon after leaving a police station would lead to an investigation.

'Not sure yet, we should know more soon.' Laughter echoed from the inside of the van: something had amused Dr Shepherd. They both looked over. Lorraine shook her head. 'I couldn't do crime scene, it's too grim.'

'What do we know?' Robyn's hand was filthy where she had touched the van.

'We had an anonymous call from an unregistered mobile just before two.' Lorraine shivered. 'When the first response got here, the van was unlocked and the back doors open.'

There was a swishing sound and a technician in full protective gear shuffled through the gap. With a mask on, it was impossible to tell who they were. A gloved hand held out something in a plastic bag. 'Dr Shepherd found this in the deceased's pocket.' The voice was female.

Robyn took the bag in both hands, conscious that the bandages made it hard to hold on to things. She peered through the plastic to see a nylon wallet, the Spurs logo almost obscured by dirt. 'So his wallet wasn't taken? Interesting.' She managed to pull open the wallet through the plastic, seeing a thick wad of twenty-pound notes jumbled with business cards. As she turned the bag, a photo slid to the bottom: a young woman holding a baby, both with big smiles. She handed the wallet to Lorraine. 'Reasonable amount of cash, too.'

'From his file, he actually lives in New Town.' Lorraine sneezed.

'Bless you.' Robyn reached into her bag for the stash of tissues.

'Thanks. You're prepared for anything.' After wiping her nose, Lorraine tucked the tissue into her sleeve. 'A plumber goes places at all hours. Could be an emergency job?'

'Possibly.' Robyn looked left and right. 'This car park is used by both Fleet and Flotilla blocks. Let's hope we can find a diary, otherwise we'll need to run house-to-house calls through both towers to see if anyone called him out. His mobile number's on here, we can find out recent calls.'

A voice came from the back of the van. 'Hey, Lorra, check this out.'

Lorraine looked away, as if embarrassed. Her gesture made Robyn bite back the question of why she was happy to have her name mangled. Her predecessor, DI Prentiss, would have demanded to know all the details: he had loved mocking his juniors. 'Shall we see what Kelly's found?'

They had to edge along the side of the van in single file, Robyn in front. She rounded the bonnet of the truck to where Kelly stood by the back door. 'Hey, Robyn, I didn't know you'd arrived.' Lorraine edged into view and Kelly regained his breeziness. 'I'm always stoked when I get a call for Meresbourne, you do keep handing me some doozies.'

Robyn hesitated, not wanting to admit she wasn't sure exactly what he was talking about.

The body lay on the van's metal floor. 'Deceased is a white male, no point in me estimating how old he is because you already know his name. All I can say is he's had a really bad day because he seems to have been beaten up twice. Look here.' Kelly directed his torch beam. 'You see the cut on his lip? Done just before or even after death because there's no bruising. However, this …' He angled the beam lower. '… was done a number of hours before.'

In the poor light, Robyn had to lean forward to see. Visible above the neckline of Newman's t-shirt was a dark, irregular mark.

'He was caught by a mob earlier. He didn't stay around for treatment, so I don't know whether he was hurt or not.' As a reflex, Robyn checked her watch. 'This was between five and six o'clock this afternoon. I guess there could have been internal injuries.'

Kelly leaned against the van. 'OK, useful to know. I'll check everything tomorrow.' He pushed back the sleeve of his coverall to show the big sports watch with numbers glowing in the dark. 'I mean today.'

'How long has he been dead?' A gust of wind hit the tent; Lorraine huddled into her coat.

'At least a couple of hours, I'd say. Oh, he was covered with this when we looked at him.' Kelly shone the torch at a grey piece of fabric now in a large plastic bag. 'Looks like a dust sheet. Certainly a few interesting stains on it. There's also one minor detail I want to know.'

Robyn could also feel the cold and wished he'd stop being so cheerful. 'What's that?'

Kelly took off his gloves. 'I don't know what killed him.' He ran the beam of his torch up and down the body. 'Sure he was beaten up but all of the wounds look superficial and he's a young, strong lad, so none of them should have been fatal. I need to open him up. Anyway, if you want to take a look before we get everything bagged up, he's all yours.' With a wave, he slipped out of the tent.

11

Jake Newman's body lay diagonally across the floor of his van, legs curled to fit into the space between the racking on either side. His head lay on his left hand, pillowed on a pile of rags, the face peaceful.

'He doesn't look dead.' Lorraine's torch beam was shaking a little. 'Just like he's asleep.'

'So the question we have to answer is did he crawl in here himself or did someone put him here?' Robyn shivered again. 'If you'd been beaten up, why would you sleep in your van when you've got a home to go to?'

They moved around to the cab. Receipts, invoices and catalogues were scattered across the top of the dashboard. Under a day-old copy of the *Daily Journal* on the passenger seat, Robyn found a sweatshirt and a clear lunch-box, empty apart from one brown apple core. In the corner of the windscreen was a Meresbourne Town sticker. 'Tart.'

'What did you say?' Lorraine looked up from her search under the seat.

'I said he was a tart.' Robyn was annoyed for having spoken aloud and having to explain herself. 'Local people will see the Dockers' sticker and think he supports the team when in fact he supports Spurs. It's all for show.'

'Maybe he does support Meresbourne and also wants a team that wins occasionally?' Lorraine squinted back down under the seat. 'There's something under here.'

Robyn shone her torch into the door pocket. She lifted out chocolate wrappers, a tub of chewing gum and a half-used pack of hand wipes. Scrawled across a piece of Lady Ann-crested notepaper was an address in the industrial estate and the figure £350, underlined three times.

Lorraine was crouched in the foot well, stretching her arm under the seat. 'Something's under this seat. It feels like a gun.' Wriggling further in, she gave a grunt of satisfaction and slid her arm out, turning to sit with her feet hanging out of the door.

'What have you got?' Robyn leaned over.

With a gulp of laughter, Lorraine held something up. 'OK, maybe he's not a master criminal.' She turned, bringing her hand into the light, pointing something shaped like a pistol into the air. 'Bang.' She opened her fingers: the lime green and orange colouring didn't look like a firearm.

'What on earth?' Robyn picked the thing up finding the back legs and torso of some plastic animal. There was a moment of silence. 'Did you find any kind of diary or a phone?'

Lorraine shook her head. 'The diary will probably be on his phone.'

'Yes. There doesn't look to be any more we can do here.' After saying goodbye to Kelly, they sat in Lorraine's car. 'Has he been reported missing?' Robyn held her hands to the vent where warm air was finally starting to flow.

'Not as of an hour ago, Guv.'

'We'd better do the call tonight.' She thought of the jeans she was wearing. 'Would you mind doing the talking? I'm not really dressed for this.'

'OK, Guv, I'll meet you there.'

Robyn trudged across to her own car. More than anything, she wanted to go back to bed and sleep. She was grateful for the sat-nav telling her where to go because the New Town estate was a confusing maze of identikit blocks of boxy houses and low-rises. She parked next to Lorraine, who was leaning against her car chatting into her phone.

'Hi, Guv. Just checking something with Kelly because we couldn't see his left hand. Our man was wearing a wedding ring but didn't he say earlier he lived with his girlfriend? He likes complicating things.'

'Like the football – all for show. Let's get this over with.' The temperature was dropping with the clearing skies.

'I had a look at the numbers.' Lorraine pointed up to a lighted window on the top floor of a three-storey block. 'Good thing we came as it looks like someone's waiting up for him.'

When Lorraine pressed the buzzer, the front door clicked off the latch after a couple of seconds. On the top floor, Lorraine rang the bell of number sixteen. There was a small cry, then a second of muffled speech before the door was opened. A young woman in a dressing gown stood with a baby in her arms. She stared at them, one hand tense on the door. The baby made another whimpering cry, struggling in her arms so she had to let go of the door to contain it.

'Mrs Newman? I'm sorry to disturb you so late.' Lorraine held out her warrant card. 'May we come in?'

The woman's eyes dropped for a second before turning into the flat. Robyn followed her, edging past the clutter lining the hall; a push-chair, toolboxes, packets of fixings. The television was on in the living area: people in bikinis sat around a pool sipping cocktails, the sound muted. The girl settled at one end of a sofa, laying the baby on her lap. 'I'd just got him to sleep.'

Lorraine stepped into the pool of light from a standard lamp. 'Mrs Newman, I'm afraid –'

'I'm not Mrs Newman. Just Miss Land. Don't be fooled by this.' She held up her left hand, a cluster of diamonds catching the light. 'He didn't want to get married, even when this one was born. Said if we wore the rings, what was the difference?' The baby twisted, grizzling. 'He's teething. Every night the same.' She reached for a bright green plastic ring on the side table.

'Miss Land.' Lorraine waited until the woman's eyes lifted from the baby. 'I'm sorry to have to tell you, Mr Newman is dead.'

A curtain of hair hid Land's face. 'Dead?' After two quick breaths, she wrapped the baby into her arms, causing a whimper of protest which became a stuttering cry as she clutched him. When her face moved into the lamplight, tear tracks showed on her cheeks.

Lorraine sat on the other end of the sofa, placing a hand on Land's shoulder. 'I'm afraid we don't know how he died yet. We will find out.'

Feeling redundant, Robyn moved into the tiny kitchen area and put the kettle on. There were mugs on the draining board and she found tea bags in the second cupboard she opened. She added milk and sugar and carried a cup over to the girl.

'That's J-J-Jake's mug.' The girl's eyes lost focus in tears.

Robyn retreated, nearly standing on a fluffy toy. She found a plain mug in another cupboard and transferred the tea over the sink. When she returned, the baby was in Lorraine's arms and the girl was curled into a ball, knees to her chest, hugging a cushion. It was hard to tell who was least comfortable, Lorraine or the baby. She was holding him with exaggerated care away from her body, causing the baby to lean towards her.

Robyn squatted down in front of Land, feeling her leg protest at the movement. 'Is there someone we can call – a neighbour, your mother?'

'Cassie.' The voice was muffled by fabric. Robyn looked around:

the phone was easy to spot in a gold and crystal-studded case. 'Could you unlock it for me and I'll call Cassie?' She put the phone down on the edge of the sofa.

One hand reached out as Land uncurled a little, her hand flicking over the keypad.

When Robyn took the phone back, the screen showed a picture of Newman holding the baby up, making him wave.

Robyn scrolled through the contacts until she found a number for Cassie. The phone at the other end rang and rang. When the line cut, she rang again. This time it was picked up in a few seconds.

'What the? It's the middle of the night, babes?'

'Cassie, I am sorry to disturb you. I'm a police officer. I'm here with Miss Land. I'm afraid she's had some bad news and needs a friend. Could you come over, please?'

'Whaaaa? Say again – something's happened to Jess?'

'No, Miss Land asked me to call you. She's very upset.'

'No way, this is a wind-up. Jake, if this is you messing around.'

'No, miss, this is DI Robyn Bailley.' Now was not the time to worry that her voice had not passed. 'We're here because Jake has been in an accident.'

'Let me speak to Jess.'

Robyn turned. 'I'm sorry, she'd like to speak to you.' She placed the phone next to the cushion.

It was lifted slowly and the girl spoke. 'Cassie.' The phone dropped from her hand.

When Robyn picked up the phone, the line was dead. She looked across at Lorraine. 'I hope that means she's coming.'

'Guv.' Lorraine looked down at her shoulder, where the baby had dribbled. 'Can you take him? I'm going to clean myself up.'

Robyn just had time to arrange her arms before Lorraine passed him over and went to the kitchen. Looking down into his crumpled face, Robyn remembered what had soothed Becky when she'd been a baby and began humming, holding the baby close so he could feel the vibrations through her chest. Beside her on the sofa, Jess's phone was still unlocked. With a quick glance towards the prone form, Robyn picked the phone up and began flicking through the multiple messages. There was a contact, 'J'. The last message had been sent just before midnight: *when are u coming home?* There was no answer. She scrolled up: the previous messages had been sent on Thursday.

Back in half hour.

pick up milk when you come.

After an hour: *Where are u?*

Met Axe still in pub lol xx

There was a knock at the door. Lorraine turned the tap off and went to answer it. There was a brief exchange in the corridor and a young woman in a tracksuit charged in. Without glancing at Robyn, she sat on the edge of the sofa and flung her arms around Jess.

Robyn stood up, careful not to wake the baby who had subsided into sleep.

From the sofa, there was a low murmuring. 'Sweetheart, I just heard.' Cassie held Jess's face, looking into her eyes. 'There now, there now. You'll be all right, you've got your mates. We'll look after you.'

Lorraine caught Robyn's eye then looked at her watch, then the door.

Robyn considered. The questions they needed to ask could wait until the morning. She nodded to Lorraine, then looked down at the baby.

Lorraine was already in the hallway. Robyn leaned over the back of the sofa. 'Miss Land. I'm very sorry for your loss. I'll give you my card so you can call me if you need anything.' Shifting the baby to her left arm, she tried to open her handbag one-handed, causing it to swing forward, knocking against the back of the sofa and dislodging her make-up bag. 'Damn.' It was lucky neither of the women on the sofa seemed to be listening.

'Lorraine, can you do this?'

Lorraine stuck her head around the door. 'Do what?'

'Put the baby in the buggy.' Robyn wondered why she was whispering.

Shaking her head, Lorraine stepped back.

'Just take him.' Robyn was in no mood for squeamishness. 'I need to finish here.'

Lorraine took the baby back, eyes wide. Robyn laid her business card on the table. 'We're leaving now and will be back in the morning.'

Jess broke from Cassie's arms. 'Those bitches, did they attack him again? That was your fault! You made people think he'd done something he didn't.' She grabbed a cushion, swinging it towards Robyn's face.

Recoiling, Robyn tried to hide the stabbing pain in her chest from the sudden movement.

'It's all your fault.' Jess swept something off the table and flung it. 'If you hadn't pulled him in.' The baby's teething ring hit the wall behind Robyn's head.

'I'm sorry for your loss.' Robyn hurried into the hallway.

Lorraine was struggling to get the baby's limbs through the straps as they flopped, heavy with sleep. She stood up with a sigh. 'Why do they make these things so complicated?' As Robyn held open the door, she walked out into the lobby. 'That was a bit uncalled for. Are you OK?'

They started down the stairs. 'All I need is some sleep.' Robyn kept her hand on the bannister to keep herself in a straight line. 'We've got lots of obvious conclusions we could jump to and they're probably all wrong. Tomorrow.'

'Sure. Oh, Guv. Can I ask you something?'

'Of course.' Robyn hoped this was going to be quick.

'Would you support me going for sergeant?' For once, there was no hint of humour in Lorraine's face.

'Where did that come from?' Robyn stood up straighter, willing herself to concentrate. 'Yes, yes I would certainly support your promotion. You're an excellent officer. Now can we discuss this more in the morning?'

Lorraine grinned. 'Thanks, Guv. I'll meet you at the station at, say, ten-thirty?'

SUNDAY 18 SEPTEMBER

12

The alarm buzzed at six as usual because Robyn had forgotten to turn it off. After the bleary acknowledgement of what time it was, the racket the birds were making meant she didn't think she'd get back to sleep. In the bathroom, the morning light full in her face was not flattering. Her chin and neck were red and blotchy from the electrolysis, merging into darker patches of bruising across the top of her chest. Reaching into the cabinet for toothpaste brought a dull ache rather than a sharp pain: this was positive though she wondered whether she would have to cancel the full body wax arranged for the following week. It would be a nuisance because the newly visible hairs across her chest would become more noticeable and she would no longer be able to wear her favourite blouse, the red one with a slight cleavage.

Most disappointing was her hair which was a flat mass where the shaping had grown out. An insipid line at the roots showed her natural hair colour. Of all the relief and happiness Robyn was enjoying from now being able to be express herself as she wanted, there were some things she thought she would never understand. One of them was how women considered going to the hairdresser to be a pleasure when you were stuck in a chair for hours with something foul-smelling on your head. She added buying a home hair-dye to her mental list along with rebooking the missed manicure for when her hands were out of bandages.

Restless, Robyn drifted downstairs to get a cup of tea. At the kitchen table, watching a blue tit cling upside-down to the bird feeder, she tried to convince herself it was a good idea to have got up early as she still could do all of the things she'd planned before going into the station. Trying to look on the bright side, she reasoned the best way to deal with whether she would see Becky or not was to act as if the visit was going ahead. She retrieved the shopping bags from the car and set to work. When she had finished, the spare room was transformed. Everything looked co-ordinated, even though the new sheets still had creases from the packet. Standing in the doorway, Robyn was ashamed to realise she had no idea whether purple was still her daughter's favourite colour or whether she had grown out of it. She decided to call Becky later because it was impossible to convey how much she missed her by text message.

Her flush of energy spent, Robyn put the radio on and a gentle burble about gardening was the backdrop as she made breakfast. The pips sounded and she turned up the volume.

Seven o'clock on North Kent FM and here's the news with Stacey Betters. A young woman remains in a coma after falling from a balcony at the Lady Ann Hotel during a family wedding on Saturday. There was a second of silence. *In Meresbourne, a protest outside the police station by groups associated with feminism took place on the opening day of a festival celebrating the author Edmund Napier Loveless. The commemorative week was formally launched at the town hall yesterday by the leading broadcaster and academic Dr Felicity Bergmann.* Another second of silence. *The Docker's new manager, Craig Hellaway, defended his squad after the first three games of the season have produced only one point. He emphasised the squad's youth and remains confident of a top-half finish.*

And now the weather, it looks like the current unseasonable cold will be with us for a few more days.

There was a thump from the hallway. Robyn fetched the *Meresbourne Sunday Gazette*, wincing as she bent to pick it up. The headline promised an exclusive, *Horror at the Hotel* under Ady's by-line. Two photos filled the front page: the bride and groom walking into the ballroom, Shazia circled in the crowd, mouth open, one arm in the air, petals of confetti frozen as they left her hand. The other was of guests leaving the hotel with their heads down, walking past the taped-off area where Shazia's body had lain. Ady had been thorough: he had a member of staff describing how the room looked after the forensic teams had left and words from an unnamed 'close friend', probably Jade, describing Shazia's ambition to open a beach bar in the Maldives.

She opened the paper. There was a fuzzy shot taken of the demonstration and a long-range picture of the paramedics loading Clyde into the ambulance with a terse comment from Fell. Robyn's attention was caught by the words underneath a shot of two pensioners holding a RAW banner between them.

'We were there to protest about the shockingly low conviction rates for rape', Philippa, 67, told me. 'It was all calm until some radicals turned up and everything became violent. I saw what they were doing to that policeman', added Sue, 64. 'That's what gives protests a bad name. We've been all over the place and it has always been peaceful protests that get results.' Philippa and Sue have a long history of protest. 'We were at the nuclear sites and it was all about standing your ground. You didn't need to sink to the fascists' level of violence.'

There was a double-page spread on events for the Loveless celebrations. Activities were taking place around Meresbourne and the villages and Robyn felt a twinge of sympathy for Matthew trying to cover them all when there was even an event in Willingdon nature reserve, where someone was holding a Gaia-worship ceremony. The report of the launch at the Town Hall had a picture of Dr Bergmann giving the camera a fierce look over her glasses. The column described the speech as 'robust' and highlighted the closing statement.

What was true at the time of Loveless is true today: at every turn, women are under attack. Physically, psychologically, the world is a constant barrage of oppression. It is time we held those who abuse to account, in the only way they understand.

Folding the paper over, Robyn started reading the back page, losing herself in the report of the Dockers' Saturday performance.

A battery warning beep from her phone drew Robyn's attention. Her eyes felt heavy and the main section of the paper had slipped out of her hands to the floor: she had dozed off in the chair. The short sleep had not refreshed her and, as she prepared to leave, thoughts seemed to take a long time to cross her mind. She kept it slow as she drove to the police station.

'Morning, Guv.' Bounding up the steps, Lorraine joined her, looking her up and down. 'Are you sure you're OK?' There was no clue she'd been up half the night apart from a hint of darker skin under her eyes.

'Morning. I'm fine, thanks. Did Graham get back to you any time?'

'Not heard from him at all. Maybe he's hungover from the excitement of your team scoring a point.' Lorraine heaved open the door.

'That's not funny.' Robyn frowned, counting the likely number of missed calls without a response. 'I haven't heard anything about Newman's body on the local news yet. Guess it's only a matter of time, though – I suppose they don't normally have this much going on.'

'Yeah, a rape leading to an attempted suicide and now a suspicious death. You wait ages for a good story and then three come at once.' There was a hard edge to Lorraine's voice. 'Where do you want to start, Guv?'

'We start by taking the lift.' She pressed the button for the second floor. 'I want you to lead on Shazia's rape. It's the sort of case you need to have under your belt to move up to sergeant.'

108

Lorraine was grinning as they walked into the CID office. At his desk, Ravi was hunched over a computer. From under the hood of his green sweatshirt, there was the outline of headphones and a steady, thumping beat. When he glanced over to them, there was still a smear of red dye in the centre of his forehead.

'Ravi.' Robyn paused, wondering how approach things in a neutral way. 'You weren't due to be on call today.'

Only Ravi's eyes moved as he scanned his screen.

'Ravi.' Robyn raised her voice and realised it was futile. She moved in front of him and mimed taking off the headphones.

Reaching for his phone, Ravi turned off the music. He pushed back the hood, sliding the headphones around his neck.

'How are you, Ravi?' Robyn moved closer to be able to read the sheets he was working on.

Shrugging, Ravi looked back at her without speaking.

'What are you doing?'

'I'm going through the guest list and checking everyone for criminal records.' Ravi tapped the page in front of him. 'Found four so far.'

'I appreciate you are anxious to help.' Robyn found herself tensing. 'But, because we are talking about your cousin, you cannot be involved.' There was no sign of acknowledgement as Ravi began typing again. 'Lorraine and I are here, on Sunday, to continue the investigation. If you don't believe we're going to give this case the attention it deserves, then you don't know either of us very well.'

Turning over the sheet, Ravi began scribbling on the other side.

'I gave you a direct order, Ravi.' A stiffening of his jaw was the only sign he might have heard. 'You cannot work on this case because you are a suspect.'

Ravi stood up so fast, his chair cannoned backwards, spinning into the one behind. 'A suspect? Me, attack Shazia? If you think something twisted like that, I really do need to do this all myself.'

Lorraine stepped forward. 'Don't be so precious, you know what she meant. Just like any crime, everyone who was in the hotel is a suspect until we eliminate them. The fact that you can't accept you're included shows why you can't be involved.'

'You didn't know Shazia! She had big plans, wanted to go places.' Ravi ran his hands through his hair. 'I have to try and convince her parents someone will get punished when there are loads of cases which just got dropped when things were difficult. I've seen them on the system.'

Losing patience, Robyn fetched the nearest chair and moved it to the centre of the floor, then pulled her own forward. She wanted some of the tension to dissipate before trying to answer. She sat down. 'Ravi, come here, sit down and we will talk this through.'

Lorraine shuffled her chair next to Robyn. 'Come on, Ravi. You aren't Batman. We've got to do this as a team.'

Glowering, Ravi slouched forward and slid into the empty chair, crossing his arms.

'You've raised a serious allegation, that I do not investigate cases properly.' Robyn saw Ravi's mouth open and her hand rose to stop him.

'You've had your say. Now listen to me.' Robyn paused, watching Ravi's eyes widen as he stared at the bandages. 'You know full well the cases you're referring to were dropped when DI Prentiss ran this team. Since then, we have only given up on a case when there are no more leads to follow, not because we can't be bothered or because the girl isn't pretty enough.' She took a perverse pleasure in seeing Ravi wince. 'Justice for Shazia means dealing with evidence without prejudice and without making any assumptions. You are off this investigation, and there is no room for discussion. Lorraine will lead it with my support.' She paused. Ravi's head had fallen: he was staring at the floor.

A burst of music cut through the silence. Lorraine scrambled for her mobile. 'Sorry, Guv. It's Kelly.' Pushing the chair back, she headed for the corner of the room.

Ravi watched her go. When he swivelled back, his eyes met Robyn's for the first time. 'What am I supposed to do then?'

'Last night, we were called out to a suspicious death.' Now was not the time to mention who it was. 'Graham will lead and you will support.' She paused again. 'Just to make it clear: if you intrude in any way onto Lorraine's investigation, I will suspend you, which will be bad for your career. Do you understand?'

A loud laugh from Lorraine made Ravi's mumbled reply inaudible. 'Sorry, I missed that.'

'What am I going to say to my family?'

'You tell them the truth. To make sure the investigation is robust, we have to have an independent officer. It's nothing to do with how good you are, you're just too close.' For the first time, Robyn felt sorry for him. 'Would it help if I were to meet your family, tell them what we're going to do?'

Before she had finished, Ravi was already shaking his head. 'No, Guv. Thanks but no. Probably better Lorraine does that.'

'Because your family don't approve of what I'm doing.' It came out before she could stop herself.

Ravi pressed his lips together, his skin paling.

'Whew. Kelly's got a cause of death for Newman and you'll never guess what it is.' Lorraine plonked herself back onto her chair. 'Come on Ravi, your starter for ten. Male found dead, lying in the back of his own van: he'd been in a scuffle earlier but all the visible injuries were superficial. What killed him?'

It was tempting to pull rank and cut across Lorraine to finish with Ravi though when she looked across, she saw Ravi's shoulders had relaxed. It was a confrontation Robyn hadn't been looking forward to and now the moment had gone.

Ravi gazed at the ceiling. 'I don't know – strangled?'

'No!' Lorraine rolled her eyes. 'You'd have bruising and marks. I said only minor stuff visible.'

'OK. Poison.'

'Nope. Try again.'

'Heart condition, one of those undetected things?'

111

'Nope.' Lorraine smiled. 'One more guess and if you don't get it, I'll tell you because this could take all day.'

Ravi appeared to concentrate, brow furrowing. 'He – was – he was electrocuted.'

'Better but no.' Lorraine inclined her head. 'He choked on his chewing gum. Kelly found a lump of it in his wind pipe. Looks like my mother was right all along about not swallowing gum.'

Ravi laughed, a weak sound which tailed off after a second.

'We found gum in the cab.' Robyn looked at Lorraine. 'Is Dr Shepherd saying there's something suspicious about the death?' She knew how perverse it was, hoping the death was at least manslaughter because it would keep Ravi occupied.

'He just said he believed this wasn't a natural death.' Lorraine shrugged. 'He hasn't done the full autopsy yet, just said he was curious because he didn't like not knowing how someone died so he did some outline checks. He's got a whole load of toxicology tests he wants to run too.'

'When will we get the full report?' Ravi uncrossed his arms.

'Tuesday afternoon.' Lorraine smiled at him. 'You know, the more I think about it the odder the situation was. What's been bothering me –'

'OK. Here's what's we're going to do.' Robyn held up her hand. 'Ravi, go home and get some sleep. You and Graham start this case fresh on Monday. Meanwhile, Lorraine and I will keep working.'

Ravi's attention was on the papers across his desk. 'What about the records I've checked?'

Robyn looked him full in the face until he had to look away. 'We'll use the work you've done and that is the limit of your involvement. Understood?'

'Yes, Guv.' His head dropped. There was a second, two quick breaths, before he began pulling the sheets together into a pile. He took his time aligning the corners before he held the pack out to Robyn.

'Thanks.' Robyn took the papers. 'Now go home.'

Without enthusiasm, Ravi stood up. 'What did you do to your hands?'

'There was a riot here yesterday and the Guv was right in the middle of it.' Lorraine leaned forward to switch on her computer. 'Didn't you know?'

'A what? Here?' Ravi paused in pulling his jacket off the back of his chair. 'I was up at the hospital last night, didn't see any news. What the hell?'

'Goodbye, Ravi. We'll see you in the morning.' To get him to go, Robyn made a point of collecting his papers and putting them into her in-tray, then was surprised to see Ravi frown. She glanced down. Her in-tray was, as usual, full to overflowing and the notes had spilled onto the desk. Gathering them, she crossed to Lorraine's desk and placed them in the centre. 'As soon as you go, we will start.'

There was a second's pause. Ravi hadn't moved.

'Bye, Ravi.' Lorraine held up her hand. 'Take it easy.'

With slow steps, Ravi slouched out. As the door swung shut, Robyn allowed herself to relax. 'You are going to have to tell me if he tries to intrude. I am serious about suspending him.'

Lorraine looked as if she wanted to say something, then dropped her eyes. 'Yes, Guv.' She fanned out Ravi's notes.

'Right.' Robyn rolled her chair back to her desk. 'Let's start with the hotel's CCTV and pick up movements in and out of the room, then we can cross-check it against the photos from the ballroom.'

'Are you sure we can really separate the two investigations, Guv?' Lorraine had her head on one side. 'After all, we'll need to go over all Newman's movements for the Saturday including the wedding.'

'As Newman left before Shazia was attacked, there may not even be any connection.' Pausing, Robyn felt her eyelids drooping and wondered whether her judgement was impaired. 'For me, the big question is what took Newman out from home again so late?' She wondered what she could say to remove the doubt from Lorraine's face. 'Is there anything useful on Ravi's list?'

'You can tell where he's coming from. He's focused on the groom's relatives even though three quarters of the guests were from the bride's side.' Lorraine looked up. 'We're going to have to look into them though. I was doing a bit of searching last night and it seems rape is a real problem in India.'

'In India, maybe, however, we're in Meresbourne.' Robyn stifled a yawn. 'What about the criminal records Ravi talked about?'

'Petty stuff, shoplifting, an insurance fraud, apart from one case of assault. Let's have a closer look at that one.' Lorraine flicked through the list. 'Ah, here it is. Well, well.'

'What?'

'The one with the assault conviction is another one of the ushers, Trudwick. These boys get everywhere. Let's have a look.' She tapped details into her computer. 'Tum-te-tum – is there a handle I can turn to make this go faster? Right. So, he was a bouncer working at Quiksilva. Threw a girl out of the club and then beat her up in the street. Charged with using excessive force, found guilty, fined and had his door licence suspended for six months.'

'Nothing sexual?'

'Nothing so far.'

'Every offence has a first time. Let's start with the CCTV.'

'This is becoming a habit, Guv, you and me watching CCTV together. Like an episode of that programme, *Square Eyes*.'

It felt good to laugh, even if her chest twinged. 'Thanks. Join the police and see the world.'

Lorraine checked her notebook for a web address, then cursed when the password was rejected. 'If that useless manager gave me the wrong details for the security camera access – oh, hang on, maybe that's supposed to be an underscore – there.' She swivelled her screen so they could both see. 'OK, here's the list of cameras – which one do you want to start with? We've got one from the first floor corridor and one from the lobby showing the main stairs.'

'Let's go with the corridor, because we already know lots of people were in the lobby.' She thought back. 'Bugger. I've just realised I didn't ask Eldon whether there was anyone else in the room. I was about to then Ravi burst in and …' She realised how weak it sounded.

'Oh well.' The corners of Lorraine's mouth turned down. 'Surely he would have said if he'd seen another person?' She chewed her lower lip for a second. 'It's possible though, isn't it? When Eldon went into the main part of the room, if someone was in the bathroom, they could have sneaked out while he was looking at Shazia.'

As a welcome distraction, the screen filled with the black and white image of the Lady Ann's first floor. Robyn peered at the screen. 'OK, the camera must be at the far end of the corridor.' She fast-forwarded the film through a period of emptiness. There was movement on the screen when the time-clock showed thirteen forty-seven. A number of people appeared almost directly under the camera. One small shape detached itself and ran down the corridor, followed by a woman who grabbed the child's hand near the top of the left-hand branch of the stairs. A man with a smaller child followed them and they trooped out of view.

'From the register, they must be the Barkers.' Riffling through the papers on her desk, Lorraine pulled out a print-out. 'We've got their address in Birmingham.'

'Nothing out of the ordinary so far.' Robyn fast-forwarded again. At fourteen ten, two shapes appeared at the end of the corridor.

'Where did they come from?' Robyn kept her eyes on the screen. As they walked towards the camera, their shapes grew clearer: a man holding a Panama hat and a woman with a walking stick. They stopped at a door before the far stairs and disappeared from the screen.

'The lifts are up there.' Lorraine pointed to the top of the screen. 'They must be the couple in 106. Shame they couldn't tell us more.'

They had been so close to missing these important witnesses. Robyn shook her head, thinking how much she had allowed her personal problems to interfere with the investigation. 'Yes – hang on, who was that?'

A shape had appeared on the screen. 'Ah, there's Newman.' The time showed fourteen twenty-one. They watched as he galloped up from the stairs and into 108. Less than three minutes later, he came out wearing a t-shirt and jeans. After looking both ways, he jogged towards the camera before ducking out of sight to the right.

'He didn't want to be spotted, so he went down the fire escape.' Lorraine mimed hitting her head. 'Of course, that's why no one saw him leave.'

The film was still running. 'And now here's Shazia.' A small figure stepped up from the stairs. Her movements looked hurried and jerky and she seemed to struggle with the lock of 108 before the door closed behind her. A minute passed. A figure filled the screen, getting smaller as a man walked down the corridor, collected a tray from outside a room at the far end before walking towards the camera again.

'And the staff use the fire stairs because it comes out near the kitchen.' Lorraine reached for the remote. 'Can we watch the last bit again? This angle is really annoying – I want to check if that was Keith Eldon.' The figure walked up the corridor. 'Yep, definitely him, his bow-legged walk is quite distinctive.'

The screen was empty while the timer ticked from two twenty-eight to twenty-nine. Robyn found herself holding her breath. A figure appeared at the top of the stairs. He slowed and glanced around him before crossing to 108 and knocking. He stood close to the door as twenty seconds ticked by, then he knocked again. Eleven seconds later, the door was opened. The man stood for another few seconds on the threshold, then stepped inside.

Lorraine reached for the controller. 'Got him.' She began to rewind.

'No, let's watch to the end. I want to see whether he was in the room when she jumped.'

'OK.' Lorraine pressed the button and the film ran again through the scene on the doorstep before the door closed behind him. 'This is horrible, knowing what he's doing in there.'

'I know.' Robyn forced her breathing to slow as another minute ticked on. A pair of people appeared from the lift. They walked towards the camera, two women in saris, one leaning on the arm of the other. They went into one of the rooms before the farther staircase.

Robyn checked the notes. 'Room 106 made the complaint around now.'

The younger woman of the pair left her room and walked alone up the corridor towards the camera before turning down the stairs. At fourteen thirty-six, the door of 108 opened. The man, tie undone, looked up and down the corridor before starting for the stairs. At the top, he stopped, retied the bow-tie and took the first steps down and out of screen. Barely a minute later, Keith Eldon plodded up into view and stopped outside 108. He knocked on the door, waited, knocked again then used a card to open the door. The seconds ticked past for nearly three minutes before the screen filled with people: the manager; the older receptionist and another porter.

'So many chances.' Lorraine pressed to pause. 'If Newman had been just a couple of minutes later. Or if the two women had turned up earlier.' She restarted the film. 'This is really clear, we can get a still from this and blow it up, Ravi's good at that.'

Robyn shook her head.

'Oh, no, not Ravi. Maybe Chloe knows how to do it.' Lorraine stepped the film back until she had a clear shot. 'There.' She leaned towards the screen. 'Hmm. I don't recognise him from yesterday – someone else must have interviewed him. Who's the best person to identify him – someone from the groom's family, I guess?'

'It could be easier than you think.' Taking a swig of water, Robyn rested her chin on her hands. 'Look at his clothes.' Even with the high angle of the camera, it was possible to see the long jacket. 'The only people wearing tail coats were the principals.'

'Of course!' Lorraine grinned. 'There were only five of them and we know Newman had changed and the groom was sat on a throne where everyone could see him. That leaves a choice of three: two ushers and one best man.' She dived across to her desk. 'Notes from yesterday, notes from yesterday. Here we are.' She extracted her book from under a pile of statements. 'Right, so from what Newman gave us, we're looking for ... Axeman, Lassie and Julian. Oh for goodness sake – it sounds like a sixties pop group.'

Robyn felt her pulse rise, the feeling of being close to an answer. 'Or a kid's cartoon. So which one have we got here?' She leaned in close to the face frozen on the screen.

'It's not the one called Axe.' Lorraine sounded confident. 'I talked to him yesterday and he's taller with lighter hair. Can you look up Julian Gage and I'll take Bartholomew, aka Lassie?'

Robyn woke up her computer, fingers poised over the keys. 'Is that G – A – U?' Her burgundy fingernails clicked on the keys. At home, she thought the bolder colour suited her. At work, it seemed too dark and dressy. 'Nothing.'

'No U.' Lorraine was looking at Ravi's list. 'We should have something on Lassie because according to Ravi's list, he had a shoplifting conviction.'

'Still nothing on the brother.' Robyn grimaced. 'What have you got?'

For long seconds, Lorraine stared at her screen. A slow smile spread across her face. 'It's him.'

13

The printer whirred, Lorraine bringing back two images: the arrest mugshot when Bartholomew was a teenager and one of him with the groom, ushers and best man all raising champagne glasses. She laid them in front of the screen. 'It's definitely him. The hairline is identical, receding with the big peak at the front.' She peered between two print-outs. 'He's changed a bit since he was fourteen. A lot bulkier and looks like he's broken his nose at some point.'

'I think we should pay him a visit.' Grabbing her bag, Robyn stood up. 'What's his address?'

Lorraine tapped into the computer. 'Oooh, now there's a coincidence. He lives in Flotilla block, back where we were last night.' They got the lift to the car park. 'Are you sure we can let Ravi work on the Newman case, Guv?'

Robyn slammed the car door, harder than needed. 'If we can nail this guy sharpish for attacking Shazia there's no problem, is there?'

On the drive across town, neither of them spoke. At the Docks estate, the tower blocks merged into the grey sky. Stepping out of the car, Robyn heard a child bawling. The front door of Flotilla block was being held open by a pushchair jammed between the heavy door and the frame. The girl in the pushchair was screaming, writhing against the straps. When Robyn pulled the door open, the girl's contortions sent a handbag draped over the pushchair's handles swinging. Lorraine bent to retrieve the spilled items, a packet of cigarettes and a bus pass. In the lobby, a woman was dragging a boy along by one arm, his trainers scuffing the floor.

Despite the grey skies, the woman wore only a vest-top, the sequinned flower pattern straining over her pregnant belly. She swept the boy up with one arm and grabbed her things from Lorraine's outstretched hand with the other. 'I don't talk to 'king coppers.' It wasn't clear whether she was talking to them, the children or herself as she slammed her trainer down on the pushchair's brake and walked away.

'I reckon she could tell we're police because you held the door and I didn't steal her cigarettes.' Lorraine pushed the button for the lift. 'Maybe all this community work we're doing is having some effect after all.'

The lift smelt of cigarettes and wet dogs. It whined upwards, juddering each time the number increased. On the sixth floor, the lobby was garish with graffiti tags. Number 36 was at the end of the corridor, the side with the clearest view of the Victorian rows of Upper Town on the hill above.

After Lorraine's knock, the spyhole darkened, followed by a hiss of whispered conversation. 'Who is it?'

Robyn clasped her hands behind her. 'Police. We'd like to talk to Colin Bartholomew.'

Whoever was there moved away and there was another hint of voices before the spyhole darkened again. Somewhere along the corridor, a bass beat was turned up, muffling any sounds from the flat. When the door opened, a man filled the narrow hallway. The singlet stretched across his frame looked as if it was a child's size. One muscly arm rested on the wall.

'Mr Bartholomew?' Robyn was hit by a cloud of smells; harsh deodorant, fresh sweat and underneath, the sickly sweet smell of some sort of rot. 'I'm afraid we have some distressing news.' She held up her warrant card. 'May we come in?'

The man didn't look at the card or move. To enter, Robyn would have to duck under his arm and squeeze herself against the wall, stepping over a black rubbish sack discarded by the front door. The knowledge of what he had done made Robyn want to puncture his arrogance. She matched his stance, her hand an inch from his on the wall. As his eyes scanned down her, she pulled her shoulders back, to emphasise the bra. 'I'll have to squeeze right past you, won't I?' They stood chest to chest: Robyn looked down on the lump marring the line of his nose.

With a grunt, Bartholomew retreated into the main living area swinging his leg over a weightlifting bench in the centre of the room. A rack of weights, rubber mats and an exercise bike filled the space: there was no television or sofa. In one corner, a laptop sat on the floor in a mess of cables. Standing behind a kitchen counter, a young woman was almost hidden behind plastic shopping bags.

'Hello. We're police officers.'

The girl's eyes flicked up to Robyn for no more than a second, then moved to Lorraine who hovered at the end of the corridor. Robyn moved so she was no longer reflected in the full-length mirror propped between two of the windows. 'Mr Bartholomew, I believe you attended a wedding yesterday at the Lady Ann Hotel?'

'Time to go.' Bartholomew jerked his thumb towards the door.

It took a second for Robyn to work out he was talking to the woman.

'You'll be late for work.'

The woman shuffled forward, hands feeling her way along the edge of the counter, as if blind or uncertain of her balance. She hesitated at the edge, looking as if she wanted to move and not sure where to go next.

'Were you at the wedding yesterday, miss?' Robyn wondered whether the woman's nervousness was caused by their presence or something else.

'She didn't come to the wedding because she wouldn't know anyone.' Bartholomew's reedy voice didn't match his bulked-up frame. Without warning, the woman dashed out from behind the counter and into the second room off the hallway, closing the door. Robyn caught Lorraine's eye and tried to signal 'catch her when she comes out'.

Robyn turned back to look at the man. In the light room, the skin around his left eye was bruised with patches of yellow and purple.

'What do you want, copper?' Hands on the back of his head, Bartholomew seemed to be trying to make himself look bigger.

'Well first, I have some bad news.' Robyn kept her tone conversational. 'I'm afraid your fellow usher, Jake Newman, was found dead in the car park outside in the early hours of this morning.'

'Dead?' Bartholomew brought his arms down to his sides.

'Yes. I'm sorry. We are trying to get a picture of events yesterday, starting with the wedding.'

'You're telling me Paul is dead? How?'

'That is what we are investigating.' Wiping the smug expression from the man's face gave Robyn a certain crude satisfaction. 'Could you tell me about the wedding?'

'It was a load of fuss. Lulu didn't want anything so big, it was all Vasanti and her family. Kept demanding more and more.' Bartholomew flexed his shoulders back and forward before selecting a weight from the rack.

'Can I use your bathroom?' Lorraine stood up and began walking towards the front door without waiting for an answer.

Bartholomew began bicep curls, the movement slow.

'Can you tell me what you did at the wedding?' If the display was meant to impress her, it was not working. The veins bulging on each movement made Robyn worry something was going to burst: even the man's eyes were bloodshot.

He switched the weight to his other hand and began the repetition again, the fitness tracker on his wrist moving in and out of the light with each motion. 'Yeah. Nothing special, just be there with Lulu. Once everything broke up, me and Axe went for a couple of beers. I don't normally drink because of training, so although he wanted to make a night of it, I came back here. Paul wasn't answering his phone.'

Robyn watched the impassive face. There was no acknowledgement he knew anything about what had disrupted the wedding. One eye was always in the mirror, watching his movements.

'So you came back here. Was anyone with you?'

'Yeah. Lyndsey.' His head jerked towards the bedroom.

'You must have been upset about the girl.'

'Yeah well, shit happens.' Up, down.

From the hallway, there was a low exchange of voices. To draw Bartholomew's attention back to her, Robyn cleared her throat. 'What happened –?'

'– you nothing.' Lyndsey dodged around Lorraine, a leopard-print plastic bag slapping against her legs. The front door banged shut.

'… to your eye?' Robyn raised her voice. 'We've seen the wedding photos – you didn't have a black eye on Saturday.'

'A weight slipped in my hand.' Up, down. 'Did it this morning.'

'Given how much it's bruised already, you should have put something cold on it.' She hoped the banality had covered her lack of sympathy. 'Going back to Saturday, you got ready in room 108?'

'Yeah.' Up, down.

'What did you do once the formal part of the wedding was over?' Moving one foot outward, Robyn found herself shifting her stance, wanting to appear more forceful.

Up, down. 'If you're asking me did I shag anyone, then yeah, I did.' The fitness tracker beeped and Bartholomew changed his

123

movement to lift vertically, bringing the weight close to his chest each time. 'Couldn't really say no, even with the colour she was.' From outside the flat came the sound of a baby screaming and a roar from a man. Bartholomew's steady movements had an almost hypnotic quality.

'Did you need to get your girlfriend out of the room before you admitted you'd had sex with someone else?' Lorraine spoke from the corridor, sounding as if she were speaking through gritted teeth.

'She's not my girlfriend. She's messed up and I'm helping her out.' Bartholomew paused long enough to shrug. 'More like a pet, 'spose.'

'And that's why you treat her like a dog?' Lorraine folded her arms.

Robyn shot her a warning look. 'For your information, the girl you had sex with is now in a coma with severe head injuries.' There was no reaction. 'You were with Shazia; tell us exactly what took place yesterday afternoon.'

The weight was switched to his left arm and the movement began again. 'Not much to tell. After the speeches, the dancing started. We was supposed to do this dance and then get everyone out on the floor. She ended up dancing near me.'

Robyn waited until it became clear he was not going to say any more. 'How did Shazia end up in your room?'

'She wasn't feeling well. Don't think she was used to champagne. I knew no one would be in our room, so said she could go and lie down.'

'Did you go up with her?' Robyn felt herself tensing: she knew the answer to this question.

'Nah. Think she wanted to be sick, so just gave her the key.' Bartholomew put down the weight and flexed his shoulders a couple of times.

'Why did you go up there?'

'Thought I'd better see if she was OK.' A flicker of a smile passed across his face. 'Didn't want her passing out.'

'And was she?'

Bartholomew stretched out for a towel hanging over a weight stand. He wiped his face, neck and underarms before turning back towards Robyn. Close to, his skin tone was uneven, livid red veins and bulging tendons.

'She must have felt better because she grabbed me.'

'She grabbed you – can you be clearer about what you mean?' Robyn saw Lorraine tense, rocking on the balls of her feet.

'Christ, you're enjoying this, you sick bastard.' Bartholomew put his hands to his head, elbows out. 'I've already told you what I mean. I went up to the room, we shagged. What was a bit weird was there was a suit hanging up.' He wrinkled his nose. 'I couldn't work out who'd left. Anyway, I cleaned myself up and went back down because she was worried about people finding out.' He looked towards the window. 'They're a funny lot. All pretending to be nice girls when underneath, well.'

'So you had sex with Shazia.' Robyn took a breath. 'Did she consent to intercourse?'

'You kidding? She jumped on me.'

Lorraine took a half step forward. 'Despite the fact she was sick?'

'Yeah, she could have done with some mouthwash, know what I mean?' Bartholomew laughed, scratching the back of his neck. 'It must have been to thank me for being a gentleman.'

'You think it's being a gentleman to take advantage of a woman when she's drunk?' Lorraine took another step forward. Robyn tried to catch her eye again but she was staring at Bartholomew.

This time, Bartholomew made no attempt to conceal a smile. 'Why do most women get drunk? Because they want to have a bit of fun. She had a chance to relax a bit and must have liked what she saw.'

'Was there anyone else in the room while you were there with Shazia?' Robyn kept her voice neutral. Bartholomew knew what he was doing, trying to be as offensive as possible, winding them up.

'Nah, I'm not into those kind of things – are you?' His eyes narrowed. 'With your type, do you get hard or wet?'

Beside her, Lorraine gasped. There was no way to let her know she was finding Bartholomew's attempts to shock almost cartoon-like.

'How was Shazia when you left her?' Lorraine's hands were balled into fists.

'Properly shagged.' The man scratched a hairless armpit. 'Never had it before and now she's had the best.' His lips pulled back from grey, irregular teeth. 'She must have realised she'll never get it that good again and maybe that's why she jumped.' He picked up a red stick and began rubbing at a point near the top of one thigh, a smirk on his face.

As he applied the liniment, Robyn struggled to keep her nose from wrinkling at the smell. She was so focused on keeping her face steady, she jumped when the front door slammed. Lorraine had gone. The look on Bartholomew's face was like a child who had got his way.

'Mr Bartholomew. You seem very confident your attention was welcome.'

'I told you – she started it.'

'Did you use a condom?'

'Christ, are you getting turned on by this, tranny?' Bartholomew pulled his legs closer together.

Robyn smiled and leant forward. She relished his wriggle backwards along the bench. 'Just part of routine enquiries. Did you?'

Bartholomew stood up, walking in the widest circle possible around Robyn and into the kitchen area, pulling open the fridge. 'No. Didn't have any with me.'

'That's taking a risk, isn't it?' Robyn tried to put a caring note into her voice. 'What will your girlfriend say? You might expose her to something.'

Bartholomew took out a fluorescent bottle and took a swig.

'You have got a girlfriend, haven't you?' Robyn up and stepped onto the lino marking the edge of the kitchen. By resting one hand on the far counter, she was blocking him in.

'Enough! Get out, piss off. Don't come near me.' Standing as far away as he could, Bartholomew began shuffling from foot to foot.

'Tell me what I need to know, or come with me to the station.' Robyn stood square in the aisle, arms folded.

In the silence, Bartholomew's trainers squeaked against the lino. 'All right. I don't have a girlfriend.' He squeezed the bottle. 'Not because they're not interested just I've never found one who understood the training comes first.'

The close air of the flat, the sweat and her suppressed anger was making Robyn feel light-headed. 'Where were you when you heard Shazia had fallen?'

'Shazia. Right.' He took a swig from the bottle. 'With Lulu. He was gobsmacked, stuff like that on your wedding day.'

'Did you tell him you'd just had sex with her?'

'Course not.' Bartholomew tipped the bottle to get out the dregs. 'Anyway, we didn't know what had actually happened for a while, just lots of people shouting.'

'What did you do when you found out it was her?'

'What could I do?' The smug expression was back. 'Anyway, I heard someone came into the room and that's why she jumped. He's the one you want to be talking to.'

'I need a formal statement and a DNA sample from you.' She breathed in. Bartholomew's sweat now had a bitter, pungent tang. Her grip tightened on the counter as she tried to keep her breathing shallow.

'Why?' Bartholomew crushed the bottle in one hand. 'Well, I ain't giving one. I've told you what I done.' He threw the bottle, which hit Robyn on the shin. 'Whoops, missed the bin.'

'We will check your story.' The sting of the impact had cut through the fog in her mind and given her an idea. 'We already have your fingerprints on file: if you won't give me a DNA sample, I will get a warrant.' She smiled, letting the words hang in the air for a second before walking towards the front door. She stopped and turned back to him. 'Tell you what, to show you I'm here to help, I'll take the rubbish downstairs for you.' The door slammed behind her.

The air in the corridor smelled of damp which was a welcome relief after the stifling flat. Robyn took a deep breath as she walked to the lobby.

Lorraine stood by the lift, eyes down. 'Sorry, Guv. He really managed to play me, didn't he?'

'At least you realised what he was doing and took action. It would have been just what he wanted if you had lashed out.' She pressed the button for the lift. 'He really didn't think he'd done anything wrong.'

The lift doors hadn't even closed before Lorraine started. 'Why couldn't we arrest him? He admitted it!' She banged the side of the lift with the flat of her hand. 'He must know we believe it's rape. Why let him go?' The lift clanked. 'And why are you carrying his bin bag?'

The lift doors opened. Outside, the weather had closed in, rain driven in different directions by an irregular wind. Wet leaves were plastered to the windscreen.

'Think it through. He had just admitted having sex with Shazia. Are we really certain it was rape? We don't have a lot of physical evidence to go on because the doctors were too busy saving her life. A lawyer could pick the point apart in a few minutes. Bruises – oh, she liked it rough. We need evidence.'

Lorraine slammed the car door. 'She threw herself off a balcony.'

'When he was nowhere near her.' Robyn put the bag on the back seat and settled into the front. 'We should check the wedding pictures and confirm his story but it sounds like when she jumped, he was in the perfect place to make sure he was seen and remembered.'

'Which is exactly what you'd do if you'd done something wrong. That bag really smells.'

'Unfortunately, I don't think things are so simple.' Robyn heard part of the car creak as they went over a speed hump. 'This time, we do things in reverse. We know who did it, now we do the investigation and in his bin bag, which he was happy for me to take, I think we'll find some DNA we can match.'

'And I bet he thought he was being so clever refusing to give a sample. Nice one, Guv.' Lorraine laughed. 'And then we can press some charges?'

'And if we can, yes, we will press some charges.' She glanced across. 'It's frustrating so we have to be better than that. Finding other ways to get results is a big part of moving up to sergeant. It's only in films where a cop hands in his badge and then catches the bad guy.'

'Or bad woman. Should we tell the family that we know what happened?'

'Not yet.' Robyn hadn't considered it but the reaction was automatic. 'We can't prove anything yet. I don't want to get their hopes up then for something to go wrong, even though I know it looks clear cut.'

'When are you going to talk to Fell about me going for promotion?'

'I wasn't planning to do it this week.' She could feel the force of Lorraine's glare without looking around. 'I should have said. With this sort of thing, you've got to pick your moment and now just isn't the time to mention anything like this to Fell. He's so stressed without Tracey organising everything for him, anything that caused more paperwork, he would veto right away.' Lorraine braked too hard for a junction. 'Don't worry, it's a week's delay, no more.' As soon as she was back, she would write a note to remind herself to speak to Fell: what Robyn had done recently to jeopardise her own career was one thing but she couldn't justify stopping anyone else's. She searched for a safer topic. 'Did you get the impression Bartholomew and Lyndsey are a couple?'

'No. Or at least not a regular one. Are you sure there isn't another dead body in the bag?' Lorraine coughed and opened the window. 'Although it's a one-bedroom flat, there's a mattress in the corner of the bedroom. I think Lyndsey sleeps there.'

'So if they're not a couple, what do you think they are? I would have thought if he's so dominant, they'd be sleeping together.'

'Things have moved on a bit, Guv. I know there's a lot of concern about porn and stuff but for most people, they just have friends, doesn't matter if they're male or female. It isn't all about, well, sex, any more.'

'What do you mean?' This was one of the times when Robyn wondered if her team were embarrassed talking to her about certain subjects.

'What I mean is, well, it's like when my band goes away for a gig and has to stay over.' Lorraine was talking faster than usual. 'To save money, we just get a couple of family rooms and all muck in together. There's nothing rude about it.' Lorraine slowed for the roundabout. 'I guess it's because girls and boys mix much more when they're young, there isn't this sense of, oh I don't know, of the opposite sex being something exotic and special, they're just your friends.' She drove the car into the police station, reaching for her pass. 'The irony of all this is parents still see contact with the opposite sex as being scary, when in fact it seems to be the other way around. The more time boys and girls spend together, the more relaxed they become. And modern boys and girls aren't so different anyway.'

'Right.' Robyn didn't like where this conversation had gone. One way of interpreting Lorraine's comment was that everything she had done was unnecessary. 'Is there anything else relevant to the investigation?'

'The bathroom was incredible. As well as being a fitness freak, Bartholomew must be a complete hypochondriac.' Lorraine shoved the pass back into her bag. 'The medicine cabinet is crammed with things for any sort of sniffle or pain then stacked against the wall are loads of big tubs of those supplement things body-builders use and there are also a whole load of pill boxes. When you look inside, they're drugs of some sort though they can't be from the UK because they don't have proper labels and all the writing's in some language with lots of consonants in it. I got a picture.'

'Interesting. I wonder how he affords everything? Those pills and potions are expensive.'

'Dunno. What do you think Graham's up to?'

Robyn took her seatbelt off. 'I don't know. I wish he'd check in: we could have used him yesterday.'

'He'll turn up.' Lorraine kept the engine running. 'He tells these amazing stories about when DI Prentiss was in charge, how they used to go out on these benders when they caught someone. They'd be in the pub and send the youngest officer into the office to keep moving stuff around about every half hour and make cups of tea for everyone so it looked as if they were all working.'

'It wasn't so funny when you were the officer that had to face the Superintendent.' She had a memory of having to come up with a series of excuses for where Prentiss was: the bathroom; the canteen; getting something from his car. 'It's one of the reasons why I left Meresbourne and went to Bristol. One time, and I am not making this up, a bloke holding a bloodied baseball bat was caught standing over an unconscious man. Prentiss questions the guy, lets him go because he was "provoked" and when I go over to the pub later, there were the two of them playing darts together.'

'The way Graham describes it, it sounded like the Wild West and they were all that was standing between the townsfolk and pesky bandits.'

'Surely you don't believe everything Graham tells you? After all, he does like a joke.' Robyn opened her door. 'OK. We've moved things on. Enjoy playing your gig then get some sleep. We'll build the case tomorrow then finalise things with the forensic evidence.'

It looked like Lorraine was trying to muster arguments, then she nodded once. 'OK. I know I'm going to play really badly when I'm wound up like this.' She moved the car into gear.

'Forget about everything until tomorrow.' Robyn tried to smile. 'Otherwise you end up carrying so much around with you, it will wear you down.' She shut the door.

14

Robyn considered opening the rubbish bag in the incident room, decided not to risk it and bagged the whole thing up for analysis. Through the thin plastic, she could feel the outline of drinks bottles, which she was certain would contain DNA from saliva in the residue. Trying to stifle yawns, she filled in the necessary forms to allow the lab to match the DNA to Bartholomew's record. Although she searched the computer, she could not identify Lyndsey. Her plan had been to spend the afternoon reviewing the rest of the Lady Ann statements; when she found herself trying to read a sheet upside-down, she decided to call it a day at two o'clock.

The clouds had thinned enough to allow a pale sun to break through by the time Robyn got home to a cold, dark house. Aimless, she cast around for a task to occupy herself and decided on the ironing. Setting up the board in her bedroom, the bed looked very inviting. A few minutes of rest would be fine. She undressed, pulled the duvet around herself and tried to force the ugly thoughts out into the pillow.

When Robyn opened her eyes, the patch of sky she could see from her window was already darkening. She checked the clock – she had slept through the afternoon. Tempting though it was to stay in the warm cocoon, she knew she would have to get up if she wanted to sleep tonight. Making an effort she pushed the duvet aside and headed for the bathroom.

At the top of the stairs, she could see into what was now Becky's room. The relentless co-ordination and its overall newness made it look like a hotel room rather than a real place where someone would stay. The effort she'd put into the room seemed greater than the effort she'd put into trying to communicate with her daughter. She needed to call Becky immediately and understand what it would take to bring her down so that they could talk, face to face, father and daughter.

Pulling on a jumper, she grabbed her mobile from the bedside cabinet and started scrolling to Becky's number. Frustrated by the jerky process, she changed her mind and headed downstairs. In the kitchen, she reached for the whisky. The bottle almost slipped through her hands, the heavy base thudding on the counter. She stopped: she should not be a coward. If there was something to celebrate after the call, she would allow herself a proper drink. For now, she would make do with water. In the lounge, with her thumb over the green button, she took a sip. The ring tone began in her ear as the liquid caught at the back of her mouth.

'Hello?'

Her throat constricted as she tried to swallow. A gasp of breath met the remaining water, causing some of it to go up her nose.

'What is going on there?'

Robyn coughed because not enough air was reaching her lungs. She held the phone away as another cough turned into a hiccough. 'Becky, sorry, something caught in my throat.'

'Dad, is that you? I thought it was a dirty phone call, all the heavy breathing.'

134

Robyn hiccoughed again, a small noise escaping. There was a possible giggle from the other end. 'No, just I've got hiccups.'

There was a proper laugh this time. 'Do you want to call me back when you're in one piece?'

Part of Robyn did. The other part said now she had her daughter on the phone she should not let her go. 'Now's fine. Becky, everything's ready for you here. Are you coming down tomorrow?'

There was a pause. 'No, Dad, I'm not.'

Robyn tried to suppress another hiccup. 'Will you tell me why?'

'Because, I'd rather be on my own. Can you imagine what it's like when I don't know who either of my parents are at the moment?' Becky drew a shuddering breath. 'Mum's just been lashing out over the least little thing and you, well, where do we start?'

Robyn waited in case she went on. The pause got too long. 'You're right, of course, I can't imagine. It just feels like the best way for you to find out who I am is to come here and see me.' She left another gap for an answer although there was no acknowledgement. 'I am worried about your mother though. I don't remember her being so angry before.'

There was a loud sniff from the other end. 'She's been like this for a while now. I didn't go home for the summer because I didn't want to be in the middle of it all.'

'Becky, I've got to tell you because you need to understand. Your mother was very close to being charged with assault.' Now she had started, Robyn wanted to make sure she finished. 'When you said you wouldn't visit unless I released Julie, there was no way I could agree to that because she was involved in a crime.'

'I don't think she means any of it.'

'Whether she meant it or not, she was involved and people got hurt.'

'She's having a really hard time of it at the moment. Apparently, the university isn't even sure whether it's going to be running Women's Studies courses next year.' Becky sniffed again. 'I think she's been joining all these movements to try and prove she's still relevant.'

Robyn had to fight back an urge to laugh. 'I don't think she'd be happy to have you doubting her motivations. There was this author she used to quote all the time. Something like the only thing worse than not doing something was doing something you didn't fully believe in?'

'Oh, give over.' The line was cut.

Robyn stared at the phone, not able to accept the call had ended. She replayed the conversation, now thinking about how brittle Becky had sounded. Her complaint that nobody was there for her seemed unfair – there was a new room upstairs waiting to welcome her until she realised Becky didn't know about it. Driven to her feet, Robyn stamped upstairs. Pulling out her phone, she stood in the doorway of the spare room and took a picture. On the screen, the room looked even more impersonal. She hurried back downstairs and looked around. All her parents' old ornaments had gone to the tip and she had not replaced them, enjoying the lack of clutter. Over the fireplace was a framed picture: of all the photos she'd taken, this was her favourite and it had been commended in the Kent Print Cup. She marched upstairs and set the frame on the mantelpiece – she'd need to put a proper hook up. She looked around again – there was still something missing.

From the top shelf of her wardrobe, she retrieved Puppy, the soft toy dog with half an ear and bare patches in the purple fur, and set him on the bookcase. She hoped Becky would remember him from visits to her grandparents and would realise this was a room for her. Taking another photo, she kept the message short:

Hello sweetheart, your room is all ready for you. Dad.

With the evening stretching ahead, Robyn faced the chores needed to be ready for another week. Because she hadn't bought any new clothes, she spread out the two suits she'd bought at the beginning of her transition. It seemed very unfair: one of Roger's suits had been fifteen years old and never attracted a comment, then the second time she had worn a particular blouse, someone had remarked on it. The decision was made when she found a seam unravelling on the grey suit. She ironed the black one, hoping no one would notice the strains in the jacket where the shoulders were a little too tight.

Neither would last much longer, so in an attempt to give more purpose to the day, Robyn switched on her laptop. At least this time when she bought online, she knew to look out for some of the ways purchases could be wrong, like finding the sleeves were too short, exposing inches of forearm. The browser opened up at the local news site, which was covering the Lady Ann case. She was surprised by the number of reader comments on the story: as she watched, the number clicked up. The latest comment was by someone calling themselves Woodsman.

Medway Mike got it bang on. Women gotta make up there minds whether wannt it or not. Cant be tits hanging out 1 minit an then cry as somewon raped them. Anway Meresbourne gals like it ruff.

Somewhere, nearby, there was someone who had just insulted all the women in Meresbourne. She scanned to the bottom of the comments; the messages had started with women leaving messages of shock and sympathy for Shazia.

She scrolled through a series of posts and found the tone hardening.

Once again women trampled beneath the twin oppression of religion and culture. Real women should fight back.

Gaia-Girl2 compared marriage to slavery and Feminicki described the arrests as police oppression. Then she found MedwayMike's comment.

Can someone explain this to me? If I left my valuables on display and my front door open, police would say it was my fault when they were stolen and wouldn't investigate. Why is it different for a woman who wears almost nothing, gets really drunk and then complains because she gets attacked?

From there, the messages became angry, everyone trying to shout louder. For comparison, she looked at the story of the riot. There was only one comment on here, a 'wouldn't happen in my day' rant from someone who had capitalised every word. Despite her revulsion, Robyn went back and read the thread again. There was a common theme of women being viewed just as pieces of meat.

Revolted, she pushed the chair back and stood up, grabbing her handbag. She didn't bother with a coat, welcoming the fresh, damp air as she stepped outside. She didn't have a destination, just intended to walk around the block, to clear her mind. The streets were deserted, the only sound was music just audible from the Moon and Rainbow pub on the corner: a poster with running ink was advertising 'Elvis night'.

At the corner, she turned left, the only figure on the street of nose-to-tail parked cars. She had to admit to herself, she would never agree with some of the views on what it meant to be female. Potentially, Julie was right and someone who had spent most of their life in a man's body would never understand fully what it meant to be a real woman. Car noise intruded on her thoughts as she turned onto the main road. She was sure none of the women in her team had thoughts like this: Lorraine and Chloe just got on with being women without thinking about what it meant because they had done it all their lives, whereas she had to conform to society's ideas of what a woman was supposed to be.

She carried on around the block by taking the next street on the left, now walking between pools of white light and the dark gaps between the smaller streetlamps. There were lights in the upstairs windows of houses though many were already dark – people went to bed early in Barton. An engine sounded behind her. Robyn glanced over her shoulder, then shut her eyes, dazzled by the headlights. She found her pace quickening, taking her into a patch of shadow. The car seemed to be taking a long time to pass and she had a sudden thought of what Khalid had said about street attacks. They had all started like this, a woman walking on her own, late at night. She was halfway down the street: if she needed to run, home was ahead but to get away from the car it would be better to go back towards the main road, forcing the driver to leave the car or reverse. She risked another glance: the car was drawing level. The windows were shiny blocks: her reflected face looked yellow and ghostly. Her image was erased by the window sliding down.

'Excuse me. Could you help us? We're looking for a petrol station and the sat-nav sent us down here, which doesn't look right.'

The woman's voice was plummy; she was probably from Gaddesford or Upper Markham. Robyn took a deep breath and squeezed through the gap between two parked cars so she didn't have to raise her voice in case it gave away her nerves. 'Of course. There's one a couple of minutes away. At the bottom of this road, turn right. You get to a T junction and if you turn left, you're on the Maidstone Road and there's a petrol station on the right.'

'So right, left, on the right. Thank you so much.'

The car drove away leaving Robyn feeling idiotic. Everything was fine, this was exactly what normal people did. It was ridiculous for her to feel so vulnerable. It wasn't very late and she was bigger than the average woman – not an easy target. There were rape alarms at the station and she considered picking one up, then wondered again why she felt she needed one. The night felt cold all of a sudden and she started moving again, swinging her arms both to keep warm and reinforce the space around her as she rounded the final corner. There was an agonising fumble with the keys before she could get the front door open. With the chain on the front door, her pulse began to return to normal.

MONDAY 19 SEPTEMBER

15

Walking into the police station, Robyn felt as if she'd not been away for more than a few minutes. Her sleep had been fractured, punctured by a moment of sudden wakefulness, convinced someone was calling for help. She had sat up in bed, straining her ears against the silence. When it came, the scream was right outside, a yowling mix of fear and rage: the neighbourhood cats were fighting again. The normality of the crush in the canteen was welcoming and she merged into the crowd, happy to be invisible. In the queue, she thought she felt a couple of looks: the story of Saturday would be doing the rounds. She kept her eyes fixed on the display boards behind the counter, not wanting to make eye contact with anyone. While waiting to pay, she scanned a poster announcing 'Diversity Day': someone had written 'today' across it. Walking out with her tea, the posters seemed to be everywhere which proved she hadn't been fully awake when she'd arrived. The HR manager and two of her lackeys were waiting by the lift, thrusting flyers into the hands of everyone passing.

'Ah, DI Bailley, good morning.' The woman flicked a length of hair over her shoulder. 'You are coming to our Diversity Day workshop.' It was not a question.

'I have two serious crime enquiries which started over the weekend – there's a lot to do.' Robyn had to fumble her cup from one hand to the other as the heat became too much.

The woman's narrow brows came together. 'You, of all people, are such an advocate for diversity, I'm sure everyone will be expecting you.' She turned her professional smile on a couple of uniformed officers, who quailed under her gaze and took a sheet. 'I'll see you in the main conference room at ten.'

Superintendent Fell strode through the lobby towards the lift. Turning her back on Robyn, the HR Manager held out a leaflet. 'Good morning, Superintendent. These are the final preparations for the session. We're expecting a good turnout.' Her voice had become deeper, with a warmer tone.

'Good, good.' Without stopping, Fell walked into the lift and turned. 'We need to be seen to implement all of the recommendations in the Public Services Equality bill.' The doors closed before the HR manager could comment. She turned back, eyes moving over Robyn.

'How's Clyde?' Robyn pushed the lift button, waiting for the HR Manager's eyes to return to her face. She was getting used to being scrutinised: what amazed her was that the people never seemed to realise they were doing it.

The HR manager seemed surprised to be asked. 'Sorry, what did you say? How's who?'

'Clyde.' Robyn paused, waiting for a sign of recognition. 'The officer who was hurt on Saturday.'

'Ah.' The woman forced a leaflet into the hands of an officer walking towards the stairs. 'I haven't heard.'

'Ah.' The stairs seemed a very attractive option. 'I thought you might have kept track.' She walked away. At the first landing, she found two of the diversity flyers screwed up. Kicking them both into the corner was a satisfying, if childish moment.

In the safety of the incident room, Robyn set down her cup of tea next to the slick of papers on her desk. Yesterday, she'd planned to at least put things in piles and hadn't got round to it. She stirred the tea. Today would be a day of difficult conversations. There was no telling what state Ravi would be in and she needed to find out what was wrong with Graham. Fell and Khalid would also expect updates. She regretted not picking up a bacon sandwich but those indulgences had been rationed, along with a number of other treats in the quest to get herself into a size fourteen blouse. There was an apple in her bag: she set it on the desk in a prominent position. Even if she didn't eat it, at least the guilt might stop her indulging in anything else.

Chloe stuck her head around the door. 'Morning, Guv.' She cast her eyes around the room. 'Ravi not here yet? Good, I'll nip to the canteen – you want anything?'

Robyn's phone rang. She held up her cup to show she was OK and Chloe disappeared. 'Hi, Khalid.'

'Robyn, good morning. An eventful weekend. No long term damage from Saturday, I trust?'

She was not going to tell Khalid about the bruise on her chest which sat directly under the bra strap. 'I'm fine, thanks. Have things calmed down for you yet?'

Graham walked in, giving a muted greeting on the way to his desk. Robyn raised her hand to him. In her ear, Khalid continued. 'Mostly. Annoying how the press hasn't given Clyde's injuries more coverage.'

'I saw the *Gazette* article yesterday – I thought that was reasonably balanced?' Robyn was only half-listening while studying Graham. The skin underneath his eyes was an unpleasant greyish-yellow colour.

'Mostly, yes. What annoys me is I keep seeing comments where what those women did was presented as "fighting back against oppression" – you'd hope papers would challenge such rubbish, not

145

just regurgitate propaganda.' Khalid tutted. 'One other interesting thing: Bergmann's talk to close the Loveless festival has moved to the football stadium. She must be expecting a bigger crowd.'

'I'm amazed Bergmann would go anywhere so associated with men.' The oddness of the image made Robyn smile.

'Like I said, she can draw a crowd. Anyway, the reason I was calling.' Khalid's tone had become brisker. 'As well as the panel this evening, Fell wants to do a briefing later today to call for calm so, can you give me anything you've got on the Lady Ann case?'

'What time is it?' If she'd known she was going to be doing a media briefing, Robyn would have worn a different blouse.

'Ah, don't worry about it, it's not going to be a big number.' Khalid sounded less assured than usual. 'There's a bit of a concern about causing offence to certain sections of the community, so best it's just him.'

Once again, she was seen as a potential risk. Swallowing, Robyn told herself it was nothing personal though all the same, she didn't think this would have happened to Roger. 'OK. We've got movement though it's nothing we can talk about. We have a suspect who admits he was there and we're waiting on the forensic reports for confirmation.' Even though the only other person in the room was Graham, she found herself turning away and dropping her voice. 'The big question will be, even though there is circumstantial evidence, can we prove the sex was rape? The girl can't talk to us and, even if she recovers, there's a chance she may not be able to remember anything.'

'Hmm.' There was a sound of typing at the other end. 'We'll need to bring it to some sort of resolution though. The case is still getting a lot of attention on social media.'

'Yes but are activists just tweeting to other activists? How many real people are reading?'

Khalid laughed. 'Probably not many. And you're right – I thought you didn't do social media?'

146

'I don't.' Here, she had no hesitation about lying: her online explorations were private, allowing her to ask the questions about her transition she couldn't ask in person.

'That's a good thing.' Khalid paused. 'Some of the things they've been saying about you aren't very, ah, charitable, especially after the film was published.'

Robyn picked up her cup and began pressing in the dimples with her thumbnail. 'I know what they say about people like me. I don't see why they should stop me doing my job.'

'Yes. You're right.' Khalid didn't sound convinced. 'Look, call me if you get anything else, bye.'

Robyn sat back, putting the phone back into its holster. She allowed herself a brief moment with her eyes closed, trying to think of how to open the conversation with Graham, who sat hunched at his desk, head buried in a report. To give herself purpose, she stood up. 'Morning, Graham. Have you got a minute?'

Graham looked up. There was a tiny rasping noise as an unshaven patch under his chin rubbed against his collar. 'Can it wait, Guv? I've just got these reports in from Maidstone.'

'No, it needs to be now.'

As Graham got to his feet, the door swung open and Lorraine marched in holding a coffee cup. 'Morning. Ooh, nice pendant, Guv. Is it new?'

Robyn's first thought was Lorraine was joking: nothing Robyn owned was more than a couple of months old. Then she decided to just be grateful for the compliment. 'Thanks. I got it from one of the craft stalls in St Leonard's Square.'

In the moment of pleasure, she hadn't noticed the door had opened again. Chloe walked in, followed by Ravi who was pale and hadn't bothered to shave. He went to his desk, sat down and switched on his computer without a word.

Graham walked over and laid a hand on his shoulder. 'I'm sorry, Raver. No one should have to go through something like that.'

147

Shaking off Graham's hand, Ravi whirled around. 'You weren't there. I called you, asked you for help and you didn't answer.'

Robyn sat back on her desk. She was torn between intervening and wanting to see what Graham said. She saw his hands clench once, twice: his nails were bitten down and she moved forward. 'Enough, Ravi.' She was close to him now, smelling his angry sweat. 'This is not the time or the place to discuss it. We have two serious cases and it will not help if we are at each others' throats.'

Ravi, with his desk behind him, couldn't move. Graham took a step backward. 'I'm sorry.' He turned and walked to the far corner of the room, pulling out a drawer of a filing cabinet without looking at the label.

Robyn turned back to Ravi as he threw himself back down on his chair. Lorraine moved beside him. 'Look, stuff happens. What's done is done. Now channel it.'

'Are you quoting a line from one of your Scandi cop dramas?' Ravi kicked at the floor. 'This isn't TV.'

Robyn opened her mouth. Before she could say anything, Lorraine gripped one arm of the chair, wrenching it around so Ravi faced her. 'No, you're right, it isn't. We're police officers. We deal with crap. You're supposed to be on the fast-track which means they think you're going to be better at dealing with crap than the rest of us. A bad thing happened and we're all really sorry but we can't make anything unhappen and it would be a lot easier for us to investigate if you weren't acting like the victim.' She spun the chair so Ravi was facing his desk and shoved it forward until the arms jammed against the wood.

In the silence as Lorraine returned to her desk, Ravi's noisy breathing was a harsh sound.

Robyn snapped to attention. 'Right, everyone.' Even though heads turned, she could sense the reluctance. From the tension in the air, there were still things unsaid which would come out when she wasn't around. She had to keep them busy. 'Has all that made anyone feel better? Has shouting helped us solve any of our cases?' She looked around the faces. 'One point you might want to keep in mind is this team is going to be under scrutiny. We were lucky in July: the Professional Standards' investigation concluded we had done nothing wrong but after this weekend, my guess is we'll be back under the microscope, with another inspector crawling all over us. If you have to shout at each other, fine, go ahead if you've got the energy. But that's only in here. Nothing gets out that this team is anything other than united. OK?' She looked around the circle. The nods from Lorraine and Chloe were immediate; the one from Ravi sullen. 'OK, Graham?'

A phone rang. After a second, Robyn heard Chloe answering the call. She kept her eyes on Graham.

'Ah, Guv, it's the Superintendent for you.'

'Tell him I'll speak to him in a moment.' She had to be sure Graham agreed, like the others.

'OK, Graham?' In the background, Chloe could be heard telling Fell that Robyn was just finishing a call.

Graham looked up. 'Yes, OK for Christ's sake.' Shoving the filing cabinet closed, he sloped through the room and out.

16

Robyn took the phone from Chloe. 'Good morning, Sir.'

There was a grunt at the end of the line, which was as much small talk as she had expected. 'Bailley, I need a briefing on your cases.'

'Certainly, sir. When?'

'Now.' There was the sound of another phone ringing in the background. 'Come up and bring me a cappuccino, will you?'

Robyn stared at the phone for a second, then allowed herself to smile. It meant a good excuse for another trip to the canteen. Spending extra time in Fell's office would not be pleasant though if he waffled or she got an urgent task assignment from the meeting, there was a good excuse to miss the diversity seminar.

'OK. I've got to go upstairs. I want this place organised when I get back. We have two major cases. There should be evidence boards for both.'

With two cups in her hands, Robyn was grateful someone had already pushed the lift button, until she saw the shaven head of DS Phil Flagg with a young officer she didn't know.

'Morning, Phil.' She kept her tone light, with the certainty he would find her familiarity most annoying. 'Are you here as part of the cover for the Loveless festival?'

There was a nod and smile from the rookie officer but Phil recoiled. Without looking where he was going, he stepped sideways onto the toes of a civilian worker, who yelped.

'Sorry, love, sorry.' The creases across Phil's forehead deepened.

Robyn made sure she smiled at the rookie. 'Hello, I should have introduced myself. I'm DI Robyn Bailley. How long have you been on the team?'

'Six weeks, ah, ma'am.' The rookie stood up straighter. 'DC Clements, Ricky.'

'Welcome, Ricky. How are you finding things?'

'Good, thanks, ma'am. I heard about what you did on Saturday.'

The lift arrived. Robyn gestured for the woman to go first, who stepped forward with an exaggerated limp. Robyn followed. Ricky looked at Phil. Robyn heard the comment even though she couldn't see his face. 'We'll take the stairs.'

Robyn smiled at herself in the mirrored walls of the lift. Phil's obvious discomfort reinforced her suspicion that it had been him who had made a formal complaint about her soon after her return to work. Baiting him was harmless fun. On the fifth floor, the outer door of the office was open. From inside, Robyn could hear Fell's voice and he did not sound in a good mood.

Robyn showed herself at the inner door. Fell looked around, the phone in his hand and nodded her to a chair.

'To repeat, I have no one spare at the moment to undertake such an investigation, so I would ask you to continue the review and, at the point you find something specific of concern, I can reconsider.'

Robyn sat, keeping her breathing shallow. There was no acknowledgement of the coffee.

'Yes, the new budget will be with Finance by Thursday, as agreed. We have covered the agenda? Yes? Goodbye.'

Fell swung his chair to face Robyn.

'Right, Bailley, what is going on?'

Robyn took a quick breath. 'We have progress on the Lady Ann case, sir. A man has confessed to having sex with the victim. We are anticipating a charge of rape or at least sexual assault.'

'Those are difficult to bring to a successful prosecution and we are in danger of losing the trust of two sections of the community.' Fell looked over his steepled fingers. 'I would like to see the Lady Ann case resolved in a way that ensures citizens maintain confidence in the police.' His eyes seemed to be fixed on her necklace.

'There's something else you should know, sir.' Taking a deep breath, Robyn kept going. 'The initial suspect was found dead in suspicious circumstances on Saturday night.'

A sharp intake of breath cut her off. 'How long between his release from custody and his death?'

'Between six and eight hours, sir. The cause of death appears accidental and we're waiting for the full post mortem to confirm the circumstances.'

Fell sighed. 'I will have to inform Professional Standards. This is the second time, Bailley, since you, since your, your new start that it has been necessary to call them in regarding one of your cases.' He paused, shifting his gaze from over Robyn's right shoulder to above her head. 'I hope those two elements are not connected?'

Anything she came back with at this point would only lead to problems. 'No, sir.'

Fell raised his eyebrows. 'You may think this is just bad luck, Bailley, I have to consider the consequences for the reputation of the division. The investigation may conclude nothing improper took place but it is the need for an investigation which will be remembered.'

'Yes, sir.'

'However, I have just received a piece of good news. You will be pleased to know our officer has been released from hospital. After a period of recuperation, he is expected to make a full recovery.'

'That's really good news, sir. I was worried Clyde was seriously hurt.' The bruise on her chest chose that moment to twinge.

The clock next to the portrait of the Queen showed five to ten. Fell must have spotted the movement of her eyes because he checked his own watch. 'Right, I have to get to the conference room.' His eyes narrowed. 'I am hosting our first diversity seminar in five minutes – I take it you are attending.'

There was no way out. 'Yes, sir.'

'Right then.' Fell stood up. 'This is an important meeting. The first in Kent. This is exactly the sort of initiative which will help us to retain "Division of the Year".'

With a sense of resignation, Robyn followed Fell into the corridor and along to the conference room. The chairs had been stacked in a corner and a series of stalls set up around the edge with banners and posters proclaiming "Women's Network"; "Police Parents" and "Benevolent Association". Fell approached a tall, black officer in uniform who was scanning some notes. 'Good morning, good morning. Thank you for coming today. We're all looking forward to your talk.' The officer looked around the almost-empty hall and Fell seemed to become conscious of the gap. 'Superintendent Prince, may I introduce DI Bailley? Prince works for the Met.'

They shook hands. 'I understand you found evidence of a drugs shipment recently.' Although Prince was shorter than her, he had a sense of solidity.

'Yes, sir. We were searching an abandoned warehouse and found activity.' Robyn wondered why the Met was showing an interest in a two month-old find. 'One of the forensic technicians recognised the type of packing material from a previous shipment he'd examined in another location. When the items were tested there were traces of heroin.'

Prince nodded. 'We believe this is one drop from a large, well-organised international operation. We've found similar packaging along the Kent, Essex and Suffolk coasts, so we're confident the drugs are coming in by sea for sale in London. By using a range of landing locations, they reduce the risk of detection. We've managed to intercept individual shipments and the intention is to work our way up the chain of command.' From his belt, there was a discreet buzz from a slim phone.

Over his shoulder, Robyn saw Fell look at his watch and glare at the HR manager.

Robyn reached for her phone, turning away as if to look at a stand.

'DI Bailley's phone.'

'Chloe, it's me.' Robyn kept her voice low. 'I'm up in the main conference room. Could you do me a favour: get the team to come up – it's a bit sparse in here at the moment which will make Fell look bad. And hustle anyone you find on the way, will you? Thanks.'

With a confident smile, she turned to Prince. 'My team are just on their way. They're looking forward to your talk.'

Like Fell, Prince didn't appear to do small-talk. 'To tackle the smuggling, we are in the process of setting up a cross-border team to share intelligence. Could you nominate an officer to feed in data from Meresbourne? This has a high priority at the Met as recent shipments appear to be purer than before and we are aware of at least two linked deaths.'

'Yes, sir.' She thought for a second. 'My choice would be DC Lorraine Mount.'

There was a tiny movement across Prince's forehead. 'Only a DC?'

Fell's heavy footfall sounded behind her. Robyn made sure she spoke up. 'It's my view DC Mount is ready for promotion and a case working with the Met would be ideal experience for her.' She held her breath. She couldn't put Fell on the spot as his natural reaction would be to object. The best thing she could do would be to make Fell think it was his idea.

On the other side of the hall, Lorraine and Ravi straggled in and behind them, a couple of civilians. A second later, Chloe arrived, with a pair of officers in Uniform.

'Ah, here's DC Mount. I can introduce –'

'Well, as this is looking a bit more healthy, shall we get started?' Fell bustled to the microphone. 'Is this on?' He looked around. 'Can you hear me? Good. Without any further ado, I'd like to welcome you to Meresbourne's first diversity celebration and I'm delighted to welcome Superintendent Prince from the Met Police, who's going to talk about his experiences.'

With a minimum of movement, Prince stepped up to the microphone. His speech was short and to the point, the stories of discrimination told without emotion. Robyn found herself thinking of Meresbourne's previous DI, Kenny Prentiss and his ever-so-amusing range of names for various ethnic groups. When Prince finished, the applause was warm.

Robyn turned to Lorraine, planning to introduce her but she had already approached the Superintendent.

'Hello, sir, you won't remember me. You came to give a talk to my intake at Henley.' With her eyes wide, Lorraine looked a little starstruck. 'You were brilliant, really inspiring.'

'Thank you.' Prince reached for his phone.

'Sir, this is DC Mount who would be my nomination to provide our information to the drugs operation.' Robyn was hoping Lorraine would follow her lead.

'Ah.' His hand stopped on the holster. Prince's look towards Lorraine became more appraising. 'Are you aware of what DI Bailley has suggested?'

'Bailley.' Fell's voice cut through the conversation.

'We have a need for a Meresbourne representative –'

'DI Bailley.' Fell's voice had a growl to it.

Robyn gave Lorraine what she hoped was an encouraging smile and moved across to join Fell and the HR manager.

'Sir?'

'Bailley, I think this has been rather a success.' Fell paused for a second to wipe a small piece of fluff from his lapel. 'We will be doing this again and thought at the next one you could speak about your experiences.'

'That's an interesting idea, sir.' While trying to keep her face neutral, Robyn racked her brain for good arguments why she shouldn't be involved. 'However, given there is a real focus on gender equality at the moment, I wonder whether a senior female officer's experiences may be of wider interest, to really appeal to the biggest audience?'

The HR manager was pushing her lips together into a thin line.

'We shall see.' Fell checked his watch. 'Something to consider though. I must say goodbye to the Superintendent.'

It seemed a good chance to escape. Robyn nodded to the HR manager and scanned around the room for her team. Lorraine was still in conversation with Prince, Chloe was chatting with the stall holder for the Benevolent Association, Ravi beside her flicking through leaflets. Robyn walked over.

'– what we should do? We could get a football tournament going. We had a league up in Doncaster across the station with mixed teams. Everyone chips in to play and it all goes to the fund. How about it?'

'Shall we?' Robyn smiled down at Chloe. 'I think your football idea would be popular.'

Together, they walked along the corridor. 'Oh yes, it's such a good cause.' Chloe walked past the lift to the stairs. 'The Benevolent Association helps a lot of people. When my dad was hurt, I don't think we would have managed without them.'

'Your dad is an officer?'

'Was. He was in the force all his life. He got hurt in a crash, a drunk driver. And, well, he wasn't so good after. That's why I always support the Benevolent Association.'

Robyn saw Ravi's arm brush Chloe's, which could have just been an accident as they bumped shoulders at the turn of the stairs.

17

When they walked into the incident room, Graham was at his paper-strewn desk. 'Oh there you all are. It's past eleven. I thought I was the only one doing any work around here.'

Robyn looked around. The evidence boards were still in the corner, bare.

'Someone give me a hand here.' Robyn got one end of a board. Chloe jumped to her feet and manoeuvred the other end over a cable. Between them, they wheeled the board to a position in the centre. 'Thanks, Chloe.' She turned to the room. 'Right, I want all the details of Newman's death on here. Lots of questions we can be working on while we wait for the post mortem. What was he doing in the Docks estate? Did he run into the feminists again? Let's get on with it.'

Chloe fetched a scrap of tissue and began wiping the board.

Robyn held up her hand. 'Not you, Chloe. You're working on the Lady Ann case.' She turned. 'Ravi, Newman's death is your case. Can you get this board up to date, please?'

At the sound of his name, Ravi lifted his head, blinking as if he had just woken up. He glanced around the room, then met Chloe's eyes. She gave him a tiny nod. He stood up and took the tissue from her. 'Call this clean?'

'Yes, well, I struggle to reach the top.' Chloe looked back at him, chin up. 'You should try being short some time.'

Graham looked around his screen. 'I don't think the powers that be knew what they were letting themselves in for when they removed the height restriction.'

Robyn was relieved when Chloe laughed. 'When I was in Uniform, we had a child trapped in a house when his mother locked herself out. Guess who was able to get inside by climbing through a fanlight? We should be considered a specialist unit.'

'Are you suggesting Ravi and I only get cases involving giraffes?' Lorraine dropped into her chair.

'How many crimes are committed by giraffes anyway?' Ravi held his hands out.

'Loads.' Graham cracked his knuckles. 'They can't stop sticking their necks out.'

Amongst the groans, a paper ball flew across the office, missing Graham by several feet. He watched it pass, not even bothering to move. 'Feeble. Who said girls can't throw? Oh, just about everyone.'

Lorraine was about to retort when Robyn spoke. 'OK, settle down.' She groped for words. 'That was the whole point of the diversity seminar we just went to, we've got to accept differences and think what everyone brings to the team.' The silence that followed made Robyn wonder if she had just managed to upset everybody.

'And that's exactly why I didn't come. A diversity seminar? What kind of rubbish is this?' Graham waved his hand around the team. 'We don't need a seminar because we're doing fine. We're about as diverse as you can get, we've got pink people and brown people and even different shades of brown. We've got you, Guv.' He pointed at

159

Chloe. 'And we've even got a northerner for Christ's sake, what more do they want?'

There was a second's pause. Robyn knew she should say something: it was a relief when her phone rang. 'Hello, Sir.' She mouthed 'Fell' to the team.

'Right.' It was the news she had expected. 'Yes, sir.'

She put the phone down, conscious of the team's interest. 'The Superintendent has confirmed Professional Standards will be investigating the death of Jake Newman, given he was released from our custody only a few hours before.' She looked at Graham. 'As this is your case, I'll expect you to be the primary liaison with them.'

'Me?' Graham raised his eyebrows.

'Yes.' Robyn scanned his face. 'Any reason why not?'

'None.' The word came out very quickly. 'Just I was guessing they'll send an inspector and they'd want to work with an equivalent rank.'

Robyn had not enjoyed being the focus of Professional Standards' scrutiny and had no wish to do it again. 'He will have to interview me as I was the last person in the station to see Newman alive, so it's better you do the day-to-day handling.'

'And I thought today was going to be a good day.' Graham sidled back to his desk.

'It will be a good day.' Lorraine looked up. 'Kelly's just emailed through the outline pathology report so we've got some details for the board. I'll send it across.' She scanned her screen. 'OK, one of the last things in Newman's stomach was instant porridge.'

'So he was killed by a Scotsman?' Ravi gave a weak smile as he stuck a picture to the board.

'Porridge sounds like a woman's weapon to me.' Although Graham was clowning, Robyn heard a brittle note in his voice.

'No true Scottish person would ever eat instant porridge. This is an attempt to frame northern people.' Amid the laughter, Robyn thought how quickly Chloe had become one of the team.

'Hmm, certainly plausible.' Graham held up a finger. 'We're looking for a Sassenach. The real worry is if they are armed with golden syrup.' He allowed a moment for laughter, then seemed to sober. 'Right. Let's get this show on the road. We'll need to tie down Newman's movements, Raver. Let's make a list of everyone in his life, starting with his girlfriend.'

'Before that, is there anything else we need to ask Kelly at this stage?' Lorraine stopped typing.

'You can ask him what those pills in Bartholomew's bathroom were – always useful to know.' Robyn saw another email arrive with the subject 'Budget'.

'Righto. And just one other thing.' Lorraine stood up. 'Everyone had better still be on for the Jazz Jam tonight, seeing as it's my birthday.'

There was a second of silence: it looked as if everyone had forgotten their planned team evening. Chloe was the first to speak. 'Oh goodness, I forgot your card.' She dived into her drawer, pulling out a big, blue envelope. 'I meant to give it to you when I got here. Happy Birthday! I'm really looking forward to tonight. I can't wait to hear you play.'

Robyn had a horrible moment of doubt when she wondered whether she had signed the card, then remembered Chloe collaring her the week before.

With Ravi settled, Robyn thought it was time to tackle Graham. 'Right. We need to talk about a couple of things. It's nearly lunchtime so a meeting room should be free.'

Graham's eyes darted left and right looking for an escape until his sagging shoulders showed acceptance. 'OK then.'

With the people in the lift, Graham's usual persona seemed to reassert itself and he laughed with someone about the latest roadworks. They found a free meeting room. Graham remained standing, his hands gripping the back of a chair.

Robyn waited for him to sit down, then gave up. 'I want to talk about how we run these two cases because there are going to be a lot of crossovers but first, tell me what's going on with you.'

Voices from the next room carried through the wall. Graham was still staring into space.

'You can't tell me everything is all right when clearly it isn't.' She banged the table with the flat of her hand. 'Sit down and talk to me.' She looked into his face until his eyes met hers. 'At the moment, I have an officer who doesn't answer his phone over a weekend when he's on call and appears to be distracted all the time. I don't think that's because he's a bad officer, I think there's something wrong and I need to know what it is.'

Graham cracked the knuckles of one hand then the other. 'Had a lot on my mind recently.'

'What is it?' She had to lean forward to hear him, a gaggle of HR workers had just occupied the next-door office and were being noisy.

'My wife is dying.'

'What?' Robyn's first urge was to reach over and put her hand on his: a second thought told her this might not help.

'Cancer.' Graham sniffed. 'She had it before and she'd beaten it, so they told us.' He slid down into the chair. 'After her operation, the doctors said they'd cut out all of the tumour and she was clear. She seemed like her old self. Then she started getting these new pains and they ran a test. That's when they told us there must have been a secondary.' He shut his eyes. 'Because they'd missed it, it's spread. Everywhere, into her lungs and her spine. Now they say it's gone too far to treat and there's nothing they can do.' The last words had come out as a whisper, as if Graham didn't want to say the words out loud.

'I'm sorry.' Robyn tried to meet Graham's eyes but he was staring at the table. 'Why didn't you tell me before?'

There was a shriek from the HR room followed by laughter.

'Shall we go somewhere else and talk about this?'

162

Graham stood up. 'Actually, I don't want to talk about it at all.' He headed for the door.

Robyn caught up with him at the lift. 'I want to help you. I appreciate this isn't easy so tell me what I can do. What about special leave arrangements? You can't feel like working.'

The lift was full with people heading to lunch. They walked in silence past DI Pond's office next to the incident room. 'Come on, we can talk in here.' Matthew's empty office was tidy to the point of sterile. 'What do you need? Do you want a leave of absence?'

'Nah.' Graham shook his head.

'This is going to be hard.'

'Don't worry.' Graham scratched his nose. 'I can manage Raver.'

'Are you sure?' Robyn jerked backward as the chair back had no resistance. She felt her cheeks warm. 'Well, we can review this at any time.' She swallowed. 'What are they saying about, ah, timescales?' She hated the way she sounded like Fell trying to avoid a difficult subject.

'Months?' Graham shrugged. 'Weeks? They really don't know very much for all their white coats.'

'We can handle things here, it's not a problem.' She wondered how he was staying so calm. 'You take leave, be with her.'

'No.' Graham brought his hand down on the desk. 'You don't understand. She doesn't want me around.' He looked up to the ceiling. 'Can you imagine, no you probably can't. The hardest bit is my wife does not want me around because she says if I get upset, it makes her feel worse.' He looked back at Robyn. 'Have you ever seen someone you love in so much pain and there's absolutely nothing you can do to stop it? It makes me so angry.' He folded his arms. 'She's spending what time she can with her friends and our daughters. Our youngest is back from Australia this week, so that'll make her happy. It's best I'm out of the way.'

'OK.' Robyn struggled to find words. She was thinking of the pain she had caused Becky. 'You must let me know if you need anything.'

'The last thing I need is some tosser from Professional Standards breathing down my neck the whole time.'

She knew what this meant. After assigning Lorraine to Prince's team, there would be no one else so she would have to deal with the investigator herself. 'OK.'

Graham looked happier than he had done for a while. 'And don't tell the others. I really don't want to talk about it.'

'Of course.' Robyn stayed in the empty office for a moment. The smiling faces of Matthew, his wife and their three children gazed at her from the desk photo. It reinforced how solitary she had become and walking into the bustle of the CID office was a relief. Ravi had at least got some semblance of evidence on the board. In the centre was the wedding group shot showing Newman and the other ushers, smart in their suits, raising champagne glasses. Other images showed his friends and family. Robyn picked up a marker pen and added details of the argument between Newman and Trudwick.

'This is really weird. I even talked to him on Saturday.' Ravi tapped the picture of Newman. 'He was just a regular bloke. Why would anyone want to kill him?'

Graham, looking as if the last conversation had not happened, pointed to another image of Newman, head lolling, skin bleached white by floodlights. 'That is exactly what we are here to find out. Right. Raver, suspicious deaths. Rule number one: know who's dead. Get on the phone to the girlfriend and get her over to the morgue to identify the body.'

'Why do we have to ID him?' Ravi frowned. 'Surely we know all that already. The Guv and Lorraine were with him before he died, we've got his mugshot, fingerprints, everything.'

'Because details matter.' Graham adopted his lecture tone. 'His girlfriend might notice something we haven't, like "why doesn't he have his lucky Gonk with him, he never travels without it?" Two, it shows her we're serious about investigating and a handsome chap like you might get her to open up a bit about things we need to know. Chop chop.'

Out of the corner of her eye, Robyn could see Lorraine doing a bad job of hiding her giggles.

Half an hour later, Graham and Ravi left for the morgue. Robyn waited until she was sure they would not be popping back for a forgotten item, then stood up, going to lean on the front of her desk. 'OK, now is a good chance to talk about the Lady Ann case. Chloe, has Lorraine told you what we found out on Sunday?'

Chloe nodded. 'Yes, Guv. I still don't see why you didn't arrest Bartholomew at the time.'

'As I said, we need evidence.' Robyn saw outrage cross both faces. 'I know we've got the doctor's view but rape is unlike anything else. It comes down to one person's word against another's. Even getting a case to trial is hard and conviction rates are tiny. We have to think like a defence lawyer.' She walked to the blank whiteboard, found a pen and drew two vertical lines.

'Right. This column – facts suggesting it was rape.' She began to write: the felt-tip squeaked on the board leaving almost no mark. 'Bugger. Is there another pen?'

Chloe got up and fumbled in a drawer. 'Try this one.'

The pen was supposed to be red and came out pink. 'Thanks. OK. "Evidence". Then we put how the defence would challenge it over here.' She labelled the second column "Attack". 'And then we need to work out how we counter those points here.' She wrote 'Proof' in the third column. When she turned back to face Lorraine and Chloe, she saw determination in their eyes.

'OK, what facts have we got?'

'Bartholomew admitted he had sex with Shazia.' Lorraine's voice was cold.

Robyn wrote 'Confession'. 'Now the Defence would say it was consensual.' She wrote the word in the second column – the new pen was barely legible. 'And how do we prove his story isn't true?'

'She jumped off the balcony!' Lorraine spread her hands, jabbing the air. 'Doesn't Shazia trying to kill herself mean anything?'

Robyn took a deep breath. 'It tells me she was upset, yes.' She was conscious of the smell of her own sweat. 'It doesn't tell me what she was upset about.' She met Lorraine's eyes. 'Any lawyer could come up with a hundred things a nineteen-year-old girl might consider the end of the world. Let's see – she was jealous of the bride, angry because she hadn't been made a bridesmaid or just guilty because she'd been caught when someone walked into the room. And because she can't talk to us, we have to find another way of proving things.' She tapped the board. 'Come on. What else do we have?'

'Bruises on her body.' Lorraine leaned forward, elbows on her knees, chin cupped in her hands.

'Bruises.' Robyn wrote it down under 'Evidence' then added something to the next column. 'Caused by the fall, I think the Defence will say. How do we prove not?'

'What about the fact she didn't have a boyfriend and was probably a virgin?' Chloe sounded rather apologetic.

Robyn wrote it down, then added in the next column, 'Gagging for it'. Both Lorraine and Chloe snorted.

'Look, I don't like this any more than you do but this is what we will be up against. We have to do this to be able to build a case the Crown Prosecution Service will consider worth taking forward.'

The silence built up. Robyn recapped the pen, waiting for someone to speak.

'Are you saying everything we've found doesn't prove anything?' Lorraine slumped back in her chair. 'He's just going to get away with it?'

'No, of course not.' Robyn sighed. 'I'm just saying we need to think about this in a different way.'

'So what do we do?' Lorraine was turning a biro around in her fingers.

'We have to provide Shazia's voice, represent her as she can't do it herself. We need to talk to her friends, her family, show she wasn't the type who would have casually picked up a bloke and gone upstairs with him.' Robyn began wiping the board. 'Also, we need to get as much as we can on Bartholomew – his background, habits, previous behaviour, so his shoplifting is relevant here. What do his mates think of him, the girl he lives with? Get out there and talk to people.'

At last, her words seemed to have generated some response. The pair bent over the guest list and began muttering together. Robyn watched them for a moment then went back to the monthly budget report she had to complete for Fell, already a week overdue.

She was lost in the figures when a noise made her look up. Lorraine and Chloe were on their feet. 'We're off to get started on the interviewing, Guv.'

Desperate for air, Robyn decided to stretch her legs and pick up some lunch. She reached for her bag. 'Great.'

There was an awkward silence.

'Ah, Guv, we were going to start with the family and, well, maybe as it's already a difficult time?' Lorraine twiddled her handbag strap.

Swallowing, Robyn tried to look as if the rejection hadn't hurt. 'Yes, well get on with it then. I'm going to lunch.' She made a point of checking the catch on her handbag. 'You two still here?'

The pair of them hurried to the door. Alone in the office, Robyn stretched back and let her eyes slide out of focus. The administrative side of policing bored her rigid and she knew she wasn't very good at it. Now, if she couldn't interview people because she would offend them, there was a real question over what she was supposed to do.

18

The beginning of a headache was tightening around Robyn's temples and the quiet in the incident room seemed more oppressive than its usual buzz of chatter. She had given up on the budget and skimmed through emails, declined a number of meetings and waited for her appetite to return. Her phone ringing was a welcome distraction until she saw the name on the screen: Prentiss. Robyn had last spoken to the ex-DI at his retirement party two years ago. It was a bad memory: one of the funny stories he had dredged up had been one of Roger's first cases as a rookie police officer when he had nearly arrested a transvestite after mistaking him for his wife. Guessing the call might be to do with Graham, she let it go to voicemail. A second after the ringing stopped, it began again and curiosity got the better of her.

'Hello, Kenneth.' Using his full name was a moment of pleasure because Robyn knew everyone called him Kenny.

'Rog – ah, DI Bailley, where are you? I need to talk to you.'

There was the same note in his voice, the way you were expected to drop everything at a moment's notice. 'I'm at the station. This is a surprise.'

'Can you get away?'

'What's this about?'

'I've got some information. OK. I'll meet you in the petrol station on the roundabout in ten minutes.' Before she could ask another question, he had hung up.

Much as the summons irritated her, it was no loss to abandon the emails. She was curious about why Prentiss wanted to speak to her when he was mates with officers like Graham. She and Prentiss had never been close and the choice of venue was also odd. The garage was an anonymous place across the other side of the roundabout from the police station, the last place to buy fuel before the motorway. She could walk to it, though it meant a dash across the dual carriageway. Retrieving her handbag, she walked out of the station. The muggy air outside didn't help her headache. As she climbed over the crash barrier waiting for a gap in the traffic, she wondered again why she was doing this. A lorry turned off the roundabout, throwing up gravel from its wheels into her face. A gap opened and she started to cross. Halfway, a car turned without signalling, coming fast. She ran for the other side, having to leap onto the kerb, feeling her foot skid on the loose gravel. The car's horn blared as it raced past her, gone too fast for her to see the number plate. She picked her way across the rough grass to the forecourt of the petrol station. Looking up, she saw Kenny Prentiss sitting on a high stool at a plastic bar next to a coffee machine. Next to Prentiss, a woman with two-toned hair seemed to be trying to inhale the contents of her paper cup.

Robyn pushed open the glass door and walked around to stand at the end of the counter. 'Well, I'm here. What was the panic?' She thought retirement seemed to be suiting Prentiss: he had lost some of his belly and looked tanned as if he spent a lot of time outside.

A flash of a smile passed across Prentiss's face, broadening when he got to her chest. 'Bailley, good to see you.' His hands moved as if he couldn't decide between clapping her on the shoulder or shaking hands. 'You look – well. Very glamorous.' His lips pressed together before he became more serious. 'Thanks for coming. You need to talk to Dominika.' He inclined his head at the woman on the next stool. A pair of kohl-defined eyes flicked up before returning to a contemplation of the bottom of the cup. The movement brought hair down over her face, as if there was something to hide.

'Why do I have to talk to her, why now and why here?' Robyn looked hard at Prentiss. Even with the air-conditioning blasting down, her skin prickled with heat.

'I know, it's a bit irregular – relax. Believe me, you'll want to hear what this woman has to say and she refuses point-blank to report it formally so this is the only way.' Prentiss gestured around. 'This place seemed as good as any.'

Her old boss had always made her feel uncomfortable but this was new, something she'd never noticed before. Robyn kept her breath shallow. Whether it was aftershave, fresh sweat or the combination, he was giving off a scent that was almost aggressive, like a man about to throw a punch.

'You OK? Right. You know my wife was a nurse?'

Robyn nodded. She'd wondered how Prentiss had found someone to put up with him and when she'd found out his wife was a professional carer it made a lot of sense.

'Well, we were driving back from the golf club Friday night, about one am, and June sees this girl crying at a bus stop. Well, she insists we stop, see if the kid's all right, you know?' He shook his head. 'Would do it when she's on her own as well. I keep telling her she can't be mother to everyone, hey, she doesn't listen to me.' He jerked his thumb over his shoulder. 'Anyway, it was Dominika. June got her talking. Turns out, she'd been attacked. She was grabbed and dragged into a car, only just managed to get away.'

'Why doesn't she want to make a formal complaint?'

'Well let's just leave it by saying she was out on her own late at night.' The look of scorn from Prentiss was one she remembered well. 'So then I remember a couple of stories in the *Gazette* and think this isn't the first time. Had a quiet word with a few people.' He tapped the side of his nose. 'And it looks like you've got someone who's targeting young women. This girl can give you a description of him.' When she didn't reply immediately, there was impatience in his voice. 'It took a lot of persuasion to get her here. Talk to her.'

The girl's hand trembled as she poked the straw around the cup. It was enough to convince Robyn there was a story. 'OK.' She walked to the far stool and put her hand on the ridged plastic. 'May I sit down?' She didn't want to move too quickly, making the girl any more nervous than she already was.

Prentiss followed, clapping Robyn on the back. 'There you are love. Bailley always was the kindest bloke I knew.' He stopped, arm still resting on Robyn's shoulder. 'Well, come on, I did know you as a bloke.'

The woman was gripping the cup between her hands. 'You told me a woman.'

Prentiss smiled, the insincere beam Robyn remembered. 'And she, Robyn, yes, she is a woman. As good as. Look, you're here now, just talk.'

Biting her lip, Dominika glanced again at Robyn.

Robyn slid onto the stool, arranging her body to mirror Dominika's. 'Hello. I'm Robyn. I know I may not be quite what you expected.' She paused, smiled: there was no answering movement. 'I really want to hear your story. Will you talk to me?'

One of Dominika's feet tapped against the cross bar of the stool. 'I wanted talk with a woman.' She didn't seem to be opening her jaw fully.

'Come on, sweetheart.' Prentiss was standing at her shoulder. 'It's the closest thing to a woman we've got. It's going to have to do, yeah? You're both here now, might as well talk to – them.'

Keeping her voice soft, Robyn ignored him. 'I'm used to being judged by people too. We can talk, Dominika, wherever you feel most comfortable. Would it help you to talk about it?' Where sunlight fell on the woman's face, the heavy patches of foundation couldn't quite hide the dark bruising around her jaw.

There was a sharp exclamation, the sound of things hitting the ground. An angry man's voice yelled something. Dominika's eyes flicked towards the sound. A child began wailing. Robyn kept her eyes locked on Dominika's, willing her to look back at her. 'Talking about this might make it easier to deal with.'

The girl blinked a couple of times, meeting Robyn's eyes for the first time. She gave a tiny nod.

'Good. Now, you start any time you want.'

In anticipation of the story, Prentiss lolled against the counter, slurping the last out of his own coffee. Dominika's shoulders hunched forward; her foot was tapping again. Robyn turned to Prentiss. 'I really appreciate you doing this so maybe you could leave us alone?'

'I already know what she said.' The tone was one Robyn remembered that had never failed to irritate her. She hated the way Prentiss was always so sure of himself.

'I know you do. But clearly, having to say it again is making her uncomfortable, so let me talk to her on her own.'

'Christ's sake, OK, I'll wait in the car.' Prentiss marched away, throwing his cup at a bin. He didn't stop when the cup missed and bounced across the tiles.

'I'm sorry.' Robyn let the seconds pass wondering if the girl had changed her mind. It was only when her lips moved she realised Dominika was whispering.

'– and he grab me round the neck.'

She couldn't move the stool forward without entering Dominika's space. All she could do was try to block out the surroundings and create an aura of safety around the two of them. 'Go on.'

'He squeeze my neck, scratch me –' The child's scream rose in intensity. '– thought I was going to die.' Her shaking hand pulled down the scarf around her neck showing the edge of a yellow mark.

Still struggling to hear, Robyn risked leaning closer. 'Go on.'

The door opened, Dominika's eyes flicking to the movement, her body tensing. Under the fear, Robyn detected a hardness about the woman's looks. The most likely reason was she was a prostitute. It would explain Prentiss's sarcasm.

'He pull me to car, back, off the road to New Town.' Dominika stared down again into her empty coffee cup. 'He start, he start …' She choked off a sob and mimed hands tearing at clothing.

Robyn reached for her handbag, keeping the movements slow. In one of the outer pockets was a packet of tissues. She lifted the first one and held out the packet, shocked when the woman flinched away from her outstretched arm. The certainty of Dominika's situation and a suspicion of what she had to endure made Robyn more determined to get her story.

From the edge of the stool, Dominika glanced up. When she focused on the tissue, her shoulders lost their hunch, her lips pressing together. She took the tissue: her nail varnish was chipped, showing yellow underneath. After wiping her eyes, Dominika seemed able to continue. 'He start to try and not ready.' She held up her hand, little finger crooked down and there was a hint of a smile. 'Then a car went past. He duck down so not be seen. I manage to get my bag and spray him.'

'What do you mean –?'

The woman mimed using an aerosol.

'You used a pepper spray on him?' It had come out sharper than Robyn intended.

Dominika tensed. 'I knew things be like this. Exactly is why men like him on the streets and not arrested because women not allowed to defend themselves.'

Robyn shook her head. 'Dominika, I'm sorry. I was just surprised. I know it's not easy to get hold of those things in England.'

'No. My …' She stopped, blinking. 'My friend he buys it at home and brings it here.'

'What else can you –?'

Robyn stopped as Prentiss got out of his car and walked towards them. He pushed open the door.

'Just getting a paper. Didn't know you two were going to take so long.' He paid for a *Daily Journal* and left, casting a searching look at Robyn.

'Take as long as you need.' Robyn smiled at Dominika. 'What else can you tell me about him? Did you see what he looked like?'

'All in black. With hood up and a scarf over face. Just his eyes. Blue, blue eyes.'

'What about his build?' Robyn saw a flash of uncertainty cross Dominika's face. 'His body – was he tall?' She sat up straight, one hand over her head. 'Fat?' She puffed her cheeks out, bulking her arms around her body.

The smile lasted longer this time, a crinkling around Dominika's eyes softening her face. 'Not too tall. With my heels, less than me.'

'This is very good.' Robyn nodded to encourage her.

'His hands. His hands had tight grip but were small. Didn't go round my wrist.'

The girl was observant, she just needed prompting. Robyn allowed herself to smile. 'What else?'

'This was odd thing.' Dominika turned over one palm in front of her. 'He smell intense.' She turned over the other. 'And car smell dirty.'

'What do you mean by intense?'

The girl shivered. 'Strong. Like when you use chillies and smell hurt your nose.'

'This is really helpful. You said the car smelled dirty – what sort of dirty?'

The girl's eyes drifted over Robyn's right shoulder. After a couple of seconds, she blinked, her focus returning. 'Old smell.' She angled her head to the right. 'Earth but not country earth. Old places.'

Robyn nodded again. 'Can you remember what sort of car it was?'

The girl shook her head. 'Had a back door.' She looked like a child trying to please. 'He put me in one side and I ran out other.'

'I'm glad you got away. I think a doctor should look at your jaw.'

The girl shrugged. 'You going to stop him?' She pulled her handbag onto the counter.

'I'm going to try.' Robyn sensed the girl was anxious to be gone. 'You could still make a formal complaint.'

Dominika's face closed in on itself as she zipped up her bag. 'I go now.'

'Will you take my number?' Robyn held out a card. 'If not for this, in case there's any trouble with your friend or anyone he introduces you to.'

There was a second while the girl processed this then her eyebrows shot up. Pulling her bag to her, she hurried to the door. She ignored Prentiss in his car and ran across the forecourt in the direction of the lorry park. Robyn followed her outside.

Prentiss had got out of his car. 'What did you say to her?'

'Just asked again for her to report the attack.'

'What, a girl like her? You know what she is?' Prentiss had been an expert on vice because it had been an area of work the Dearmans, a local crime family, had specialised in.

'I know.'

'Did you get anything useful?'

There was something about Prentiss which always made her feel like a junior. Robyn rubbed her forehead; foundation left marks on her fingers. 'She gave a description.'

'I read a girl was put in hospital by someone last month. D'you think this could be the same guy? Have you got any leads?' He sounded as if he was enjoying himself.

175

'A couple of things we're following up.' Robyn wanted to scream how she was still clearing up cases Prentiss had just abandoned because they were too hard but she had no energy for a fight. Desperate to end the session, she stuck out her hand. 'Thanks for bringing Dominika. Do you think she'll be all right?'

Prentiss paused for a moment, looking at the coloured nails, before taking her hand. Robyn braced for a bone-crushing grip; instead it was a more delicate touch, his fingers just taking hers with a light squeeze. 'She'll be fine. Probably turning a trick for a trucker as we speak.' He laughed. 'Right, I'd better get on. Say hi to everyone for me and tell Graham I'll call him.'

He crossed to his yellow Nissan sports car, beeped the horn once and pulled away.

Robyn went back into the garage and picked up a meal-deal lunch as some kind of acknowledgement for the time she had spent there. The man behind the counter gave her a filthy look. As she put her change away, she saw him give the same look to the next person, an inoffensive middle-aged man in a grey suit.

'Hello, Guv. Canteen not cutting it today?' Graham paused in the doorway, sunglasses pushed up onto his forehead.

'I was meeting someone.' The cashier gave a loud tut. 'I'll explain later. You've just missed Prentiss. He asked me to tell you he'd call you.'

Graham took a quick breath. Before he could respond, the queue cleared and he went to the counter to pay. He and Robyn walked back to the car, Robyn slipping into the back of Graham's Vauxhall.

'Hi, Ravi. How did the identification go?'

'Oh hello, Guv. Didn't expect to see you here. It was not good.' Ravi craned around in his seat. 'You know where the morgue is, on the edge of the hospital site?'

'Yes.'

'Woah.' Ravi's head jerked to one side as Graham accelerated across the roundabout and up the slip road to the police station. 'Well first of all, we couldn't get parked anywhere near, so we had to walk about a mile with Jess and the baby and her mother. Her mother is a big lady.'

'And he means big, like a beach ball on legs.' Graham nosed the car into a space.

'Yeah. So we had to go past the sexual health unit and there was another group of protestors.' Ravi undid his seatbelt. 'This time I think it was about men using prostitutes. Anyway, they gave Jess and her mother some abuse as they walked past because they wouldn't join them. As if they needed any sort of grief on a day like today. Do those people do anything except protest about stuff?' He led the way across the damp car park.

'It's what feminists do instead of shaving their armpits.' Graham swiped his pass on the door reader and they filed into the lobby. 'So what were you doing talking to Prentiss?'

The corners of Robyn's mouth were turning up even though part of her mind said she should be shocked. 'Now, now. Prentiss wanted me to meet a girl who claims she's been attacked in town. Because she won't come forward formally, he brought her along informally.'

'Sounds like Kenny. Always doing his civic duty, especially if it means picking up attractive young ladies.' Graham's raucous laugh filled the lift.

There was a muffled sound of a gunshot. Ravi reached for his mobile and began swiping the screen.

'Really?' Graham shook his head. 'They're only fun in the films.' He checked his watch. 'Yikes. OK, Raver. We need to get those details and look sharp, we said we'd be at Gaddesford by two.'

'Did Jess Land identify Newman?' Robyn sank into her chair.

'Yeah. And no big surprises unfortunately. Raver, you tell the Guv.'

Ravi looked up from his computer. 'It was definitely him. We asked about the day.' He took a deep breath. 'Jess Land didn't go to the wedding because she didn't think they'd welcome the baby. She wasn't expecting Newman back because he was planning to get drunk with the boys and stay over at the hotel, so she was surprised when he came home ...' He flicked a page of his notebook. '... just as *Fact or Fiction* was finishing on TV, which makes it about nine o'clock.' Ravi looked up. 'She described him as drunk and angry. She picked up about the points on his licence, though apparently he wasn't making a lot of sense. Something bad had happened which he didn't want to talk about.' He looked around. 'She went to bed at ten after watching *Ward Nine*, leaving him pacing up and down, still agitated. The baby woke her around one o'clock and because Newman wasn't in bed, she thought he was in the baby's room. When the crying didn't stop, she got up and realised he'd left. It took a long time to settle the kid and the next thing she knew, you and Lorraine turned up.'

'There was one thing.' Graham lowered his voice. 'She said he seemed to be in pain. He tried to pick the baby up at one point and couldn't. When she asked him what was wrong, he swore and said he'd been attacked by some mad women.'

'Anything else worth knowing?'

Ravi shook his head. 'All very ordinary. He'd always been a plumber, started out on his own about a year ago, doing all right. They seemed happy enough, she said he loved being a father, was proud he was the first of his friends to be a dad. His life was going to work, playing football, taking his son to the park.' Ravi turned over another page. 'There was one thing, Guv. Land said Newman couldn't have been called out on a job on Saturday night because all his tools were still in the flat. He kept them there overnight after his van was broken into.'

Robyn wondered why she hadn't made the connection when she had walked along the crowded hallway.

'So we need to know why he went out.' Graham tapped his picture on the board. 'We asked Land if she knew why he might have gone to the Docks estate.' He raised his eyebrows. 'Then she got angry.'

'Angry?' Robyn looked up from opening the sandwich. 'Not upset?'

'Nope. An ex of Jake's lives in Fleet block on the other side of the car park. Land suspects they got back together again for a short time while she was pregnant. When she heard where he was found, she immediately believed the worst. Having a competition with her mother for how many names she could call him.' He walked towards the door. 'It's not a bad theory. Newman has a really awful day, wants a bit of fun. His girlfriend is tired out because of the baby and isn't in the mood. He goes to see his ex not knowing the ex has a new boyfriend. There's a fight.' Graham mimed a big punch. 'Newman staggers off to his van to go home and the combination of beatings means we've got a body.'

Ravi stood up. 'What about the argument he had with the other usher, Trudwick? You could build a story there too: they have an argument earlier in the day, Trudwick gets angry because Newman is lecturing him on being sensible and then does a runner, they have a fight and, well, same outcome.'

'Hmm.' Robyn stretched out her shoulders, relieved the pain was now more of a dull ache. 'Both are possible and need to be checked out though don't forget Dr Shepherd said his injuries were superficial. The big question is, did he get into the van himself or did someone put him there? We'll have to see what the forensic report comes back with. Also, did Newman tell his girlfriend what happened at the wedding?'

There was silence before Ravi flicked back through his notes. 'No.' He looked up, his movements jerky. 'She didn't mention anything.'

'Would you tell your girlfriend you'd been pulled in by the police for rape?' Graham shrugged. 'I don't think so.' He tossed his car keys into the air and caught them one-handed. 'Right. First, we're going to see Newman's father who lives in Gaddesford and then his mother. She and Trudwick both live in Lower Markham so we'll finish off with a cosy chat with him.' He paused in the doorway. 'I wonder why Kenny didn't come in and say hello?'

179

Ravi grabbed something off the printer and followed Graham. 'See you later, Guv.'

Alone again, Robyn picked up the drink before putting it down again. Although it had come out of the fridge, it was barely cool. She ripped the plastic off the sandwich, wondering what must have been added to the coleslaw to make it so bright. Taking a first bite, with her other hand, she typed 'assaults on women' into the computer.

19

With printed records of all the unsolved assaults on women in Meresbourne and the villages in the last two years, Robyn arranged the sheets by date across her desk. When she had finished, she had three rows of paper, sitting on top of all the other clutter. Picking up a highlighter pen, she started at the top left, taking the sheet balanced on top of her in-tray and skimmed through the case summary: a teenage girl had been beaten up when she held onto her mobile during a street robbery. The sheet was filed on the floor. The next case was a young woman coming home from a club who had been groped in the street. Robyn marked the sheet with a green '1'. She dismissed the case of a woman in Upper Markham who'd been hit with her own fire irons by a burglar and a case where the attacker was related to the victim. When Robyn had skimmed the last sheet, she rearranged what was left into a single row, including her handwritten summary of Dominika's case. She read through them again. Now, when they were together, there was a clear pattern in the cases: women walking alone late at night had been grabbed then assaulted. As the dates advanced, the violence of the attacks had increased. Robyn rubbed her eyes. She could remember the last case: only eight weeks ago, a clubber had been found battered and half-naked. Tests showed she had taken ecstasy and her last coherent memory was of stumbling out of Quiksilva after arguing with her boyfriend. The street she was found in had no CCTV and, with no witnesses, there had been nothing to go on.

Robyn asked herself again how she had missed the pattern. One attack had been just a few streets away from her own house in quiet, middle-class Barton. The earliest case in the line-up was just over eighteen months ago, when Robyn had been in charge of the team for six months. Her head sank into her hands. She could not blame this omission on DI Prentiss and his sloppy ways.

'Afternoon, Guv.'

Robyn jumped a little as Chloe and Lorraine walked in. She glanced at her watch: nearly two hours had gone past. She took a swig from the open cola bottle and grimaced at the sweet, flat liquid. 'What have you got?'

'Not enough to nail Bartholomew.' Lorraine scrunched a piece of paper on her desk and hurled it towards the waste paper basket. 'We've got more of a picture of Shazia's life, though. She's the youngest of three, another sister living at home. No problems, or at least none they were admitting. She and her sister seem to be close and when we were being shown their bedroom, she even mentioned about a potential boyfriend which she didn't want to say in front of their mother. Nothing suggests Shazia would pick up a stranger at a party. I guess it's not proof.'

'It all builds the picture. Ravi wasn't there, was he?'

'No, though I saw him in some of the photos around the place. They look like a close family.' Lorraine's hands knotted. 'Her sister asked what happened to Shazia so I told her it looked as if there had been some form of assault and that might be why she jumped.'

'That was information we shouldn't have released yet.' Robyn frowned. 'How did she take it?'

'She got angry. Angry with whoever did it.' Lorraine spread her hands, palms up. 'She asked me directly – I wasn't going to lie to her.'

'No one's asking you to lie. You can tell them we are still gathering evidence, which is true. I didn't want to give them information until we can be more certain.' Robyn sat down. 'Well, it's done. Was there anything from the wedding itself?'

'Again, not much. We've seen some more photos of Shazia. She looks like she was having fun.' Chloe held up a picture of a group of girls, a happy mix of bright silks, gold and smiles. 'In most of them she had a glass in her hand, so she probably did drink more than she was used to. Surely that means she was in no state to give consent?' Chloe ran her hand through her hair.

'You've got to remember, in cases of sexual assault, things don't work logically.' The pencil Robyn was spinning between her fingers hit the desk with a clatter. 'What you've just said confirms Bartholomew's story. For the rest, it's still his word against hers, so we need to give the best possible impression of her. We have to convince a jury who will unfortunately judge a woman's behaviour more harshly than a man's. For example, how serious was this boyfriend?'

'Not very – they probably weren't even a formal couple.' Lorraine sounded weary. 'According to her sister, there was a boy at college she liked who was a cousin of a cousin, nothing serious and probably her family would approve.'

'Now we're getting important things.' Robyn stepped towards the evidence board, then stopped. 'If we can't have a board, we need a way to store these facts.'

Lorraine looked as if she had a bad taste in her mouth. Robyn remembered the first rape case she'd worked on and the constant feeling of embarrassment from having to put yourself into someone else's sexual fantasies. 'Has the crime scene report come through?'

'Not yet, Guv.' Chloe scanned through emails. 'Let's hope that gives us something to work on.'

'So what's your plan?'

Lorraine sighed. 'We haven't really got one.' She gestured at the notebooks. 'We've got a whole load of evidence but we're not trying to prove what happened are we? It's why, or maybe how?'

'Exactly. Once we've got the forensic evidence confirming Bartholomew's story, I think it's worth a discussion with the Crown Prosecution Service.' Robyn knew they might also say there was no chance of getting the case to court. Given the sensitivities, she would be glad to have such responsibility taken from her. 'The CPS will be able to give you a view of the evidence and tell you what else you need.'

'What other evidence could we get?' Chloe's voice had a plaintive note.

Robyn made sure she sounded positive. 'You need to think about what you're trying to prove. Physical evidence will only take you so far – you'll need psychology to either force him into a more honest confession or paint him so …' She realised she had been about to say 'black'. 'Paint him so bad people will want him locked away whether they believe he's guilty or not.' She hoped neither Lorraine or Chloe had noticed as both seemed intent on their screens. Robyn let the pause lengthen. 'So – what are you going to do next?'

There was silence for a few more seconds before Lorraine raised her head. 'We could talk to the couple in 106 again. See if they can give any more details about what they heard.' Her face screwed up as if she were tasting something bitter.

'Good.' Robyn smiled. 'What else?'

'We can trace Bartholomew's ex-girlfriends.' Chloe leaned forward. 'If he's got any. Then we can find out if he's been violent or if he likes things rough, even if nothing has been reported?'

'Yes, good scene-setting for the jury. What else?'

Lorraine looked as if she were holding her breath. 'What about …'

184

She stopped, breathed in. 'We could find out which gyms he's used, see who he hangs out with. It might be good to see if there have been complaints against him – there may be something in why he trains at home.'

'Good. Now you're thinking like a sergeant.' Robyn clapped her hands. 'Well, get on with it.'

The pair converged around Lorraine's computer and began a low conversation. Watching the intent on their faces, Robyn wondered about herself. She wanted this case solved, to bring Bartholomew down but she could detach herself from it while Lorraine and Chloe seemed to be taking the attack very personally. She hoped her calm came from longer years of experience and not something inside her that could never understand being a woman.

The urge grew to check her make-up, reinforce herself. As Robyn stepped out into the corridor, Matthew was walking towards her, biting down hard on a chocolate bar. This seemed like a good opportunity to make up for lost time. 'Hello, Matthew. Have you got a second?'

Chewing, Matthew put his hand over his mouth.

'Thanks, finish your food, there's a couple of things. First the bad news. Fell said this morning he's referring Newman's death to Professional Standards.'

Matthew's eyes closed briefly. He crammed the rest of the bar into his mouth.

'But, there's also some good news. We got an outline of the post mortem early and Dr Shepherd's stated, without a doubt, the cause of death was nothing to do with the time in custody or the riot.' Their eyes met in shared relief as it was likely to limit the scope of any investigation. 'There's one other thing.'

Matthew held his thumb up, then down, still chewing.

'More thumbs down, I'm afraid. I think we've got a serial attacker in town.' Robyn saw lines appear on Matthew's forehead. 'I've been going through old cases. I don't think the attacks on women over the last eighteen months are isolated incidents, there are too many and there's a pattern. Can you brief this out to your team and get them paying extra attention to men hanging around late at night?'

Matthew swallowed. 'Sure. What's the description?'

'He's white, of medium height, stocky, those are all the things we do know.' Robyn ticked points off her fingers. 'He's careful, keeps his hood up, wears gloves and covers his face with a scarf. One person said he had blue eyes.'

'Not a lot.' Matthew shook his head. 'With the weather so cold at the moment, lots of people are wearing gloves at night. Is there anywhere he operates?'

'The fringes of the town centre, quiet residential areas. The last two were in New Town and Barton and, after one girl fought back, he's started using a four-door car. I'm sorry it's so patchy – I've only just started working on it but it looks serious.'

'We'll keep an eye out.' Matthew crumpled up the wrapper and shoved it into his pocket. 'Just to warn you, regular patrols are down to a minimum for the next couple of days because of all the events and there's the Loveless birthday parade tomorrow.' He snorted. 'All leave is cancelled.'

'Good luck.' Robyn searched for a positive. 'I heard Clyde was out of hospital.'

Matthew gave a small smile. 'He'll be off the frontline for six weeks but has already asked for a desk job as, according to him, he's coming back next week.'

Robyn smiled in return. 'I'm so glad. Thanks, I'll get you more details as soon as I can.'

The toilets were at the end of the corridor by the lift. A red bar showed on the lock of the disabled cubicle. At least the ladies' and gents' toilets had basin areas where you could stand if everywhere was occupied. For her, there was nowhere to wait except the corridor. As she hesitated outside, the desire for privacy was overridden by a real need to use the toilet. She fidgeted for a moment, feeling the pressure in her bladder increase because now it was all she could think about. Crossing her legs provided only momentary relief. Becoming impatient, she tried the handle, in case the sign was wrong. The door didn't move.

'All right. Keep your hair on.'

She recognised Phil's petulant tones and decided to cut her losses and go down a floor. There was a moment of pure happiness when she found the disabled toilet empty, followed by relief. Looking at herself in the mirror as she washed her hands, Robyn was ashamed. About eighteen months ago was when she had first acknowledged to herself that transition might be both what she needed and wanted to do and it looked like a number of women had suffered in that time because she hadn't been paying enough attention. Her positive mood faded. Talking to Matthew was just the beginning: she needed to warn people.

As she walked onto the second floor, Graham and Ravi appeared from the lift.

'Taking the stairs, Guv? Far too keen.' Graham was being jolly: to Robyn, it sounded forced.

'Hello. What have you got?'

'We've got plans for a nice cell and we're going to write "Trudwick" on the door.' Graham grinned, then held the incident room door open for Robyn with exaggerated courtesy.

20

When Robyn, Graham and Ravi walked into the incident room, Lorraine charged forward. 'Guv, did you hear the radio?'

'No, what was it?'

'Let me find it on catch up.' Chloe dived for her computer. A familiar jingle filled the room.

This is the three o'clock news on North Kent FM. A prominent Meresbourne businessman has accused the police of racism. We have obtained details of the complaint made by Durbesh Johar, who runs local company Grove Foods. He states the police force behaved unsympathetically after the recent tragedy at the Lady Ann Hotel which has left his niece in a coma. A police spokesman stopped short of an apology. The announcer sounded outraged on the family's behalf.

We have a duty to investigate when we believe a crime has been committed. We will, of course, investigate Mr Johar's concerns seriously and do what is needed to resolve them. Khalid sounded his usual measured self.

The Dockers' new manager has shrugged off crit –. Chloe shut off the sound.

'He might say the right things, we've still only got one point from three games.' Graham sat down.

'You ...' Mouth open, Lorraine stared at Graham. 'Is football all you can think about?'

Robyn heard Graham start to speak but her attention was focused on Ravi. A sheen of sweat glazed his face. As she started up from her chair towards him, he staggered, fingers scraping along the edge of a desk. Catching his arm, Robyn was able to steer him into a chair. 'You OK?' Close to, Ravi's skin was tinged with yellow. 'Get him some water. And open a window.'

Ravi slumped forward, Robyn managed to get an arm around him and held him in an awkward hug to stop him sliding from the seat. A perverse part of her hoped Ravi really had fainted as he would be embarrassed to find himself so close to her.

'Is he OK?' Chloe's voice was higher than usual.

'He's OK.' The pulse under Robyn's finger was racing. 'Just needs a quiet moment.'

'We should get him on the floor.' Lorraine's anger seemed to have evaporated. Taking his other arm, they laid Ravi in the recovery position.

When Robyn stood up, she looked around for Graham, who was sat at his desk, looking unconcerned. 'What did you do to him?'

Chloe took her place on the floor, fanning Ravi with a file.

'Me?' There was a slight shrillness to Graham's voice. 'Nothing. Just solved his case for him.'

Ravi moaned and shifted position. After a second, he tried to push himself up, bracing himself against a pedestal unit. He murmured something, eyes flicking around then dropping to the ground.

'You've got nothing to be sorry about.' Chloe smiled, offering a cup. 'It's very hot in here.'

Ravi grimaced as he took a sip. 'What is this?'

'Elderflower cordial. Just drink it.' Chloe refused to accept the cup back.

189

'Here, this might help.' Robyn offered the remainder of the choco-late bar she'd got as part of her meal deal. It had melted, the wrapper covered in dark blobs. Ravi tried to break off a piece and ended up licking it off his fingers.

Chloe offered a tissue.

'I'm OK, stop fussing.' His voice was stronger.

'Does this mean?' Lorraine stopped, her fists clenching. 'Does this mean they won't be pressing any charges?'

'It's because Shazia jumped.' Ravi brushed Chloe away. 'Suicide really makes a family look bad. They won't want that to come out.'

'Are you able to tell us about the person who spoke to the radio?' Robyn could feel the warning look from Chloe.

'My uncle.'

'Can he decide what happens?' Lorraine spread her hands wide. 'Is he Shazia's father?'

Ignoring Chloe's protestations, Ravi hauled himself up onto the chair. 'No, but it doesn't matter. He's the eldest brother, head of the family. He thinks they're all still back in India the way he bosses eve-ryone around.'

'Was he the one who objected to you joining the police force?' Settling back into her own chair, Robyn saw Ravi's tiny nod and felt the implicit appeal. It would have been so easy to say everything was all right and they were close to nailing Shazia's attacker. 'And we're glad you followed your own ideas and joined up.' It was as much as her conscience would allow.

Ravi seemed to sense the hesitation: he narrowed his eyes, not able to hold her gaze.

'OK, we're going to get you home.' Robyn was glad to change the subject.

'I'll take him, Guv.' Chloe stood up.

'No. I'm not going. If I can't help Shazia, I need to help other people.' Ravi gripped the arms of the chair and pushed himself to his feet. One stagger and he seemed to balance, a hand hovering by the back of the chair.

'Be sensible, Ravi. We've got everything under control here.' Robyn was trying to sound positive even though she didn't believe what she was saying. She sat down, to encourage Ravi to do the same.

Graham wheeled over a chair. 'Sit down, Raver, you're making the place look untidy.' He pushed it into the back of Ravi's legs, who swayed, then sank into the seat. Graham perched on the desk next to him. 'The excitement of finding a killer, eh Raver? That feeling never goes stale.'

'Have you made an arrest?' Robyn felt she was missing something. Graham grinned. 'Tell 'er, Raver.'

Ravi looked around for his satchel, sliding the chair across so he didn't have to stand and pulled out a notebook. 'It was something from Newman's mother gave us the clue. He'd told her he was going to give up the football club, because, now he was a father, he was getting bored with all the laddish things. He was going to break it to the team after the wedding and stop after the groom came back from honeymoon, 'cos it wasn't fair to leave the team two players down.' He looked around, picking the cup off the floor and taking a deep swallow. 'Yuck.'

'So then we went to see Trudwick who, like so many young rascals, loves his mother and lives with her in Lower Markham.' Graham seemed determined to keep himself in the limelight. 'Ex-council place, pretty run down. No car, just a learner scooter, which is registered to Trudwick.'

'Yeah. His mother answered the door …' Ravi turned over a page of his notebook.

'And didn't seem too surprised to have a couple of police turn up on her doorstep.' Graham tapped the side of his nose.

'She says Trudwick's still in bed. We waited, watching the back door though and eventually, this bloke comes down in just a t-shirt and boxers.' Ravi looked up. 'Being fair, he did look like he'd just got out of bed. He's very vague about where he went on Saturday night – said as he had the night off anyway for the wedding, he thought he'd make a night of it in London. He visited some clubs, mates on doors got him in for nothing so of course he can't say where because he'll get them into trouble. He got back about ten on Sunday morning, worked last night and is still catching up on sleep.'

'There's just one problem with this heart-warming little story.' Graham held up a finger. 'His moped was caught on the automatic number-plate cameras jumping a red light on the Maidstone Road just after one am on Saturday night. About the time Newman died, Trudwick was heading into Meresbourne.'

'Good work, both of you. Did you challenge Trudwick?'

'Nah. Only found out about the image when we called through the plate. Trudwick's DNA's on file from the assault, so we thought we'd wait for the forensics, just to make sure it's a slam-dunk.' Graham grinned.

'Slam-dunk?' Lorraine looked up from her desk. 'You laugh at me for watching Scandi-crime – sounds like you've been watching too much of the American sort.'

'A breakthrough like this calls for a cup of tea and you can't get much more British than that.' Graham grabbed a stained box-lid used as their tray. 'No point in asking if you want one, Guv, because I know the answer.' As he passed her desk, Graham looked over at the ordered sheets. 'What's all this then?'

'Something I shouldn't have missed.' As the team gathered around her desk, Robyn described what she had done and her conclusions.

Graham whistled. 'Now you spell it out …'

'Right.' Robyn held up a pen to bring everyone's attention together. 'We are going to go back over all of these incidents, re-interview all the witnesses and treat it as a single case. Our first priority is a full description because at the moment, Uniform have got almost nothing to go on. Then we try and narrow down locations. Ravi, Chloe – I want you to work on this together.'

Hoping this would give Ravi enough to keep his mind from brooding, Robyn sat down at her desk. Now she had noticed the problem, she searched for anything else she could do to avoid another attack. Digging her phone out from the clutter on her desk, she called Khalid.

'Robyn. How are you?'

'Much better thanks. Can we get a media alert out?'

'Is this to do with the family's comments about the rape investigation? Because at this stage, the less we say about it, the better.'

'I heard the report just now. Not ideal.' She turned away from the team. 'I thought you sounded really calm, by the way. No, this is something else. What you said about the unsolved attacks. I've gone back over them and there's a pattern. We need to alert the public because there's someone targeting women in town.'

There was a short pause. 'So how long has this been going on?'

'About eighteen months.' Saying the time reinforced her omission. 'So can we get a media alert out? Speak to the nightclubs, get some posters up?'

'Unfortunately it's not quite so simple.'

'Why not? I've got the evidence here from old cases. We've not got much of a description, it's more about warning women not to walk alone.'

'If we put such a warning out today, before this panel tonight, Fell will get crucified.' Khalid sighed. 'Dr Bergmann will use it to attack him and when we've got a town full of angry women, they'll make every complaint going.'

'But,' Robyn nodded thanks to Graham who had just put a cup of tea in front of her, 'isn't that what we want? Everyone to be talking about it?'

'Not if it makes people think the police can't do their job.' Another phone sounded in the background. 'Look, I've got to take this. We'll talk later.'

193

Robyn put the phone down on the desk and glared at it. 'Well, if you won't help us, we'll have to just catch him ourselves.'

A packet of custard creams appeared in front of her nose. 'Trouble, Guv?' Graham shook a couple of biscuits onto the desk.

Scooping up one, Robyn shook her head. 'No more than usual.'

'Hey, no snacking. We're going out in a few minutes.' Lorraine missed the face Graham pulled at her because her phone rang.

'Right, Guv.' Chloe went to put a pile of paper down on Robyn's desk, then gave up. She moved back to her own desk and fanned out the sheets until she found one. 'I got the details through from the catering firm of their staff and thought I might as well check them out. A lot of very shiny new visas and no one has a criminal record.'

'Good Lord, what's Deany been up to now?' At Chloe's desk, Graham was bending over the pile of paper.

'You what?' Chloe started back to her desk.

Graham held up a picture of the hotel staff. 'This is Lee Dean – I put him away about five years ago for drug dealing. Never a major player but good to get rid of him all the same. Why are you looking at his ugly mug?'

'He's not called Lee any more, he's Lawrence and he's the manager of the Lady Ann hotel.' Chloe laughed at Graham's expression.

'Sneaky little bugger. Well, well.' Graham stood up, pulling his jacket on. 'Sounds like it would be worth paying him a visit soon to see that he hasn't slipped back to his bad old ways.'

'Ah, talking of drugs.' Lorraine stood up. 'Kelly gave me the details of the drugs in Bartholomew's bathroom. They're steroids, powerful ones, probably sourced from the internet as they're not licensed in the UK.' She stashed the phone in her bag and came to stand beside Robyn. 'Those pills sound nasty. They're intended for horses and in humans can cause liver failure, impotence and all sorts.'

'Aren't those things illegal?' Chloe gathered her bag.

'Not if they're for private consumption. You can do what you like to yourself and it's not illegal.' Graham held the door open for Lorraine and Chloe. 'Let's go.'

Ravi's face crumpled: his hand flailed out as if looking for support. Robyn stepped forward and let his weight lean against her. He took a quick breath though didn't flinch away.

'Come on you two.' Graham looked back from the doorway.

Ravi took a deeper breath. 'Coming.'

21

The team sat around a table in the pizzeria. Ravi had gobbled his pasta and now sat, taking regular gulps of water, as if timing everyone else.

Graham was on his second beer: he was reading the messages in Lorraine's big birthday card. 'Look at this. "To Lorra" – hah! "To Lorra, happy birthday, love K".' Is that our Dr Kelly Shepherd by any chance? Sending a lorra, lorra love?' Graham's accent was just about recognisable as Liverpool. 'Blimey. I thought I was the only person who knew everyone in the station. Have you been "networking"?'

'Just talking to people.' Lorraine took a sip of her spritzer.

'Anyone would think you were going for promotion.' Graham set the card down on the table.

Lorraine met his look. 'Yeah. What about it?'

More seconds of silence. Graham half-shrugged. 'About time too.'

'When does your hockey season start, Ravi?' Robyn had seen Lorraine's fingers tighten on her knife and didn't want the conversation to continue.

Ravi put down his glass with a bump. 'Sorry, Guv. Were you talking to me?'

'Yes. Just wondering when your hockey league starts?' Her new evening shoes, with proper kitten heels, were pinching. She had slipped them off under the table.

'It's started. I missed the first match for the wedding.' He stopped and his eyes dropped to his empty plate.

Robyn swore under her breath. There seemed to be no safe subjects. 'Do you think you'll do well this season?'

'Hope so. We've had a couple of players retire, so I'm playing left wing now, which is new for me.' This was better: Ravi's voice was sounding more positive. 'It's OK, I just don't get as much time in front of the goal as I'd like.'

'I hated hockey at school.' Lorraine smiled. 'It was always freezing, the mud went everywhere and people kept hitting me with sticks.'

'So why did you join the police? Now half the town wants to hit you.' Graham spoke through a mouthful of garlic bread.

'We didn't do hockey at my school – too posh for the likes of us.' Chloe laughed. 'We played football in winter.'

'Girls playing football?' Graham shook his head. 'What's the world coming to?'

Lorraine glanced at her watch. 'OK, I need to go and get ready. Our set starts at nine, so I'll see you all there.' She got her wallet out of her bag.

'No, it's your birthday. You organised, so we'll sort it out.' It had been a long time since Robyn had been out on a social evening like this and she realised now how much she'd missed the simple act of being with people.

'OK, thanks, Guv. I've asked the club to reserve you a booth. See you.' Lorraine dashed into the street.

'We've got half an hour, would anyone like another drink?' Robyn looked around. 'This is on me, by the way. We don't go out much as a team and I've enjoyed it.'

'Told you so, Guv.' Graham held up his glass towards a waitress. 'Hi, another beer for me and, who else?'

Ravi stood up. 'I'm going to go home.' He seemed to be struggling for words. 'It's been … well, I need to go home.' He grabbed his jacket from the back of the chair and the team's goodbyes followed him to the door.

'I'll have an orange juice, please.' Chloe tilted her beer bottle to get the last drops from it before handing it over.

'And a sparkling water for me.' One was her limit because she had to drive. Watching Graham drain his glass, Robyn wondered how he was getting home. Her phone rang, Becky's picture appearing on the screen. 'Bugger.' Swearing at her daughter didn't feel right: she wanted to talk to Becky so much, just not in public. 'Sorry everyone, got to take this, back in a minute.' She stabbed at the phone, anxious to catch the call before it rang out. 'Hi Becky, hang on a sec.' Dodging a waitress with a giant pepper grinder, she weaved through the tables. In the street, she walked under an awning to get out of the drizzle. 'Sorry, I was in a restaurant, I'm outside now.'

'I hope I wasn't interrupting anything?' Becky's voice was cold.

'No, no. One of the team's birthdays and we were out for a meal. It's lovely to hear from you.' There was silence from the other end. It seemed to be up to her to make conversation. 'You've done your play now, haven't you? How did it go?'

'Fine. We might even end up giving another performance.'

'Sounds great.' Robyn had the feeling she had when questioning a witness, where answers would have to be dragged out. 'Can I come this time, if your mother won't be there?'

Becky sobbed. It was a simple noise of pain and the sound cut Robyn like a physical blow.

'Sweetheart, what's wrong?' The distance between them felt enormous. 'Tell me what's wrong.'

'It's mum.' Becky took a shuddering breath. 'She and Richard are getting divorced.'

Robyn breathed out. Her first reaction was relief it was nothing wrong with Becky. 'Oh goodness. I'm sorry.' She hoped it sounded sincere. Even though she knew it was selfish, it was hard to feel sympathy for an ex-wife who thought you were a freak. 'What can I do?'

'When you arrested her it was the final straw.' There was another burst of wet sound. 'Richard said she'd been getting too extreme and he wasn't going to be married to a criminal.'

Robyn turned away as Graham and Chloe walked out of the restaurant. Graham waved so she could no longer pretend she hadn't seen them. 'I settled up, Guv. You coming?'

She covered the phone. 'I'll be along in a minute.' She waited until they were out of earshot. 'Sweetheart? Are you still there?'

'Still here.' Becky's voice was flat, miserable.

'You sound terrible. What can I do?'

'I need to come down and stay with you.' There was a long sniff. 'Mum's said she wants to come and "hang out" with me and "bond as women" – I've got to go somewhere 'til term starts and all my friends are away for the summer.'

The snub was clear: Robyn was happy to ignore it. 'And I guess my place is the last place she'd want to come, eh?' She'd hoped for a laugh and heard nothing. 'Come any time, sweetheart. You've got a brand new room to stay in. I've been decorating.'

'You've changed, Dad.' There was a new note in Becky's voice.

'Yes, I'm happy.' Robyn was grinning. 'But I'm still your dad.' She realised what she'd said. 'I didn't mean it like that. Now, just call me before you arrive so I don't leave you waiting on the doorstep if I'm out on a case.' A horrible thought struck her. 'And, if you get here and it's dark, get a cab. A proper one I mean, the sort you book. I'll pay for it. There's been a few attacks on girls.'

'Round the Docks estate?'

The casual acceptance in the tone made Robyn wince. 'No, all over town. It's women walking on their own late at night, so please don't take any chances. When you get to the station, call me. If I can't make it back, I'll send the key to you in a taxi, which you will then take.' She was trying to convey just how serious this was without scaring Becky. 'You're the most important thing here.'

'OK. Thanks, Dad. I'll call you when I've checked trains.'

'See you soon, sweetheart.' After the call finished, she found herself staring at the phone, not really believing she could have got so much happiness from it. A small, practical part of her mind wondered how Becky would react to her new appearance if she was already upset but the fear was swamped by her feeling of exhilaration.

Up the street, Graham stood outside the Black Cat Bar, talking to a doorman. Chloe, standing next to him, only reached the man's chest. 'Good timing, Guv, Lorraine's band will be on in ten minutes. See you, Stan.'

The three walked through the entrance corridor into the main bar. Clusters of people stood around swigging from small bottles. There were a lot of young men with beards. A hodge-podge of sound came from a raised stage in the back corner where men in black were setting out instruments.

'As I picked up the tab in the restaurant, think the least you can do is get the drinks, Guv.' Graham leaned over the bar. 'I'll have a – the one with the green label – how the hell do you pronounce it?' He straightened up. 'They do loads of really interesting Belgian beers here. Some of them are as strong as wine.'

'I'm sorry, how much was it? I'll get cash out tomorrow and pay you back.' Robyn peered into the darkness behind the bar. 'You're right, these do look good.'

'What are you looking so happy about, anyway?' Graham accepted his beer, holding the bottle up to the light. 'Look at the colour of this.'

'Just had some good news.' Robyn ordered herself a beer to celebrate. She told herself it would be good for her if she walked home. 'My daughter's coming to visit this summer after all. Cheers everyone.'

'Cheers.' Chloe took a sip of orange juice. 'How old is she?'

'Nineteen. Well, nearly twenty, it's her birthday soon.' Robyn looked at Chloe. 'Actually, that's a point – what an earth do you get a twenty-year-old for her birthday?'

'How about –?'

'Guv, before the band starts.' Graham spoke over Chloe. 'Just heard a juicy whisper.'

Robyn knew she should be interested in what Graham was saying but she really just wanted to relax and enjoy the moment.

'Stan on the door was saying there's a lot more drugs around than he's seen for a while. He also gave me a name.'

A man carrying a guitar stepped up to the microphone. 'Good evening, thanks for coming to the Jazz Jam, we're the Fatback Five.' Drums and double bass started a low rhythm. 'We'll be entertaining you for the next half hour, so don't be shy about getting up and dancing.' Lorraine's clarinet soared over the backing.

Robyn was looking at the stage. She jumped as Graham touched her arm. She could see his mouth moving though the music was too loud to hear the words. She shook her head.

He said something and this time she watched his lips move and saw the smug expression on his face. 'You think it's the Dearmans.' Graham's obsession with the local Dearman family had been inherited from Prentiss. She turned away and took a sip of her beer to give herself a chance to calm down. 'The Dearmans haven't committed a crime since you arrested Gabriel and Micky over three years ago. Why do you think it's them?'

'It's in their blood. They've been criminals for generations.' Graham tapped the table. 'And I know we haven't arrested any of them recently though we can't say for definite they haven't committed crimes, can we?' He sat back. 'Just means we haven't been looking at them as carefully.'

The band finished the introduction and accepted a smattering of applause. The next song was a faster number; Robyn found her foot tapping.

'Just as you did with the old cases, think I should have a look back and see whether it looks as if the Dearmans are still up to their old tricks.' Graham had raised his voice, to be heard over the music.

'Look, this isn't the place to discuss anything when anyone could hear us.' Robyn leant closer to try and avoid shouting. 'Also, this is meant to be a social – we shouldn't talk shop.'

Graham raised both hands. 'All right, have it your way, Guv. Just wanted to make sure we're doing our job of tackling crime.'

Robyn's good mood was slipping away. 'We are dealing with it. There's a new regional task force being set up to look at drugs coming in. Lorraine is our representative.'

Graham stared at her. 'Wait, it's being handed over and Lorraine is in charge?'

Out of the corner of her eye, Robyn could see Chloe pushing herself back into the corner of the booth, trying to keep her eyes fixed on the band. 'Yes. It will be good for her to get more exposure.'

'I see.' Graham sat back, folding his arms.

Robyn had no wish to prolong the argument and turned away from him, facing the stage so she could enjoy the music tonight, though she would have to have it out with Graham tomorrow. At the end of the song, her bottle was already empty. She was about to offer a round when Graham's phone rang. He glanced down at it, then hunched over, covering his ear.

There didn't seem any point in going to the bar: Chloe had barely touched her juice. A moment later, Graham tucked the phone back into his pocket. 'Gotta go.'

'Everything OK?'

Graham pushed himself up, both hands on the table, rocking the bottles. His 'see you tomorrow' seemed to be aimed at Chloe. He took a step towards the door, hesitated, then turned back to the stage, raising a hand for a second towards Lorraine, before walking out.

Robyn watched him go, then caught Chloe's eye. 'The music's great, isn't it?'

Chloe looked relieved at the attempt at normal conversation and nodded. The band finished the song and the guitar player called a greeting to some new arrivals. Robyn had a sudden urge to get drunk.

TUESDAY 20 SEPTEMBER

22

Without opening her eyes, Robyn resisted the urge to go to the bathroom for as long as possible until it became an imperative. The moment she swung her feet to the floor, her eyes jerked open. It had all seemed like such a good idea last night, to have a couple of beers and walk the mile home from the town centre. She had ended up in her bare feet because her new shoes hurt so much: the skin of both feet was a patchwork of red blotches, the soles blistered.

She wondered how long she had before the alarm was due to go off. Squinting at the clock, it took seconds to process what she was seeing. She had slept through the alarm. The headache was pushed to the back of her mind as she realised how late she was going to be. She had trouble focusing on the mirror while shaving and there were patches where the skin was scraped raw, a dribble of blood welling from a cut. Yesterday's suit was in a heap on the bedroom floor. When she picked up the trousers, there was a very definite damp patch around one knee. Touching the patch brought away a brown stain. Swallowing, she chucked them in the bath without investigating further. Her other suit needed mending: it would have to be either one of the skirts she wore around the house in the evenings, jeans or a pair of casual trousers she hadn't got round to sending back. When she put them on, they sank down her non-curving hips, exposing a large patch of stomach. The only top long enough to cover everything was a slouchy jumper that looked very casual. She didn't dare look at herself in the mirror.

The kettle seemed very loud as it boiled. When she poured, she got a dribble of water with a lot of dregs and scale. If she had forgotten to pre-fill the kettle, the walk home had not sobered her up as much as she thought. Shreds of kebab meat, lettuce and an empty paper takeaway cup sat on the counter. A brown stain ran down the front of the units to a pool on the floor. One piece of good news then was the stain on her trousers must just be cola. Although food was the last thing on her mind, she put a couple of slices of bread into the toaster and gulped down a glass of water which did nothing to take away the stale taste in her mouth. The bandages had gone from her hands, she had no idea where. The toast was taking so long, she began to wonder whether the machine was even working. Popping up the tray to look, the bread hadn't even begun to colour. Pushing it back down, she put the radio on.

Eight o'clock on North Kent FM, the news headlines, I'm Jenny Falconer. The leading feminist, Dr Felicity Bergmann has attacked an 'erosion of female consciousness' during a debate in Meresbourne last night. Bergmann described the media as 'letting anyone believe they can be a woman as if it were a fashion state-ment'. The event, held at the town hall, was trouble-free though there was a heavy police presence following the disturbances at the weekend.

Robyn stared at the radio. Her nagging headache was replaced by a sick feeling. A dark smell caught the back of her throat: a thin stream of smoke was coming from the toaster. Robyn had to dash to the downstairs cloakroom.

As she washed out her mouth, she was struck by shame at getting into this state and a sudden fear of whether she had disgraced herself in front of Lorraine and Chloe. There was also the question of how she would get through the day when all she wanted to do was go back to bed. The idea of taking a sick day was out of the question so she called for a taxi.

Abandoning the burnt toast, she forced down a couple of slices of plain bread with two glasses of water. She slipped into her work shoes. The laces put more pressure on the tops of her feet though at least they were not rubbing on the same points. As the taxi honked outside, she hurried up to the bathroom and grabbed a packet of paracetamol.

'Good morning.' The formal greeting was in a thick, Eastern European accent. 'To the police station, yes?'

'Morning. Yes please.' Robyn settled into the back of the cab and spent a minute trying to click in the seatbelt. Once done, she reached into her handbag for her make-up pouch. She had seen women putting on make-up in all sorts of places: she didn't see why it should be any different for her. She uncapped the foundation. As she squeezed the tube, a bubble of air popped, sending small drops of fawn liquid over her trousers and some onto the car seat.

'Bugger!'

She was conscious of the cabbie's eyes flicking to the rear-view mirror. Putting the cap back on the tube as fast as she could, she reached into her bag for tissues and began dabbing at the smears. The motion of the car was not helping her stomach and the air was too hot: she fumbled around the door.

'You try open window? I do here.' He pressed something and the window slid down. They were out onto the ring road now in stop-start traffic and the air smelled of diesel.

'I'm sorry, could you pull over? I think I'm going to be sick.'

'You no sick in my car.' The driver had half a car's space in front of him and lurched the wheel to the left, bumping onto the verge. Robyn pushed open the door and leant out, not even managing to undo the seatbelt. The sickness travelled up her throat until she retched, lumps of bread clogging in her mouth. She waited until she was sure there was no more. She tried not to think about the faces in the cars passing and hoped there was no one from the station. When the shaking stopped, she shut the door. 'I'm sorry. I'm OK now.'

'I'm adding money for cleaning.' The cabbie forced the car back into the line of traffic. At least he kept quiet for the rest of the journey while Robyn tried to piece together exactly what she had done last night. Chloe had left straight after the set finished. Robyn remembered sitting down with Lorraine and the band, sticking to beer. She was sure it was no later than ten-thirty when she'd left. There was a moment's relief that she had done nothing bad in front of her colleagues. It had been on the way home when she had run into Ady who was on his way back from covering the Loveless panel debate at the town hall. Because both of them were off duty, one of them had suggested a nightcap: she had a horrible feeling it might have been her because she finally had something to celebrate. They had ended up in a bar with a Scottish landlord and a great selection of whiskies. She remembered laughing when Ady quoted some of the speakers' more ridiculous statements and his impression of Fell had been hilarious.

The taxi pulled up outside the police station, the cabbie making a point of changing the meter to a higher rate. With no energy to argue, Robyn accepted the addition to the fare and reached her wallet from her bag. When she opened it, there were no notes, just a few loose coins. She must have bought a lot of drinks last night.

'Ah, do you take cards?'

'What? No, no cards. Cash only.'

'OK, I'm sorry about this. Could you drive me to a cash point?'

'You have no money?'

'No. Well, yes, I have money. Just not on me.'

Her phone rang as the cabbie made a pantomime of reversing before shooting onto the roundabout, sending Robyn slamming into the door. She shut her eyes and let the phone ring out. The man kept up a constant stream of indistinguishable words under his breath until they screeched to a halt outside a bank. Robyn clambered out gratefully: the cabbie got out of his own door and loomed by her shoulder as she inserted her card.

She stood up straighter: annoyance was a great cure. 'Do you mind?' Her fingers hovered over the keypad until he turned away. The journey back to the police station passed in silence. With the new notes, Robyn didn't have change, even for the inflated fare and sat, resolute, while the man huffed over counting out coins. Walking up to the front entrance brought back memories of the angry mob and she quickened her pace. The lobby was empty apart from one person standing by the desk, his back to the entrance.

Robyn felt a lurch in her stomach and forced her raw throat to swallow. The close air of the lobby had brought a taste of sickness back into her mouth.

The desk sergeant put down the phone. 'Ah, there you are ma'am. I was just trying to call you. Here's DI Bailley now, Superintendent.'

'Bailley.' Although Fell never seemed to look directly at anyone's face, Robyn could feel his appraisal of her appearance. 'I looked in at the CID room and you weren't in yet.' Fell frowned. 'I trust you are aware of the complaint made against the Lady Ann investigation?'

'Yes, sir.' She tried to make her voice sound brighter than she felt, then worried that she would sound flippant about the complaint.

'I am meeting the family at noon and I need to know beforehand what has been done and what you intend to do.' Fell glanced at his watch. 'Do you have enough to make a conviction stick? I do not want to give the family false hope, particularly when it is not even clear whether they will press charges.'

The room seemed very hot. Robyn licked her dry lips, tasting a bitter tinge. 'Not yet, sir.' She continued before Fell could speak. 'However, we are expecting the forensic report this morning which should give us enough to decide whether a conviction is possible.'

'Very well.' Fell picked up a slim attaché case. 'I am due at the Town

Hall now for the council meeting. Mr Johar has agreed to meet there. You will join me at eleven forty-five for a briefing.' He walked out of the front entrance.

The desk sergeant let out a long breath. Robyn was focusing on getting inside and finding a toilet. She had to wait as a large group strolled out through the inner door, feeling more and more certain she was going to be sick again. Someone called a greeting: she managed a small smile. In the corridor, a cleaner was sweeping the lino with a broad brush, a pile of full bin bags beside him. She dodged him and wrenched open the door to the disabled toilet. A waft of chemical pine hit her and she made it only as far as the sink. The bile seemed straight from the bottom of her stomach and she hoped no one had heard her retching. After she had washed her face, the sink and the cuffs of her jumper, she took time to put on her make-up. It had become her armour to face the day. With the nausea under control for the moment, she decided she needed something in her stomach.

In the CID office, the only person around was Graham, his feet up on the desk. When he saw Robyn, there was a studied pause, before he removed his feet one by one and then stood up. 'Bacon sarnie, good idea. Think I'll do the same.' He stood up, moving to the door. 'By the way, Ravi called in sick this morning.' He twisted the handle. 'He didn't say exactly what was wrong – I reckon he's been given an earache.' He pulled open the door.

Robyn forced her thoughts into order. 'Graham, hang on. Do you think this is connected with what we heard on the radio yesterday?'

Graham kept moving. 'It was Chloe he spoke to.' The door swung shut behind him.

'Why does nobody tell me what is going on?' Robyn felt a fool for talking to an empty room though at least anger was better than sickness. She sat down at her desk and downed a couple of tablets. A half-hearted look at her emails told her there were more than the day before and there was one with an urgent flag titled *Submission of budget*.

Chloe walked in. 'Morning, Guv. Hope you had a good time last night. Wasn't Lorraine great?'

The last thing she felt she could cope with was Chloe's enthusiasm. 'Yes. Look, something's come up: Fell is seeing Shazia's uncle in a couple of hours and wants a briefing. What did Ravi say when he called in?'

'He couldn't talk for long. He really sounded like he'd had to sneak away to make the phone call.' Chloe sat down, pulling her knees up to her chest. 'He said everything kicked off yesterday evening. Shazia's father is the youngest of the uncles, Ravi's uncle I mean, his mother is the only sister …' She stopped, breathed. 'I'm not making any sense, am I? Start again. There are four of them, three brothers and a sister, all married with families. Durbesh Johar is the eldest brother so he's head of the family and what he says seems to go.' Her knuckles whitened. 'And that's specially when it comes to a woman. Now everyone's giving Ravi grief and it's all because his uncle isn't keen on having the family talked about in the press because they think it brings shame but they're not thinking about what help having this sort of thing exposed could do for others.'

There seemed to be nothing Robyn could do except let Chloe's anger burn itself out. 'Did Ravi say whether the family will press charges?'

'He doesn't think they will.' Chloe hugged her knees. 'He sounded really down about things.' She held up a sheaf of paper. 'Pity because the crime scene report has just come through.'

'Anything we didn't know?'

'Eldon's clothes were clean. The room showed evidence of multiple occupancy, skin, hair and toenails.' Chloe scrunched up her face. 'Yuck. There was semen found on the sheets which we can test against Bartholomew's.' She put down the report. 'I suppose you'll just say the evidence confirms his version of the story.'

'What else?'

Chloe turned a page. 'It was Shazia who was sick in the toilet.'

Robyn tried to quell her returning queasiness with a sip of tea.

'Also signs of her presence in the bed, skin and hairs. It was her blood and it was arterial rather than menstrual, which means she was cut with something.'

'Dr Brockwell said the room suggested violence. Have you got pictures? If Ravi's not here, put them up on the board.' Robyn was having trouble keeping her eyes open. 'When you've got them up, think about where everything is and how it got there.' She positioned the budget in front of her to make it look as if she was working.

This brought a couple of blessed minutes of peace as Chloe stared at the pictures, finger tracing the position of each item in one picture before moving onto the next. 'How about this, Guv? He – Bartholomew – is let into the room and tries to push Shazia onto the bed. She runs away and the only thing to hide behind is the chair. After a struggle, he breaks her grip and throws the chair away. Then he grabs her, drags her to the bed and in the struggle, she kicked things off the bedside table?'

'Good.' She looked up, wishing she hadn't as there was a hint of the nausea returning. 'We've got one explanation. Now think of another.'

Chloe blinked a number of times. 'Don't you think I've got it right?'

'I do.' Robyn sighed. 'I'll say it again, we have to start thinking like the defence team. So how about this? Bartholomew comes up to check she's all right. Shazia answers the door then goes back to bed and invites him in. She's up for anything, the bed isn't enough so they end up using the chair, which gets knocked over and the things on the table are kicked off in passion.'

Chloe was paler than usual. 'This is vile.'

'This is what we're up against.' They looked at each other for a moment.

Graham walked in, settled down at his desk and unwrapped his sandwich, the paper rustling.

'OK, can you go through the report and give me something to tell Fell? Think about all the variants you can and lots of reasons why your scenario is the only possible one.' Robyn tried to put encouragement into her voice as Chloe was looking gloomy. She turned to Graham. 'When you've finished breakfast, let's talk about the next steps with the Newman case.'

'Mh-hmm-hmm.' Graham's reply was through a mouthful of bacon.

Robyn looked around. Lorraine's bag was on her desk. 'Anyone know where Lorraine is?'

'She got asked to join a conference call on the drugs operation.' Chloe looked at her watch. 'Must have been about fifteen minutes ago.'

'OK, thanks for letting me know.' Out of the corner of her eye, Robyn saw Graham pause just before he took a bite, then put the food down. Her phone rang. 'Morning, Matthew.'

'Robyn.' Matthew sounded impatient. 'Didn't you get my email? You know I've got a suspect for the attacks in the cells? Picked him up last night loitering halfway up Albert Avenue on the way to Upper Town.'

'Fantastic.' Robyn ignored a stab of headache. 'We'll be right down.'

23

The cells corridor was empty, which was unusual. The custody sergeant directed them into an interview room without a word.

'You're a ray of sunshine today, Martha. What's up?' Graham leaned on the door frame blocking the sergeant's exit.

Martha lifted just her eyes to his face. 'We're all under bloody review. Those women from Saturday have had the cheek to claim police brutality, never mind what they did to us, so we're expecting the Complaints here asking questions. We'll get to the stage where nobody dares arrest anyone. You're just treading on eggshells the whole time.'

Graham made a sympathetic grunt.

The tension on Martha's face didn't ease. 'They come in here thinking the worst and we've got to prove ourselves innocent. They treat us worse than the criminals – we have to start by assuming they didn't do it. I'll get your man.' She ducked past Graham and into the corridor.

'Bloody joke.' Graham slid into the fixed chair. 'Ouch.' He began rubbing his knee. 'I hate these interview room chairs. They're designed for a nursery, there's no room to put your legs.' He looked over to Chloe. 'It's all right for you.'

'We need to take this carefully.' Robyn felt hair falling over her eye and resisted the urge to run her fingers through it. 'We don't have any forensic evidence, so we need to establish the facts.'

'You want to be good cop?' Graham flexed his leg a few times. 'I think I've got a dead leg.'

'Why don't you lead?' Robyn tried to get thoughts to move across her brain. 'Chloe, you observe. I want to keep an eye on his reactions.'

The door opened and a stocky man shambled in, the policeman at his back keeping a distance, followed by a young woman in a dress printed with coloured swallows who Robyn recognised as one of the duty lawyers. The man hesitated, looked around. His eyes were a watery blue.

'Sit down.' The constable pointed. 'There. On the chair.'

The man slid into the seat, the lawyer perching on the far edge of the chair next to him. Although both were wearing black, the bright birds lifted the woman's dress, the matt cotton of his sweatshirt and jogging bottoms seemed to suck in light and gave off a musty smell as if they had been underground for a long time. Robyn nodded to Graham to start the recording and caution the man, who sat, passive, staring at the table. The lawyer crossed her legs.

'Do you know why you're here?' Graham's tone was pleasant, conversational.

The man continued to stare straight ahead. The lawyer uncapped her pen. 'My client has been arrested on suspicion of attacks on women. He has no knowledge of these and denies any involvement. What evidence do you have?'

Graham took his time unfolding a piece of paper. 'As your lawyer says, we have arrested you on suspicion of attacks. Can you tell me why you were hanging around Upper Town at …?' He checked the page. 'At one thirty-eight this morning?'

'No comment.'

The lawyer put down her pen. 'And there is no reason why he should comment. He was in a public place minding his own business.'

There was a knock at the door and Matthew stuck his head in. 'Could I have a word?'

Frowning, Graham's finger hovered over the recorder. 'Interview suspended at ten thirteen am. DI Bailley, DC Talbot and DS Catt leaving the room.'

In the corridor, Matthew looked pleased. 'Guess what we've found?' He didn't wait for them to answer. 'When we picked this bloke up last night, we ran a check on him and found he had a car, parked just around the corner. We got one of our drugs dogs down and bingo. There was a big stash hidden in the boot, heroin, ecstasy and some legal highs. Forensics are looking at it now.'

'Got the bastard.' Graham stuck his hands in the air, revealing sweat patches under his arms. 'Let's see what Little-Miss-Minding-His-Own-Business has to say about this.'

'This is more than a local dealer – this sounds like a supplier.' Matthew was grinning. 'We've been picking up some small fry. It's about time we started moving up the chain.'

'Are you coming in for round two?' Graham shadow-boxed at Matthew. 'Seconds away.'

'Inspector Pond?' Martha's voice carried from the desk. 'Call for you. It's the Superintendent.'

'He must have heard the good news.' Matthew smiled. 'Hold on before going in will you?'

As she watched Matthew walk to the desk, Robyn felt a sinking sensation. This was a more abstract concern than the after-effects of the hangover. Although the man in the cell behind them fitted the scant physical description of the attacker, she wondered why someone who was running drugs would want to draw attention to himself by attacking women. Graham started whistling, a just-recognisable mangling of "Another One Bites the Dust". At the counter, Matthew's face froze.

Robyn nudged Graham, then pointed to where Matthew had turned away, leaning both arms on the desk for support, shoulders hunching. The note died on Graham's lips.

When Matthew finished the call, he left the receiver on the desk. He was looking paler.

'What did Fell say?' Graham couldn't wait.

Jerking his head in the direction of an interview room, Matthew walked away. Graham moved to follow him until he looked back. 'Just Robyn.' Robyn followed, leaving Graham grousing to Chloe in the corridor.

Matthew sank into a chair. 'Christ, I thought this week couldn't get worse.' He pressed his fingers to his temples. 'Apparently, we've just buggered up Operation Emerald.'

'What?' Robyn gripped the back of the chair. 'I've never heard of it?'

'It's the name for a brand-new co-ordinated drugs programme. There's going to be a directive issued not to make any local drugs arrests without central clearance. They want to trace the operation to the top so by arresting matey-boy too soon, we may have put the network on guard.' Matthew sighed. 'You thought Fell was angry on Saturday, well now he's really mad.' His gaze went to the ceiling. 'It was a bit like when my daughter spilled tea on the gerbil, lots of chittering and scrabbling.'

'Christ.' Robyn's head felt too heavy between her shoulders. 'If Fell's kicking off, this must be big.'

'It was going to be announced today apparently.' Matthew sat back, affecting nonchalance.

'Well then, how the hell were we supposed to know?' This had the potential to be career-threatening and it wasn't fair on Matthew. 'Do we need to go and see Fell?' She emphasised the 'we'.

'No. No need at the moment.' Matthew stopped. 'Thanks.' He put both hands on the arms of the chair and heaved himself up so he was sitting up straight. 'We might get more when Fell's met the

219

international team.' He caught Robyn's look. 'Oh, yes, we've upset not just our own drugs' squad but ones in Holland and France as well.' This smile was a hollow one.

'So what do we do with him?' Robyn jerked her thumb in the rough direction of the cell.

'Oh it gets better and better. We charge him with personal possession and let him go.' Matthew's eyes had returned to the ceiling. 'I think if we hadn't taken his car to bits they would have just said let him go. So even though he's got enough drugs to supply a festival, he gets to walk.'

Robyn was conscious of scrutiny. She turned, catching eyes looking through the peephole, vanishing when she focused upon them. She took a deep breath. 'This doesn't change why we did what we did. There's still an attacker out there. Your guys did what I asked them to do.' The room felt hot or maybe it was her. 'Anyway, how were we supposed to know what they were planning?'

'You might want to check.' Matthew sounded serious. 'Fell said we should have known because apparently there's a dedicated Meresbourne representative on Operation Emerald. Do you know who it is?'

'Oh hell.' It was Robyn's turn to look at the ceiling. She dropped into the chair opposite Matthew. 'It's Lorraine. I thought this would be a good opportunity for her to get her name known before going for sergeant.' She stopped, thinking through the consequences. 'This wasn't quite how I meant.'

'No.' Matthew rubbed his temples. 'I don't think this is quite how any of us meant.'

There was a pause. There was half a thought in Robyn's mind she should apologise though the more she examined it, the less inclined she felt to do it. 'Look, do you want me to let the prisoner know he's free to go?'

'No, I'll do it. I need to explain about his car.' Matthew heaved himself to his feet. 'Happy days. I'll keep the brief out for my guys to look for your attacker but some more details would be handy so we don't end up doing this again.'

'I'm seeing Fell at eleven forty-five before he meets the family of the rape victim. I'll let him know it was me who asked for the pick-up.'

'Thanks.' Their eyes met for a second before Matthew left.

In the corridor, Graham was shuffling his feet. 'What are we waiting for, Guv?'

'We leave it.' Robyn jerked her head up. 'Orders from on high.'

'What? He's guilty as hell.' Graham banged the desk with the flat of his hand. 'What's Fell playing at?'

'It's all to do with a bigger operation. So, we keep out of it and focus on our business.' Robyn started moving down the corridor: she didn't want to be there when Matthew brought the man out. 'And we need to talk about Newman. I still can't see a motive.'

Graham took the bait and followed Robyn to the corridor. 'I don't think we need to worry too much about motive, Guv. We know Trudwick was the football team's enforcer. He finds out Newman is planning to leave the team and gets angry and forces something down Newman's throat, making him eat his words.' Graham shrugged. 'Maybe he didn't mean to kill him and we're looking at manslaughter. Either way, it gets a nasty creature off the streets.'

'Have you completely discounted the theory it was something to do with his ex's new boyfriend then?'

'This seems more promising, don't you think? And because we've got Trudwick's DNA on file, it should be easy to pick up if he was at the crime scene.'

They walked into the CID office. Lorraine jumped to her feet. 'Guv –'

Robyn held up a hand. 'OK, it's worth considering all angles here. Think about it: Newman might have asked Trudwick to help him out with a plumbing job or even getting the decorations out of the van on the morning of the wedding – his DNA might be in the van for all sorts of reasons.'

Graham slouched to his desk. Robyn closed her eyes for a second. It felt delicious – she could sleep for hours. There was no chance: Lorraine had crossed the office and was leaning on her desk.

'God, Guv, what's going on? We were on the Operation Emerald call talking about the information we had to share and then someone cuts in to say there's been an arrest in Meresbourne and this is going to put everything at risk.'

Robyn heard a phone ring. Graham hunched over his desk, almost buried in his jacket's collar.

'A dealer was arrested yesterday evening.' Robyn ran her hands through her hair. 'We've got orders to release him.'

'Blimey. Everybody's going to think I knew all about it.' Lorraine flopped into her chair. 'Fell will think I can't do my job.'

'It was bad luck and bad timing, nothing else.' Robyn perched on the edge of her desk. 'How were you supposed to know all of the details on your first time in the group? I'll tell Fell when I see him later.'

Lorraine chewed her lip. 'Do you really think he'll care? My career's buggered.'

'Stop worrying.' The words were sharper than Robyn meant because a headache was threatening to close down her vision. 'He matched the description of a violent attacker, so Fell can't blame us for wanting to get him off the streets.'

After scrabbling in her handbag, Lorraine pulled out a crumpled packet of sweets and shook a couple into her palm before popping them into her mouth.

'Guv.' There was sweat on Graham's forehead. The eyes meeting Robyn's were crinkled in appeal.

'Go.' Robyn searched for words which wouldn't sound empty. 'Take care.'

As Graham grabbed his briefcase and dashed through the door, Lorraine turned to Robyn, her mouth opening.

'I guess it was a bit much to expect to pick our attacker up the first night of looking for him.' Robyn wanted to stop the obvious question of what was wrong with Graham. 'After all, we know almost nothing about this guy except he seems to be strong and may have small hands and blue eyes. Oh and he smells "intense".' Her stomach rumbled. She took feeling hungry as a good sign. 'Can I have one of those?'

Lorraine passed the packet across. She raised one eyebrow. 'Intense? Didn't you say she barely spoke English – are you sure she didn't mean, say, incense?'

Robyn shook her head. 'I don't think so. She was sharp and knew what she was talking about. We need to work out what she meant.' The toffee had fluff on it but the burst of sweetness on her tongue was wonderful.

'It feels like we're getting nowhere, Guv. A rapist we can't nail, an attacker we can't describe and we may or may not have a murder.' Lorraine drummed her fingers on the desk. 'Oh and we've only got half a team.'

'And sniping at each other is not going to make anything better.' Robyn held her hands clasped in front of her to give her stability. 'Remember what you said to Ravi: we can't unhappen anything, so we focus on where we can make a difference.' She took a deep breath, turning to where Chloe sat, almost hidden behind her monitor. 'Look, both of you. If Shazia's family are not likely to press charges, then there is nothing we can do about it, except focus on the other cases. We made a mistake over the attacker – we start again with the old cases. We've got leads we can follow up. We know he's using a car now, so let's see if anything was picked up on the cameras where Dominika was attacked. Chloe, that's a good lead for you to follow up.' She waved at the board. 'Then there's Newman's death – there are still far too many loose ends. Lorraine, why don't we start by going to see Newman's ex and check whether there's anything there. Then you can drop me at the town hall to see Fell and I will tell him the problem this morning wasn't your fault.'

The fresh air of the car park was a relief. 'Can you drive? My hands are still a bit tender so I took a taxi this morning.'

'Glad you had a good time last night, Guv.' There was a knowing tone in Lorraine's voice. 'My car's just here.'

Robyn wondered whether she was fooling anyone – she knew she looked terrible. When the stereo came on, she winced, bearing the noise for a few seconds, then turned off the sound, searching for something to say to cover her action. 'I really enjoyed listening to the band. I'd forgotten how music becomes something else again when you hear it live.'

'Thanks, Guv.' Lorraine grinned, eyes on the roundabout. 'I don't know why Graham dashed off though. What is wrong with him?'

The urge to tell her the truth about Graham was strong. 'Just something he needs to deal with.' It was only a partial lie. 'Graham is a bit old-fashioned. He thinks young ladies should only play waltzes on the pianoforte rather than this new-fangled jazz music.'

Lorraine laughed without the usual volume. 'There is something else though, isn't there? He's been acting funny for a while. I think it's something to do with me going for sergeant and he won't be top dog any more.'

It was Robyn's turn to laugh. 'What, you think Graham doesn't want you to go for promotion? No way. Why would he get upset by you progressing your career? I'm amazed he hasn't already offered to give you "the benefit of his experience".'

'I know, I know. It's just something's wrong and I don't know what else it could be. And now Ravi as well. Maybe now isn't the time to start a team lottery syndicate.'

'Don't worry about it.' Robyn tried to sound reassuring. 'Graham is an expert in taking care of himself. I will speak to Fell as soon as Tracey gets back and you can put in for your sergeant's exam when you feel ready for it.'

They drove into the Docks estate where the watery sun struggled to bring colour to the tower blocks. 'Three days in a row we've been here – feels like I'm back in Uniform.' They had to drive around to find a parking space. 'Tells you all you need to know: shouldn't all of the owners of these cars be at work?'

'I guess a lot of people work shifts but yes, it's a different world around here.' Robyn buzzed doorbells until someone opened the door. 'And yet they still let anyone in.'

They were followed into the lift by three lads, all baggy tops and baseball caps.

'Oh man.' The one nearest Robyn jerked back, banging into his friend, who in turn leaned into Lorraine.

'Hey babe, sorry like.' The one in the shiny, green baseball top used the minimal space to look Lorraine up and down. He whistled, turning to his friends. 'Man, check this out.'

Lorraine's eyes were set on the indicator.

'Better than here, bruv. Reckon this one's got a dick.'

Robyn thought the lads were about fourteen though even the shortest was as tall as her. The lift was taking forever, clanking to a stop on the second floor. An elderly woman with a shopping trolley took one look inside and stepped away.

'What are you doing with this guy, babe?'

'Don't you want a real man?'

'He is a real man. I bet you.'

Lorraine yawned, leaning against the wall of the lift. 'I didn't realise the nursery was having an outing today.'

'Hey, harsh.'

'Like she's calling us babies.'

'You want babies, honey, I'll make your babies.'

The lift stopped at the third floor and Lorraine walked out. Robyn, surprised, took a second to follow her.

'Did you see how lady-boy here wiggled his ass at me?'

'He didn't wanna leave you. Wooh – on a promise.'

The doors closed, cutting off the response.

'You OK?' Robyn felt it was important to speak first. They were supposed to be going to the fifth floor.

'Fine. I was just about to ask you the same thing.' She wrinkled her nose. 'Don't know about you but I didn't want to spend any more time with those charmers, so I pushed a button – didn't see which one.'

'I've had worse.' Robyn smiled, to make sure she could still do it. She was angry at herself for not speaking up. 'You can't take something like that seriously. As you said, they're babies.'

They started up the stairs. The door to flat twenty-seven had a brass knocker and letterbox rather than the standard plastic. Robyn knocked. The light metal made a genteel, discreet tap.

The door opened a crack. Behind the chain, a woman peered at Robyn through a heavy fringe. 'Yes?' The voice was little more than a whisper.

'Crystel Marcos?' Robyn held out her warrant card: a hand came through the gap to take it. From the sliver of her face which was visible, the thick, black mascara emphasised the number of times her eyes flicked between the card and Robyn's face.

'What do you want?'

'We'd like to talk to you, miss, about an incident here on Saturday night.'

The door closed and there was the rattle of a chain. Robyn took a half-step forward, expecting the door to be opened. Instead, the door cracked open again and this time the woman slipped out into the corridor, pulling the door to behind her.

'Me fiancé does nights and he can't be having anyone waking him up at this time. What do you mean, something happened? Stuff happens all the time.'

'Are you sure you're happy to talk out here, miss?'

The woman tilted her head and took another half-step forward. 'I've got nothing to hide. And he's not much fun when you wake him up. What do you want?' The woman stared at Robyn. There was no fear, which was good and not much hint of co-operation which wasn't.

Robyn smiled, turning to look at Lorraine, who took the hint.

'When was the last time you saw Jake Newman?' Lorraine stepped closer, drawing Crystel's gaze to her.

Crystel folded her arms. 'Oh. Well at least you're doing something useful. There are people who deserve to get done in and Jake wasn't one of them. Good luck.'

'Thanks.' Lorraine smiled. 'When did you last see him?'

'A couple of weeks ago. He helped Ed get home from a stag night.' She jerked her head towards the door. 'He doesn't drink a lot and they got him on spirits and he was hopeless.' She uncrossed her arms and shoved her hands into the pockets of her jeans. 'Jake made sure he got back OK. That's the sort of bloke he is … was.' She pulled a tissue from her pocket and wiped her nose.

'I'm sorry.' Lorraine paused for a second. 'Before the stag night, did you see him regularly?'

'Around and about.' Crystel's hand went back in her pocket: the moment of emotion had passed. 'He was just one of the guys from college.'

'And your partner, you said he was called Ed?'

'Fiancé.' Crystel held up her left hand, a ring just visible in the gloom.

'Could you give me his full name, please?'

The woman's lips pursed. 'Jones.'

'Thank you. Do you know a friend of Newman's, Jason Trudwick?'

'Why are you asking anyway? You don't think he did it, do you?'

'We're just trying to get a picture of the people Jake spent his last hours with.' Lorraine was doing a good job of keeping her tone conversational.

Crystel shrugged. 'He works doors with Ed. I never knew him that well.'

'Thank you.' Lorraine paused. 'Were you and Jake a couple at all?'

'A long time ago.' Crystel laughed. 'We was kids, it wasn't serious. We're all friends now.' Her tone hardened. 'Ed knows about it if that's what you're driving at. Doesn't bother him.'

'Did you see Jake at any point on Saturday night?'

'Because he was found in the car park, you mean?' The woman shook her head. 'Nope. We was both working. When you work in bars, Saturdays is the busiest day of the week. I started at five, Ed at seven going through 'til three of a weekend.'

'No wonder you don't want to wake him up. Is that one of the clubs on Riverside?' As soon as she had spoken, Robyn was conscious of appraisal.

Crystel folded her arms again, stepping back against the door. 'Yeah. So what?'

'I can't believe there are so many clubs around now.' Lorraine spoke a little louder, trying to get Crystel's attention back. 'Paprika, The Love Lounge, Quiksilva, what's the new one called?'

'Melt.' Crystel kept her arms folded. 'It's the biggest in town.' Inside the flat there was a muffled shout. Her eyes darted to the door.

Lorraine smiled. 'If Ed's awake, is there a chance we could talk to him?'

There was another call from inside, louder now. Crystel tutted, pulled a key from her back pocket and let herself into the flat.

'I'm not buying the jealous ex angle.' Lorraine spoke under her breath.

The door was opened wider and Crystel stood aside to let them in. The flat was the mirror of Bartholomew's but everything was ordered and neat. As the man settled onto the sofa, Crystel leant behind him to square the next cushion with its neighbour. Ed was in a bathrobe, the cord double-knotted around his waist. 'So you're trying to catch the bastards what did Jakey?'

'That's right.' Lorraine nodded. 'His body was found in the car park downstairs, so we're trying to find out why he was here and who he visited.'

228

'Well it wasn't us. We don't really see a lot of him.' Ed scratched his bare leg.

'You didn't go to the wedding?'

'Nah. Bad enough having to take a night off for the stag. When you're saving for a place, you can't miss a pay cheque to sit around in a suit and have to shell out for a present.'

Crystel placed a coaster on the table and put a cup down in front of Ricky then stayed standing, holding her own matching mug.

'Can you think of any reason why Newman might have been here in the early hours of Saturday morning?'

'Nah.' Ed blew on his tea. 'Thanks, luv. Plumbing job, maybe?'

'We thought that until we found he went out without his tools.' Lorraine left a pause. 'Could Newman have come to see you?'

Robyn wondered whether Lorraine had gone too far and was relieved when Ed shrugged. 'Doubt it. He's only been here once, that time a couple of weeks ago when he sorted me out.'

'Do you know Jason Trudwick?' There was a note of eagerness in Lorraine's voice Robyn would have to warn her about.

'Jase? Yeah, worked with me on the door at Quiksilva. Still there because I needed an experienced guy who could keep an eye on things when I moved over to Melt.'

'Did you know he had a conviction for assault?'

The corners of Ed's mouth turned down. 'When someone's out of their box and tries to glass you, you defend yourself. Only thing was, because the little slapper turned up at the police station in a pretty dress and cried, you lot believed her and not us or the CCTV.'

'I thought this was supposed to be about who killed Jake?' Crystel's voice was flat.

Robyn smiled. 'It is. If someone has a previous conviction, we have to check it out. Imagine if we were talking about child abuse and we didn't follow up someone in the area who'd done it before – we'd get crucified. We have to ask.'

'Yeah, well. You tell me why a bloke would kill a best mate of his? Doesn't make any sense, does it?' Ed took a sip of tea.

'Are Quiksilva and Melt run by the same company then?' Robyn wanted to get the conversation onto safer ground.

'Yeah.' The tone was still suspicious. 'Or do you think people enjoying themselves is a crime now as well?' Ed looked up at Robyn. His face closed in on itself and even wearing just a bathrobe, he had a presence suggesting people did not often cross him.

Hoping her reaction was so normal he hadn't noticed her nervousness, Robyn made an effort to keep her voice under control. 'Is it a good company to work for?'

'Yeah. It's well run. Everything tidy, standards are important. Bloke who owns 'em, Micky, he's always got time too, says hello to everyone. Wish there were more like him spending money in this town.'

Beside her, Lorraine coughed, in a way she probably intended to be discreet. 'Micky? Do you mean Micky Dearman?'

Ed's eyebrows came down. His glare moved from Robyn to Lorraine before settling between them. A second later, he had pushed himself off the sofa and was heading straight for Robyn who rocked back on her heels, bracing herself for an impact as there was nowhere to go. He was not as muscled as Bartholomew but faster and looked more used to controlled force. Ed raised one big arm, reaching past Robyn and pushing at the frame of a film poster for Cabaret. 'Babes, does the picture look straight to you now?'

Robyn forced her shoulders to relax.

Crystel moved to stand behind Ed. 'Up a bit more, right – perfect.'

Ricky stood with his hands on his hips like a prize-fighter for a second, admiring the poster. 'What did you say?'

'You were saying Micky Dearman is a good person to work for.' Robyn let a long breath go.

'Yeah. Sees people all right.' Ed scooped up his tea cup, the mug looking small in his hands. 'Like he even gets the girls taxis so they get home safe.'

'I'm glad to hear it.' Robyn trusted her instinct. 'We know there's been a series of late-night attacks on women. Is this something you can help us with – we think there's someone out there who's behind a lot of them.'

Crystel sniffed. 'Taken your time haven't you? One of my team got grabbed six months ago and you've only just noticed.'

'Did she report it?' Robyn thought she knew the answer.

'Yeah, for all the good it did her.' Crystel's mouth was set in a thin line. 'Nothing was done and she had to quit a few months after. Works in a cafe now on half the money because she's too scared to be out late.'

'Have you heard anything about this man? Any information you've got could help us.'

Ed and Crystel exchanged a glance. She shook her head.

'Look, I realise if you did know who he was you'd have gone and had a word with him yourself before now.' Robyn spread her hands. 'All I'm after is anything you've heard.'

'Well, it's pretty obvious innit?' Ed finished his tea and handed the cup to Crystel. 'He's some mummy's boy who can't get a girlfriend who's too scared of women to talk to them, so he grabs them. Now I'm going back to bed.'

It had been hard to keep Lorraine quiet as they went down in the lift. In the car, they looked at each other.

Lorraine held up a finger. 'If Graham were here he'd say –'

'– if the Dearmans are involved, it's got to be dodgy.' They spoke in unison.

Lorraine started the car, still laughing. 'I remember my first day in the team, when DI Prentiss was still in charge. They'd just put Gabriel Dearman away and, OK, you'd expect them to be pleased about arresting the local crime boss's son but it was all they talked about for a month. I was expecting something like The Godfather but when I went and looked at the records and it's just a bunch of small-town crooks who beat a few people up. So even if the Dearmans are involved, does it mean anything at all?'

Robyn's phone beeped with a message. 'Fell's meeting has finished at the town hall. I'd better get down there.' She clipped in her seatbelt. 'And how exactly are they even involved? So two friends of Newman's work for someone with a history – so what? They need to work somewhere.' Robyn threw up her hands. 'We haven't found a reason for anyone to kill Newman and without that we can't understand if a crime has been committed at all.'

Lorraine started the car and moved towards the exit. A muffled ringing came from the bag on the back seat. 'Could you get that, Guv?'

Robyn pulled Lorraine's handbag onto her lap and opened it, feeling a small thrill of snooping. Unlike the jumble in her own bag, Lorraine's was full of pouches, each of a different size, with just one stray tissue having come loose from a pack. The phone was in a separate pocket on one side.

Robyn glanced at the screen. 'Hello, Chloe. Lorraine's driving at the moment. What have you got?'

'We've got the results back on the samples I got from the hospital on Saturday. Shazia wasn't raped.'

'What?' Robyn was aware of Lorraine's sharp glance.

'Or rather, it wasn't normal rape. There was no trace of semen in the samples even though the crime scene report says it was on the sheets.'

Robyn gripped the phone. 'So why did Bartholomew lie to us?'

'I think to cover up what he did do.' A crackle on the line took Chloe's voice.

'Hang on, I'm going to put you on speaker so Lorraine can hear.' Robyn clicked the phone into the cradle. 'Go ahead.'

Chloe's voice filled the car. 'I called the hospital. They've had a chance to examine Shazia's other injuries. This wasn't a conventional rape because there's a lot of internal damage. Whoever attacked her used something, maybe metal, because there are lacerations inside her.'

'That explains the blood on the sheets.' Lorraine crunched a gear. 'Christ.'

'So as you say, Guv, Bartholomew lied to us about what he did. I was trying to work out why and I thought about the steroids Lorraine found. If one of the side effects is impotence, maybe that's why he can't have normal sex.' There was a catch in Chloe's voice. 'She must have been in so much pain - I guess that's why she jumped.'

A picture lodged in Robyn's mind. 'The bottle.' Robyn leaned forward. 'Chloe, check the forensic report on the hotel room. There was a glass water bottle smashed in a corner – see whether Dr Brockwell's team checked the pieces.'

'Right away, Guv.' Chloe sounded determined. She cut the line.

'We have got to be able to get him now, Guv.'

'Let me get this meeting with Fell over with.' Robyn rubbed her eyes. 'Then we'll bring him in.'

24

Lorraine braked too hard outside the town hall and shot off almost before Robyn had closed the door. She walked under the vast portrait of Edmund Napier Loveless tacked to the facade, a line of pigeons perched on top, bird mess mixing with the portrait's grey hair. In the entrance lobby, there were a lot of signs for the event the night before, stuck between plaques commemorating previous mayors. The only other person was an overweight man sitting on a small stool beside the staircase.

'Could you tell me where the St Sergius room is please?'

The man's eyelids fluttered without fully opening. 'Up the stairs, second on the left.' He rebalanced his bulk on the stool.

There was no check to see whether she had any reason to be there. Robyn walked up the marble staircase. On the first floor, she tapped on the dark wood door. 'Enter.'

Fell sat at the head of a conference table littered with dirty tea cups and empty biscuit wrappers. A fan was on at the other end of the room, whining in the background. Capping his fountain pen, Fell didn't look towards her. 'We have fifteen minutes, Bailley. I need a summary of the Lady Ann case and the realistic chances of prosecution.'

Robyn sat down, pushing back the litter in front of her. The saucer tipped, causing cold tea to spill onto the wood. 'Yes, sir. We have enough evidence of violent sexual assault –'

A creak from behind was the door opening. A woman in a pale blue uniform pushed in a trolley. 'Got to clear, love. There's a committee in here next.'

'And the evidence throws doubt on the version from the person who confirmed, ah, activity took place.' Robyn wondered how long the woman was going to be there. 'This means we can be much more confident stating that the things which took place were not …' She struggled to find a neutral word. 'Were not mutually acceptable.'

The woman moved the last of the cups to the trolley and returned with a cloth and spray. She tutted when she got to the spillage.

'Are you confident you can bring a prosecution?' Fell's voice was a rumble.

'Yes.' Robyn summoned up what energy she had. 'I want to put this evidence in front of the Crown Prosecution Service.'

The woman wheeled the trolley to the door, the tea cups rattling.

'Ah, Superintendent. I am a few minutes early but I have another meeting, so if we can proceed now?' In the doorway was a slim man with white hair. The sound of the trolley receded.

'Mr Johar, thank you for coming.' Fell stood up.

The two men met in the middle of the room, shaking hands. 'This is DI Bailley who is leading the investigation.' Robyn leant over the long table to take Johar's hand: the skin gliding across hers was very smooth, like warm marble.

Johar remained standing as Fell returned to his seat. With the windows behind him, his hair glowed silver, framing his shadowed face. 'Superintendent, I know you intend to persuade me to pursue this case. You may save your breath.' His long fingers gripped the back of a chair. 'What has happened to my niece is unfortunate but cannot be changed. Any prosecution would not help Shazia.' The long ends of his burgundy silk scarf rippled as they brushed the table. 'Nothing now can help Shazia in this world. When it is just a machine keeping her alive, she has already passed on.'

Fell folded his hands together on the table. 'We have evidence your niece was the victim of assault. What we wish to avoid is the perpetrator being free to attack again.'

'You are thinking according to the way of the hunter, Superintendent. You only see your objective. I have to think of sarvodaya, the welfare of everyone.' Johar blinked once. 'Your position is that my niece attempted to take her own life, is that correct?'

'We have a witness and his statement is backed up by forensic evidence.' Fell folded his hands in front of him.

Johar inclined his head. 'And I am sure that everyone you have spoken to told you she had only the cares of a young girl. A mother knows her daughter is dead – does it help her to know she suffered beforehand? A boy has dreams of justice.' His gaze turned to Robyn. 'Does it help him to see justice fail?'

Robyn forced herself to keep her eyes on Johar's face.

'You are someone who has discovered honesty late in life.' There was no disapproval in Johar's tone: he could have been commenting on the weather. 'You say something that took place within that room made Shazia commit violence against herself. Can you truly tell me you consider prosecuting this case would do her any good?'

From the far end of the table, Fell coughed.

'The police don't think about things on a spiritual level, Mr Johar.' Robyn went with her instinct. 'The most I could give you is an assurance about the way I would approach things. I would do my best to investigate this case, then present the evidence in such a way to have the greatest chance of a successful conviction which would remove a dangerous individual from society for a time.'

Johar nodded once. 'Then maybe my nephew is not in such bad

hands.' He nodded to the end of the table. 'Superintendent, Shazia's life support mechanism will be switched off this afternoon.' There was no emotion in his words. 'We would ask for her body to be released as soon as possible. He paused. 'If a person committed violence against her, they will receive their due.'

Robyn's mobile began to ring. She fumbled to silence it but Johar had already turned away, heading towards the door. Before Fell could open his mouth, Robyn got the phone to her ear. 'Hello, Chloe.'

'Hi, Guv. We've got the forensic report on Newman.'

There was a flash of hope: the call must mean something important. 'What does it say?'

'It's clear how he died at least, though it's not very helpful. The rags he was sleeping on were covered in traces of chemicals – nothing you wouldn't expect a plumber to have mind. Anyway, Kelly's theory is the combination of being very drunk and chemical exposure made Newman unconscious and he didn't wake, even when his chewing gum became lodged in his windpipe. She paused. 'It was probably an accident.'

Robyn was conscious of Fell's scrutiny. 'Were there signs of any other person present?'

'One set of unknown prints on the back door handle and a hair caught on his sweatshirt. Short and dyed blonde so it's likely to be a woman.'

Not for the first time, Robyn wondered how she would be described if she were found dead. 'Could be from his girlfriend – we'll need to check. Anything else?'

'It looks like he was in a fight shortly before he died. There were fresh cuts on the knuckles of his left hand.'

'Interesting. OK, can you get Lorraine to follow up and we'll go through what you've found on the attacks when I get back.' She put the phone down. 'Sorry about that, sir.'

Fell cleared his throat. 'Excluding this one, how many cases does the team have at present?'

'We have the suspicious death on Saturday night and have just started working to review a series of attacks on women. It was at my request the man was pulled in yesterday, sir, I had given Matthew the description of the man responsible for the attacks.'

She paused but there was no movement from Fell.

'It was unfortunate the interrogation of the suspect happened while the Operation Emerald call was underway. Now we have a contact, we will be careful to check before future arrests.' Robyn heard a grunt but kept going. 'We are also two officers down, both for family reasons.' She braced herself. 'And if Professional Standards are coming in, that will require time.'

'They will not be coming because the post mortem satisfied them there was no link to our actions.' Fell adjusted his cuffs. 'Though they did make a number of recommendations about co-ordination across teams which I expect you to adopt.' He stood up. 'This experience has been embarrassing for Meresbourne. It does not sound as if you are overworked even with a reduced team so I expect to see you paying more attention to process and not acting unilaterally in future.'

'Yes, sir.'

'We are likely to get publicity and criticism in the media surrounding the lack of prosecution in relation to Miss Johar, though Guler assures me this will be of much shorter duration than if the man was brought to trial and we failed to secure a conviction.'

Robyn made a mental note to thank Khalid for keeping Fell calm. She was amazed she had got away without more direct criticism.

'And next week, Tracey will be back and everything will be clearer.' There was a hint of a smile as Fell put on his cap and collected his case. 'Carry on, Bailley.' At the door he looked back. 'And I expect your budget by close of play without fail.'

Stepping out into the weak sunshine on the Quayside, Robyn felt a certain release. Her phone buzzed with a message.

Dad, train getting in at 6.07. See you later, B.

She stopped to reread the message, feeling someone bump into her because she was in the middle of the pavement. Moving to the side, she muttered an apology. Given Fell himself had commented CID was not overworked, for once she felt confident about being able to get back for Becky.

B, thanks for letting me know. I'll pick you up from the station. Best, Dad.

There was a distant chime from St Leonard's and a reflex made her check her watch: twelve thirty. She turned onto Bridge Street heading for the taxi rank, checking to make sure she did not get into the same cab from the morning. The driver tutted when she asked for the police station and stopped on the roundabout in a blare of horns from behind.

'Come on, mate, can't stop here for long – we're right outside the cop-shop.'

Her annoyance at the "mate" was balanced with a desire to get out as quickly as possible. As she watched the cab speed off, another message came through.

Dad, don't worry, will get a cab. B.

25

In the two flights of stairs to the incident room, Robyn had come to the conclusion it was a good thing that the first time Becky saw her would be in private. She walked into an empty room. The summaries of the attacks now covered one of the evidence boards: a map in the centre showed the locations, arrows to pictures of the victims with summaries in Chloe's tiny handwriting. The youngest was seventeen, the oldest thirty-nine and there seemed to be no obvious link between them or any pattern in the locations.

In one corner, Chloe had summarised all of the snippets of description. A couple were no more than a few words from girls who were off their faces on drink or drugs, unable to recall anything, bruises the only proof of their stories. The man's strength and stealthy approach were the consistent themes. The fourth victim had been able to give more detail about the attack. She'd been lucky: a passing taxi driver had seen her struggling, turned his car around and driven straight for the pair, headlights on high beam. The man let go and ran. Being fat and in his fifties, the driver didn't try to follow but drove the woman to the police station. His description, of a stocky man in black, matched the others but he was able to add that the visible skin on the hands and face was tanned. There still wasn't enough to put together an e-fit.

The next attack was the first time a car was mentioned. It made sense: he'd been disturbed on the street, so realised he needed somewhere more private. No one had got a good look at it. One girl described a choking smell in the back seat.

The door swung open. Chloe and Lorraine drifted in, hands full of lunch bits.

'Hi, Guv. How did it go with Fell?' Lorraine ripped open her salad pot.

'Better than expected. This looks good, Chloe.' Robyn gestured to the board. 'When you've finished your lunch, you can talk me through what you've found here.'

From the depths of her bag, Lorraine's phone rang. Shoving a forkful into her mouth she reached down.

'Let's do it now, Guv, I've got some ideas.' Chloe stood up, leaving her sandwich on the desk.

'OK.' Robyn's stomach rumbled.

'I've been through the old cases you identified, Guv, and all the evidence we have is now on here. Once you start looking at it, we don't have a lot to go on. So, I've been trying to think laterally – what kind of person would do this sort of thing?' She slipped back to her desk and returned with a book. 'I've been reading this.' She held it out. The cover was streaks of fuchsia pink and black, the title picked out in gold. *Gender, Power, Sex – Who Goes on Top?*

Robyn felt a trace of the sickness returning. 'You're reading a book by Felicity Bergmann?' Within those pages there were likely to be condemnations of anything related to transgender people, particularly trans women like herself.

'Oh I know she's a bit of a fruitloop about some things. I saw the report of the panel in the paper this morning and she refused to condemn the violence on Saturday – said something stupid like "the war on inequality will not be won in one battle" or whatever.' Chloe opened the book at a marked page. 'But she's an expert in gender studies and some of the stuff she says does make sense. Listen to this: *The victim-male will seek to lay blame elsewhere for his own inadequacies, be they intellectual, social or sexual. Where this is combined with physical power, it creates a risk of suppressed feelings being released in a torrent, which may break legal and social taboos. The constructs of this victim-hood are typically laid early on and the architects of this are his parents, particularly the mother.*

'Mmph. Dat's wert dat...' Lorraine swallowed. 'The bouncer said the same thing earlier. We're looking for a mummy's boy, who gets so spoiled he's got no social skills but expects every woman to fall at his feet.'

'Exactly.' Chloe put down the book and reached behind her. 'That's why I think it's worth looking here. Lives with his mother, record of violence against women, regularly out late. I reckon it's him, Guv.' She held up a picture of Trudwick.

'He's got blue eyes.' Lorraine stared at the picture. 'The prostitute said he had blue eyes.'

'And when the taxi driver said "tan skin", what he could have seen was –' Chloe pointed to a photo on the evidence board showing the men in football kit with bare arms. '– freckles.' She folded her arms, looking up at the picture with a grin on her face.

Robyn looked across both. There was no beam of light telling her this was the correct solution but, given the thickness of her hangover, it wasn't surprising. There was the nagging point she had missed this whole case – she could hardly now dismiss a potential solution on the basis of her dislike of Dr Bergmann with her extreme views. Whatever she did, she had to be positive and not discourage Chloe whose smile was fading, the longer she waited for an answer.

'Good work.' She smiled, watching Chloe's grin reappear. 'I won't say I agree with all of your research methods but if they work for you, then go for it.' She glanced down at the book, still open on her desk, then gave herself a mental shake. She could not let her own self-inflicted illness affect the team.

'Can we go and talk to him, Guv?' Chloe was already reaching for her jacket.

'Hang on.' Now Robyn felt more sure of her ground. 'You've outlined a good theory but if you've got the opportunity, test it first. Before we go and talk to him, be sure of your facts. For example, does he have a car?' Robyn turned back to the other board. 'Somewhere – yes, there.' She pointed to a printout from the number plate recognition camera. 'At the moment, we believe he only has a moped. There's another one of the things we still have to follow up – why he was snapped heading to the Docks area on the night Newman was killed when he said he was in London?'

'I'll find out, Guv.' Chloe sat down and pulled her keyboard towards her.

'And another thing to check. The attacks have been between midnight and three am. We know Trudwick works on the door at the Quiksilva club, find out when they open and get them to check their shift records.'

'I'm on it.' Lorraine tapped something into her keyboard. 'Yuck. I've got the club's website up and it's enough to induce a migraine just looking at it – says they're open 'til two every night, then Friday and Saturday to three.'

There was a pause.

'So he couldn't have done anything before, well maybe two-thirty?' Chloe's voice had lost its confidence.

'We can't be certain. Those could be new opening hours, he could have had a night off. All these are things we can check beforehand.' Robyn smiled. 'Do you see what I mean about testing first? If you line up this information before you go and see him, you'll be in charge of the interview, not him.'

'OK, if I keep on with Bartholomew's contacts – can you do this?' Lorraine looked around her screen at Chloe.

'Right.' They both began typing.

Robyn frowned. She tried to remember what she had said about Shazia. 'Lorraine. There's no need to follow up on Bartholomew. The family has decided they don't want to pursue a case.'

'What?' Lorraine stood up. 'But you said the meeting with Fell had gone better than you'd thought. Didn't you mean we keep going?'

'No. I meant because Professional Standards won't be coming.' They stared at each other for a second. 'Unfortunately, it looks as if there is no chance of Shazia recovering so her life support machine will be switched off.'

'So a bloke we know raped a girl with a bottle gets to swan around because we can't touch him?' Lorraine's voice was too loud, she was almost yelling.

'And if we cannot prove it?' Robyn kept her voice low, she didn't want this to turn into a shouting match. 'If we drag the family through an investigation and then he walks free from court? What then?'

'And if he strikes again? What do we say to his next victim?' Lorraine slapped her hand on her head. 'Oh silly me, it'll be fine because she'll be dead.'

'Chloe, can you give us a moment?' Robyn kept her eyes locked on Lorraine and heard rather than saw Chloe amble to the door. She waited until the door closed, watching Lorraine's chest rise and fall as she took quick, shallow breaths. 'Two things, Lorraine and then I suggest you go home and hit something. Number one.' She paused, waiting for Lorraine to look up. 'Nothing you say is going to change the family's decision, so you are wasting your breath. I don't like it any more than you do but I've found out the hard way, you can't win them all.' Lorraine's mouth was set in a tight line. 'Having principles is good – it's what sets you apart from the people we lock up, just you cannot let them blind you to the fact we're working in the real world not *Valley Village*.' She saw Lorraine's eyebrows go up. 'Second, just because we are not prosecuting Bartholomew for the assault, doesn't mean we forget about him. You can start by letting your Emerald colleagues about his unlicensed drugs.'

'Assuming I'm still on the project.' Lorraine's spoke through gritted teeth.

'I spoke to Fell. He knows these things happen. So your start on Operation Emerald wasn't what we all hoped it would be but that's no reason to give up on it.' Robyn held up a hand as Lorraine opened her mouth. 'And this is how I will introduce your bid to be sergeant to Fell, by stressing you are the right person for this responsibility. It may be only information gathering at the moment but it's how to get the exposure and contacts you need.'

Blinking, Lorraine sat back on the desk behind her. 'Is it worth it, Guv?'

'Definitely. It's how you deal with setbacks that shows you're ready to be a sergeant. When you go in front of Fell, tell him your plan for making sure a problem like this doesn't occur again and he'll lap it up.' Robyn tried to smile, willing Lorraine to do the same. 'I told you, I think you deserve promotion and I will support you but you need to make sure you are acting like a sergeant from now on. Deal?'

The edges of Lorraine's mouth twitched before relaxing. 'Deal.' Crossing to the board, she stared at Bartholomew's picture. 'We will get you for something. Even if it's just for having bad breath.'

Robyn snorted. 'If his isn't a crime, it should be.'

26

Robyn left at five, after sending off an attempt at a team budget. She made a point of shoving a copy of Newman's crime scene report into her handbag to show she would still be working. It was a relief to leave: her headache was still a dull throb.

On the way home she stopped at a small supermarket. As she was browsing, there was the realisation she didn't know what Becky liked any more. With a growing sense of frustration, she walked up and down aisles picking up things she thought would make it look as if she was being healthy: yoghurt, brown bread, a net of lemons. It was now a habit to go to the self-service tills, avoiding someone's opportunity to stare. With everything rung through, she realised there was nothing to eat tonight and grabbed a couple of pizzas because they were nearest.

Letting herself in ten minutes before Becky's train was due to arrive, Robyn hurried to clean up the mess in the kitchen and put away the shopping. With a restless energy, she roamed the house, looking for anything out of place. A buzz from her phone made her jump.

Dad, not sure when I'm going to get there – fatality on the line so all trains stopped. B.

She stared at the screen, not wanting to believe the words. Robyn knew the drill: the lines would be closed for a couple of hours while body parts were photographed and removed. Everything seemed to be conspiring to stop her seeing her daughter. In need of something to do, she found the train operator's site on her phone. There were few details, just saying a person had been hit by a train, which made it sound like an accident rather than a deliberate act by a person whose only concern was stopping their pain.

She flung the phone down onto the sofa. There was nothing she needed to do and nothing she wanted to do. In desperation, she reached into her handbag and pulled out the crime scene report. Opening a page at random, she found a close-up image of Newman's pale face. She blinked to bring back some moisture to her eyes. His head was at an odd angle, a pile of rags the only thing between his face and the struts on the van's metal floor. She let her mind drift. Something had made the family man who was trying to settle down take the huge risk of driving his van again when he was drunk. There was a possibility Newman had realised how stupid he was being and had bunked down in his van rather than drive home but to lie directly on a metal floor with just a dust sheet for cover even though there was a sweatshirt in the cab – the man must have been paralytic. Something Chloe had said earlier rang in her mind and she flicked through the report until she found the details of the fingerprint search. She read it and read it again: there was only one set of fingerprints on the van's back doors. She remembered how dirty the van was. It seemed odd the door handles were clean. There should have been Newman's prints on the doors because that was the bit he touched most.

Even though Robyn had been expecting, waiting, hoping for the doorbell, it made her jump because her mind was still in Flotilla block's car park. The only possible conclusion was that someone else had put Newman's body in the van. The question she had to work out now was whether he was dead or alive when he was put there. The doorbell rang again. She checked her watch: it was only half-past seven so it was probably someone collecting a subscription for Neighbourhood Watch. Force of habit made her check the spy-hole. Her daughter was a few steps away, up the path, as if studying the house. Robyn had a weird sensation, as if Becky's gaze was going through the wall and examining her as well. Her hand was shaking a little as she opened the door.

'Sweetheart. How lovely to see you. I wasn't expecting you for another hour at least. Where's the cab? I'll pay him.'

There was no car outside.

'Oh, I walked from the station.'

'Becky! I told you to get a cab. It could be dangerous.'

Becky took half a step backward. Robyn could feel the full force of her daughter's stare. The hazel eyes came from her mother and there was a hint of the same judgement.

Robyn stepped forward, taking the holdall. She did not want anything to take place on the street. Already, she was annoyed with herself for treating her adult daughter like a child. 'Let's get this in.' She walked into the house, determined not to turn around, to give Becky space. 'I'll take the bag up to your room.' To give herself a second, Robyn popped into the bathroom and splashed water on her face. Her foundation was smudged and she dabbed it away with a tissue, feeling glad she had kept the make-up light today.

Downstairs, there was a noise she hoped was the front door closing. She came down the stairs to see Becky standing in the hall, looking around her.

'I'll put the kettle on.' Robyn moved into the kitchen, raising her voice slightly. 'It's all changed since you were last here.' She held the kettle under the tap.

Becky appeared in the doorway. 'They put on some buses to replace the trains. I got all kinked up 'cos the seats on the coach were so tight, so I wanted to walk. And it got my steps up for the day.' She held up

her left wrist where a purple fitness band stuck out from string brace-
lets. 'You're just like grandma.'

Robyn stared at Becky, until something cold on her hand drew her
gaze back to the sink and she realised she'd filled the kettle to overflowing so water was pouring down the side.

'I mean, putting the kettle on was always the first thing she
did too.'

Robyn gave the kettle a cursory wipe with a tea towel and set it
to boil. She leaned on the counter, hoping she looked relaxed rather
than needing support. 'It's good to see you. It's been too long.' The
moment she said it, she regretted the words. It made it sound like
Becky's fault, when, being honest, she had hidden herself away in
the long pondering towards her transition. 'Well, there isn't a lot
in Meresbourne to draw you back, is there? Nothing ever happens
around here. The usual, sleepy place.' She was horrifying herself at the
rubbish she was talking.

At least Becky had relaxed a little. She was leaning on the door
frame rather than standing rigid, a faint hum of music coming from
the headphones around her neck. She looked like any other student,
with rips in her jeans and a long, slouchy t-shirt for a band Robyn had
never heard of.

'I hardly recognise the place.' Becky looked around. 'Can still smell
the paint.'

Robyn smiled. 'This has been keeping me out if mischief for the
last few weeks. It really needed doing.'

'I remember.' Becky seemed to be looking everywhere except at
Robyn. 'The last time I was here was Grandpa's funeral. Do you
remember, it was that horrible cold day and even with the lights on,
everything was so dark?'

'That was a dismal day. I've been living here two years now and
finally got around to making some changes.' The kettle was getting
noisier now. To continue the conversation, Robyn would have to
raise her voice. Everything she could think of to say was so trivial, it

didn't seem worth the effort. She added tea leaves to the pot, waited until the kettle boiled then poured on the water. The mugs, sugar and a packet of biscuits were already on a tray: she reached into the fridge for the milk carton. 'Come and see the lounge.'

'Wow.'

It was a positive first reaction. She let her daughter roam around the room while she sat on one end of the sofa and got coasters out of the drawer in the small table.

Becky chose to sit on the floor, her back against the armchair and pulled off her ankle boots. 'You are the only person in the entire world who still uses a teapot.'

'Some of us have standards.' Robyn smiled. 'Your grandmother would never serve milk without a jug or biscuits straight from the packet. They'd have to have their own plate and napkins.'

'And a spoon to take the sugar from the bowl and another one to stir the tea with.' Becky smiled for the first time. 'I tell people at Uni and they just laugh at me.'

Robyn put on a mock-serious tone. 'You'll be telling me you don't use a separate knife for butter anymore.' She put her hand to her head, palm-upwards. 'I feel faint.'

She realised she had gone too far when she saw Becky freeze. Determined to keep going, she bent over the tea tray. 'This should be ready now.' She poured the tea, taking time over doing it to give Becky a chance to recover. She wondered if this was how it was going to be with her daughter, a constant feeling of being just a step away from disaster.

'Oh, sorry, I didn't say. I don't take milk anymore.'

Robyn stopped, the mug half-full. She hadn't seen her daughter for nearly a year: she had to get used to the idea Becky had her own tastes and preferences.

She finished pouring. 'Two for me then.' She stood up. 'You open the biscuits.' She walked into the kitchen and reached for the mug tree. Behind her, she heard a mobile ring.

'Hello, Mum.' Becky's voice was wary.

Robyn loitered in the kitchen, not wanting to interrupt.

A scrabbling sound must have been Becky standing up. 'Mum, we've been through this. I can't, I'm sorry.'

Another pause. 'No. It's not a good idea.' Robyn counted to ten. 'No, Mum, I'm sorry, it won't work. I've got to go. I'll talk to you soon. Bye.'

Robyn put the mug down and went to the cupboard getting out two wine glasses. Even though more alcohol was the last thing she needed, she grabbed the bottle of white from the door of the fridge. Becky was staring out into the garden. When she turned around, Robyn held up the wine. 'Shall we forget the tea?'

The tear tracks on Becky's face made Robyn angry at Julie for upsetting her. There was an urge to hug Becky: fear of rejection held her back.

'Sweetheart – sit down. Tell me what I can do to help.'

Becky rubbed one eye with her sleeve.

Robyn reached for her handbag where she kept tissues, then stopped. Such props might be another step too far for Becky to accept just now. She busied herself unscrewing the cap of the wine bottle. 'I hope this is OK. I hope you like white.'

'Oh white wine because that's what ladies drink?' Becky's hands were balled into fists. 'I came here to get away from mum. It doesn't mean I understand what you're doing or accept it.' She put her hands to her head. 'So don't come over all girlfriends together because we're not.' Blotches of red were showing above her t-shirt. 'Is it too much for just one parent …?' Her cheeks were streaked with tears. 'To have one sane parent?' She dodged past the table and into the hallway.

Robyn heard the door of the downstairs loo slam shut, then the bolt pushed across. Sinking back onto the sofa, she gazed upwards without focusing. She had hoped, she had dared to hope. The cap went back on the wine and she carried the tray into the kitchen, where she drank both cups of tea, rinsing the mugs and the teapot. There was a short burst of a tap running in the cloakroom tap and no more sound.

She paused in the hallway and made a decision. 'Sweetheart. Why don't we leave things for tonight? Let you rest after your journey. There's food in the fridge and you're in the room at the front. I've left a spare door key on the counter. Good night.'

Without hurrying, she prepared for the morning. Upstairs, she switched on the light in Becky's room. The glow of light showed through the keyhole in her bedroom door as she lay in bed.

WEDNESDAY 21
SEPTEMBER

27

When Robyn had been shopping for nightwear, she'd fallen for the movie images and had bought a long, silky robe in lilac. Hanging on the back of her bedroom door, it looked very fine. The reality of wearing it was rather different. Bought online, she hadn't realised the fabric was prone to static and so slippery, the panels refused to stay closed, no matter how carefully she knotted the belt. As she stepped out of her bedroom door for the first time with someone else in the house, she was conscious how little of her the robe covered compared to the comfortable, threadbare cotton robe she'd got rid of with all her male clothes. Dashing to the bathroom, she was grateful Becky's door was closed.

The bathroom reinforced another's presence: a toothbrush lying next to a spotted washbag on the window ledge and a purple towel draped over the edge of the bath. She didn't put the radio on, thinking Becky must need her sleep.

Entering the kitchen, Robyn's heart leaped when she saw the scrap pad out on the counter. In loopy script, there was a note: *What's the Wi-Fi password?*

Through the routine of breakfast, she was listening for any sound from upstairs. She thought about taking a cup of tea up to Becky then decided against it. First thing in the morning was not the time to try and have a meaningful conversation. After brushing her teeth, she laid out all she needed for her make-up. Once the foundation was on, she had to add more concealer under her eyes to hide the dark circles. She reached for the lipstick, pulling her lips back from her teeth to get a smear-free finish. In the mirror, she saw the door being pushed open – she normally had no need to lock it. Robyn jumped, feeling the lipstick slide down her chin.

There was a flash of a pale face in the mirror before Becky fled.

'Sweetheart.' Robyn checked her reflection, cursing the huge peach-coloured line. A hurried wipe removed half the colour and transferred most of it to her blouse's cuff. Part of her wanted to run after Becky. A larger part said she had to let Becky find her own way of dealing with things, however long she needed. Wiping off the rest of the mess with tissue, she reapplied the lipstick.

Once she'd turned off the beauty mirror's spotlights, her appearance in natural light made her pause. There were patches where the foundation was so thick, you could see layers at the edges. She pulled hard on the toilet roll, wadding paper in both fists and began rubbing at her face. On inspection, she looked both more like the memory of Roger and more human, so she tidied a few smears and left the rest. From the bedroom, she heard her phone ring.

'Morning, Graham.'

'Guv, I can't get in.'

There was a note in Graham's voice she hadn't heard before. All trace of his usual confidence had been stripped away. 'What's up? Are you OK?'

'It's not me, it's Sandra. She woke up in the night, pain so bad she was screaming. We're back at the hospital.'

'OK, you don't need to tell me any more. Do what you need to do, just let me know what's going on and whether I can help at all.'

'Thanks, Guv.'

'And take care of yourself. You'll be no help to Sandra if you burn yourself out.' She hoped it had come across in the way it was meant.

She took a deep breath on the top landing. 'I'm going to work, Becky. If you need me, give me a call. I'll try and be back early.'

There was no answer. She hadn't expected one. Stuck in the morning traffic, she wondered what Becky would do all day. She had left Meresbourne when was she was under two so the town was just where her little-seen grandparents lived. Apart from the *Marvellous Meresbourne* tourist trail there wasn't a lot else. As the car in front inched forward, Robyn wondered what she could say differently tonight to get through to Becky. At the moment, she couldn't think of anything.

She was glad to be the first in, wanting to get her own thoughts in order. She had made a resolution to make an effort with the backlog of paperwork. In addition to all the things she should have done, now balanced on the edge of her desk was a bundle of all of the material Chloe had collated about Shazia ready to be archived. On top was a picture taken outside the Lady Ann hotel. Shazia's emerald scarf lay on stained paving slabs, a vivid flash of green across dull grey. Robyn turned the picture over.

Lorraine and Chloe arrived together. Both seemed to be waiting for Robyn to say something. She guessed they wanted to know about Becky and determined to take the initiative. 'Morning you two. We have a change of plan. Graham called me this morning: he's going to be away for the next week or so. With Ravi off as well, we will have to focus on what we can do.' Seeing Lorraine's mouth open, she raised her voice a little. 'This is fine, we're a team, we all support each other and if someone needs a little space, we give them it.'

'Here's to the weaker sex.' Lorraine raised her coffee cup.

Thinking of what Graham was going through made it hard for Robyn to smile. 'Always remember, it might be you needing help next time.' She needed to keep them busy. 'Right, I was doing some thinking yesterday and I am now certain someone placed Newman in his van.' Robyn's phone began to ring. 'Even if he was alive at the time, whoever it was still has some big questions to answer.' She glanced down at the screen – it was her doctor's surgery. The thought of talking to either her narrow-minded GP or one of his haughty receptionists was not appealing and she swore, stabbing at the screen to cut the call. No one else spoke and Robyn glanced up to find Lorraine and Chloe still looking at her.

'How long is Graham going to be off for?' There was only curiosity in Chloe's tone.

'At least the next couple of weeks, I would say. Let's get a move on with Trudwick.' Robyn wandered back to her desk. She picked up the phone and saw the doctor had left a message. It was unlikely to be good news so it didn't provide an excuse to delay the paperwork. She pulled the nearest pile towards her uncovering the garish bulk of Chloe's book. Feeling her fingers prickle with dislike, Robyn picked it up. The hardback slipped within the loose cover and the book came open at the bookmark. At the top of the page, a header proclaimed: *The Victim-Male and Relations with Women.* Robyn read the first line. *If unchecked, the behaviour of the victim-male can include a range of anti-social and criminal behaviours, particularly of a sexual nature against the female as a substitute for the mother-figure. Examples are rape used as a weapon of war, dominant sexual practices and voyeurism.* She snapped the book shut.

'Right, we're off to Quiksilva, Guv.' Lorraine slung her bag on her shoulder. 'We'll try and get the staff rosters, then go and see Trudwick. There's no record of him or his mother having a car, so we'll have to ask him direct.'

In the quiet office, Robyn got to the second paragraph of text in a twenty-six page document on tendering for a new catering provider and found her eyes losing focus. A faint bell was ringing in her mind. She shook her head to clear it, trying to trace where she had seen this before. Looking back at the report, she reread the last sentence:

The division must achieve substantial savings and catering provision is an area prioritised for cost reductions. Apart from Dominika, the only other sober victim of the attacks had been a chef, walking home after locking up. There was a contact number.

The phone rang for a long time before a harassed voice answered. 'Hello?' In the background was traffic and gusts of wind.

'Miss Fuller? I'm Detective Inspector Bailley from Meresbourne Police. We're looking again at a number of cases, including your attack last year. Could I come and speak to you, please?'

There was silence from the other end.

'Hello? Miss Fuller – are you there?'

'I've been trying to forget about that night.'

'I'm sorry. We believe he's attacked again which means we have new evidence. I want to make sure no one else has to go through this, so if you can manage to talk to me, it will really help.'

'Look, yes, OK. I'm late for work. Meet me at Bistro Twenty-eight but I'll have to be done before eleven-thirty because we've got a big lunch booking.'

The restaurant was in one of the few remaining Elizabethan houses in Meresbourne's small old town. Robyn walked up Saints' Row and knocked on the window. The prices on the menu made her blink.

'Not open until twelve, love.' A woman in a blue house coat holding a mop had opened the door a crack. 'Best to book if you want a table.'

'I'm here to see Meredith Fuller.' Robyn held up her ID.

She was let in with no more than a glance at the card though the door was locked behind her. The cleaner picked up her bucket and elbowed open a swing door at the end of the bar. 'Meredith – a copper to see you, OK?' After a second, the cleaner jerked her head. 'She says go in but not beyond the plating area because you're dirty.'

A slight push and the door swung wide letting Robyn into the bright kitchen. Light bounced off chrome counters and walls. The air was warm and filled with a mixture of scents. The first breath was of a meaty flavour which set her stomach rumbling; then hints of a more subtle, citrus smell, with something spicy she couldn't identify. At one of the counters, a woman in a boxy white jacket and chequered trousers was spooning a pale mixture into pastry shells. One auburn curl escaped from the bandana around her head.

'Miss Fuller, thank you for seeing me.'

The woman glanced up, down and then back up to take in Robyn's face and chest. A drop of the mixture oozed down the side of a tart and onto the baking sheet. There was a muffled word under her breath before she reached for a cloth, wiped away the mixture and began again.

'Could we sit down for a moment?'

'No. I've got a party of twenty booked for lunch plus walk-ins. No time. I don't know what else I can tell you. I was walking home, someone grabbed me. A taxi driver stopped to help and the bloke ran off. I didn't see his face.' The words came out in a rush: she didn't lift her eyes from her work.

'Yes, those were the details in the file. What I'm interested in is your impressions.'

'Impressions?' Fuller looked up for a second. 'You make it sound like we were dating. He was trying to rape me.'

'That's exactly what I'm after.' Robyn leant against the counter. The metal was cold against her hand. 'What made you think his approach was sexual, rather than being after cash or your phone?'

'The way he grabbed me.' The bowl pinged on the counter when Fuller slammed it down. 'He didn't touch my bag which was over my shoulder. He came out of nowhere, lifted me off the pavement. He wanted to dominate me.'

'What happened next?'

She opened an oven, releasing a blast of heat, sliding the tarts onto a shelf. With a smooth economy of movement, she shut the door with one hand, turning a timer with the other. Back at the counter, she tipped over another bowl, sending onions rolling. Corralling them with one arm, she reached to a rack and selected a long-bladed knife.

'Miss Fuller?'

The knife blade moved in a rhythm, slice, slice, snick snick snick. 'He shoved me into a wall.'

'What did you do?'

'I managed to get my head back in time, so my shoulder hit the wall rather than my face.'

'Did he say anything to you?'

'Nothing.' Fuller's knife kept up its movement. 'Even when I hit him.'

'You managed to hit him?'

'I managed to headbutt him backwards, got his nose pretty hard. He sort of yelled through his gum.'

'How do you know he was chewing gum?' Robyn allowed herself some hope. These were things not recorded from the interview. She would have to speak to Graham, then remembered Graham would be off and not in much of a state to take things in.

'Bugger.' Fuller's full attention went back to the onions as one piece shot away from the board and onto the floor.

The cleaner stuck her head around the door. 'The butcher's here.'

'Thanks. Out in a moment.' Fuller scooped up the piece of onion and threw it away. She swept the pile of chopped pieces into a large pan and carried it to the hob.

'Miss Fuller, how do you know he was chewing gum?'

'What? Oh, he had really bad breath. When my head was back I could smell it and the gum he was trying to cover it with. Now I've got to get on.'

'One more question, please – was there anything else memorable? The way he ran, could you feel rings on his fingers? Is there anything else you can give us to help identify him?'

With a practised touch, Fuller adjusted her scarf so that all her hair was covered. 'Do you really think you'll catch him?'

'I can't make any promises.' Robyn spread her hands in front of her. 'We've spotted a pattern in the attacks and it has become a priority case.'

'Because little old me on my own wasn't a priority before? Thanks for making me feel so much better.' She wiped her hands. 'Has this sudden attention got anything to do with the town celebrating all things feminist perhaps?'

'No, no.' Robyn shook her head, annoyed at her own clumsiness. 'I'm sorry. What I should have said –'

'Whatever.' She threw the cloth to a counter. 'All I know is when I fought back, when I hurt him, I didn't think he was going to rape me anymore – I thought he was going to kill me.'

'The butcher's worried his van's going to get a ticket.' The cleaner was in the doorway.

'OK, I'm there. Officer.'

The dismissal was clear. Robyn led the way back into the restaurant where a man stood with a pile of crates full of red lumps sealed in plastic. There was a greeting, then Fuller was absorbed, checking the packets against a list. The door was open: in the street, the rain was bouncing off the pavement.

28

Robyn had no umbrella. When her phone rang, it was a good excuse to loiter for longer under the building's overhang.

'Hi, Chloe. What have you got?'

'Nothing, Guv. Absolutely nothing. Trudwick's in the clear. We're –' Chloe paused as the voice of the sat-nav intruded. 'We're on our way back now.'

'So what did you find?' Robyn watched the rain drops hitting the pavement and bouncing, letting her eyes slide out of focus.

'The club said they need time to put the shift data together so we thought we'd go over to Trudwick's place anyway. We got the conversation around to the attacks and it turns out he used to work with one of the girls who was attacked so he's furious we haven't caught the man yet. Sounded like he was planning his own posse at one point.'

'Are you sure he wasn't bluffing?'

'I'm sure. When we left, I checked his record again. He was in custody for the assault when one of the attacks took place. It's not him.'

'Bugger.' Robyn switched the phone to her other ear. 'Does it look as if he was involved in Newman's death?'

'Again, no. First he seemed really upset about it and then he got a mate to text over some photos of him in a club on the night of Newman's death, so unless he's not such a barmpot as he looks, he didn't have anything to do with it.'

'What about the moped?' Robyn saw the butcher run to his van, clipboard held above his head.

'Now there was the one thing we did learn.' Chloe's laugh was a short, ugly sound. 'Turns out, his mother's got a fancy man over in the Docks and uses the moped when Trudwick's not around. No licence or anything. We left them having a mother–son heart-to-heart.'

'OK, well, I've just got some new information about the fourth attack. We'll go through it when you get back.' Robyn put her phone into the holster and looked again at the sky, shivering. There was a little more light, the clouds beginning to break and there was a chance a few minutes' wait would be enough for the rain to stop. Her stomach was still rumbling. On an impulse, she ran a few steps up the road to the Edmund Napier Loveless museum where she knew there was a cafe. The poster on the front door flapped from one corner, saturated by the rain.

A woman with the same thin lips as Loveless looked over her glasses at her. 'One senior citizen, dear? The talk starts in an hour.'

'No, I'm just going to get a cup of tea.' Stung, Robyn kept moving, blaming the dim light in the narrow entrance hall for another thing for her to worry about. She turned left, through the archway to the new cafe which had been built onto the back of the house. As the only customer, she took her tea and scone to a corner table.

When her phone rang, she had a mouthful so was relieved it was only Khalid. 'Hi.'

'Robyn, are you in the station?'

She swallowed. 'No but I can talk, go ahead.'

'It's all go here.' Khalid tutted. 'That bloody Bergmann woman has demanded and got a meeting with the Kent Police and Crime Commissioner. It's set for tomorrow and I've got to do a briefing covering all violence against women for nine am and we don't seem to have any progress. Help.'

Robyn tried to sound sympathetic. 'Well, we've identified we've probably got a single attacker and we're prioritising it as a case. I've just spoken again to one of the victims. I'm sorry, there's no more progress. Oh, and the death of the suspect was definitely suspicious.'

'OK, well can we talk about how many officers we have assigned? Something to makes us sound like we're taking this seriously.'

'Taking it seriously?' Her voice echoed against the beamed ceiling. 'For Christ's sake, Khalid, what do you think? When I try to get someone arrested I get told to let him go again because of politics and when I ask you if we can put a general safety alert out, you tell me no.' She knew part of her anger was because of the guilt she had not spotted the pattern before.

'Yes, sorry about that.' Khalid paused. 'Is there any more you can tell me about the suspect?' His normal brisk tone had returned.

'Stocky, always wore black.'

There was a pause.

'Is that it?'

Robyn felt her anger fading. 'I'm afraid so. We're trying.'

'I know.' Khalid sighed. 'In the meantime, what am I going to say to the PCC?'

A clatter came from behind her. A waitress pushed a trolley stacked high with crockery and began laying things out on a long table at the end of the room.

'Tell her don't walk on her own at night.'

Robyn cut the call and immediately regretted the outburst. Khalid had given her strong support and she was not helping herself by antagonising him. As her phone was out, she dialled her voicemail.

265

Good morning Ms Bailley. The voice was female and young, with a slight lisp on the s. *My name is Dr Vanatu – we haven't met, I've only been at the practice for three months. After your last visit, I discussed your case with Dr Hargreaves and we've agreed that you'll move to my patient roster. I understand you are seeking a referral to a specialist gender identity clinic – I'll be honest, I haven't done one of those before but, if you'd like to make an appointment, we can go through the form and work it out together. Please call the surgery to fix a time.*

Surprised, Robyn pressed the button to listen to the message again, wanting to make sure of the doctor's name. A broad grin spread across her face as she pressed to call back.

'What the hell are you doing here, Roger?'

Startled, Robyn jumped, feeling the phone slip between her fingers and clatter against the tea cup. 'Coronation Road surgery. Hello?'

Julie stood in the doorway of the cafe. One finger twined a strand of hair around and around.

'Hello, caller? Can you hear me?' Killing the phone, Robyn stood up.

'I said, what the hell are you doing here? Are you stalking me?' Julie took a few steps forward. 'Of course, you found out I'm giving a talk and came to spoil it.'

'Hello, Julie.' Robyn gripped the back of the chair, one nail finding a ridge in the varnish. 'Don't worry, I'm not here for your talk. I was working just up the road and came in to get out of the rain.' Even though it was true, it sounded weak.

The frown lines deepened on Julie's forehead. 'You've ruined everything else of mine. Why wouldn't you want to mess this up as well?'

Robyn began to gather her things. There would be nothing she could say that wouldn't end up being twisted.

'Oh, so now you're leaving. Just walking away again when things get tough?'

Swinging her handbag to her shoulder, Robyn forced herself to

266

smile. 'Goodbye, Julie. I hope your talk goes well.' She wasn't prepared for the tears on Julie's face.

'You really don't care, do you? I've lost everything.' Julie brushed her glasses from her nose, letting them drop on their beaded chain. She ran her hands across her eyes. 'I don't even know where Becky is.'

Robyn stopped. A large part of her wanted to point out to her ex-wife that this was how she felt all the time because of the hurdles Julie had put in the way of any relationship with their daughter. That, like so many other things, was in the past now. She faced Julie. 'I know where Becky is.' Julie's eyes widened. 'She's safe. Not exactly happy, because I don't think she considers either of us is acting like a role model at the moment.'

'Where is she?' Julie's hand shot out and grabbed Robyn's forearm, her turquoise nails hard against the skin.

'I think if Becky wanted you to know, she'd tell you.' The grip on Robyn's arm tightened. 'Isn't that what you want, her to be a strong, independent woman?'

'Now you're mocking me.' Drawing away, Julie wrapped her shawl tight across her chest. Her eyes were again filling with tears.

Robyn was caught between wanting to get away and the fact that she would not leave a stranger in distress, so she shouldn't do that to her ex. She pulled out a chair for Julie and managed to catch the waitress's eye. 'Could we get another pot of tea here, please?'

Julie sank into the chair and accepted a tissue.

'So what's your talk about?' Robyn told herself she was being polite to Julie for her daughter's sake.

Still sniffing, Julie pulled a paper-filled plastic wallet from her bag. The top sheet was a poster: *Villains or Victims: The Role of Men in a Feminised Society.*

'I hope you think they have one.' Robyn saw Julie's face tighten, lips pursing into a thin line. 'I just meant, it would be hard to get rid of fifty percent of the population.'

'Such rubbish.' Julie sat up straighter as the waitress put a pot of tea in front of her. 'You have no idea what you are talking about.'

'Thank you.' Robyn raised her voice to be sure the waitress heard her as she walked away. 'Well, now you're feeling better, I'm going to go and let you prepare. Hope it goes well.' She turned towards the door.

'There's no role for people like you.' Julie's voice echoed around the room.

Robyn stopped, swallowed and turned around. 'Why did you have to say that?' The frustration of the last few days was too close to the surface to do the sensible thing and walk away. 'You may not agree with what I'm doing but, here's the thing, it's nothing to do with you and if you want to do something for women, maybe you could get out of your library?'

Julie was on her feet now. 'I did. I protested against men getting away with rape and you arrested me.'

'You were arrested because you were violent. Violence never solves violence, only makes it worse.' Robyn held onto her handbag strap: her nails were digging into her palms.

'Any woman could've told you that.' Julie scraped hair back from her face. 'You know what happens when a woman fights back against oppression? You men take it as a personal insult if a woman won't do as she's told because that makes him the victim, so he'll lash back twice as hard.'

'Good luck with the talk.' Robyn didn't trust herself to stay and she started again the door.

'Where's Becky? What have you done to her?'

Robyn gained the exit before she turned back. 'I talked to her.' She took a breath. 'Instead of shouting at her.'

'Well, what do you know about her life, what she gets up to? You weren't there when she came in late or didn't come in at all.'

Keeping one hand on the door like a talisman to secure escape, Robyn faced Julie. 'No, I wasn't as involved as I would have like to have been in her growing up.' She emphasised the words, thinking of all the times when paternal visits had been cancelled at the last minute. 'I did my best. That's all parents ever can do, their best under whatever circumstances they find themselves.'

'And you call pretending to be a woman doing your best?' Julie advanced, hand moving from chair back to chair back. 'Oh, my daughter's a woman now, so I'll be one too?'

'This isn't about Becky.' Robyn saw Julie's mouth start to open and kept talking to fill the space. 'Or about you. And what you call pretending, it's real. I do my job as who I'm meant to be. If the police can accept me as I am, why can't you?'

'Oh yes, the police.' Julie's smile was more disturbing than her anger. 'Let's see, well known for protecting their own, aren't they? And for only investigating the crimes where nice people get hurt because they don't want to go to places where they'll get their hands dirty. And can you really stand there and tell me you take crimes against women and girls seriously? What about what happened at the Lady Ann – is anyone going to be punished for that?'

'I can't talk about an active case.' It was the sort of evasive answer Fell would give and Robyn felt her own frustration. 'Not every case can be brought to a successful conclusion, just like not every problem in life can be solved. Sometimes there isn't enough evidence and we have to be sure because we've got to convince a court. The burden of proof is high because it's better to let a guilty person go free than lock up an innocent.'

'And never mind if a few more innocents suffer? If some victims get hurt, that's what they're there for, isn't it?' Julie stiffened, looking over Robyn's shoulder.

'Excuse me. Is this where the talk is to be held?'

Robyn turned. Behind her stood a short man with grey hair pulled back into a pony tail. In the confined space of the doorway, the smell of tobacco was overpowering. 'Yes, let me get out of your way.' She raised her voice. 'Hope the talk goes well.' Julie had sat down and was fumbling through her papers. Robyn hurried through the lobby and into the street where the rain had faded though the air was still damp. Marching up the street, she put the frustration and anger into movement, swinging her arms and walking fast, even when a puddle around a blocked drain soaked her shoes.

29

The atmosphere in the incident room was gloomy. Lorraine picked at a bag of crisps, Chloe was stapling pieces of paper together.

'OK, let's get together.' Robyn sat on the edge of her desk. 'I think we're close to resolving a few things. Let's start with the death. What you got from Trudwick helps to narrow things down. I'm sure if we can work out why Newman risked another arrest by driving to the Docks, we'll crack this.'

'Did Newman know about the rape before you told him in the interview room?' Chloe looked at Lorraine.

Lorraine finished chewing. 'No, he didn't. Why does that matter?'

Chloe put her chin on her hands. 'Maybe, if he only found out what happened from you, he'd want to know more, wouldn't he? He'd try to talk to someone who'd been there. Like Bartholomew, maybe?'

'Why wouldn't he just call?' Taking the final crisp, Lorraine scrunched the packet.

'Because, how about, if Newman suspected Bartholomew had been the one who'd raped Shazia, he would want to find out for sure.

If you've been arrested for a rape you didn't commit, you're going to be pretty keen to find out who had really done it.' Robyn followed the chain and her smile broadened. 'Good work, Chloe, I think you've got it. Newman gets a scare at the station, realises how people will treat him if they think he's a rapist. He goes to the pub to recover then maybe he remembers something Bartholomew said and decides he must be the guilty one. Because it's someone he thinks of as a friend, he would go in person to confront him.'

'Bartholomew had a black eye when we saw him.' Lorraine put her hand to her head. 'He told us it was an accident on Sunday morning. Newman must have punched him.'

'There were marks on Newman's knuckles.' Chloe began flicking through a copy of the forensic report. 'Yes, contusions to left knuckles consistent with striking something. Pictures, pictures.' Chloe scanned the evidence board. 'Here.' She pointed to a shot of the ushers raising their glasses in a toast. 'Newman's got his glass in his left hand.'

'So Newman comes round, accuses Bartholomew.' A sudden burst of energy drove Robyn to her feet. 'Maybe Bartholomew boasted about him and Shazia but, either way, there's a fight. Hah! Got him.' She smacked Bartholomew's picture on the board, sending paper fluttering to the floor.

Lorraine held up her hand. 'OK, Guv.' She moved forward and began gathering the fallen material. 'We get him by being sure of our facts. For a start, we need to ask questions like, if Bartholomew put Newman in the van, why aren't his fingerprints there? Instead, we've got an unknown person.' Lorraine reattached the pictures and turned back to Robyn, head cocked on one side.

'You're right' Robyn held up her hands. 'Now you're speaking as a sergeant. Between you, you have the measure of this. What should we do?'

'No doubt that Bartholomew is strong enough to carry a body downstairs: the question is, was Newman dead before he was put in the van?' Lorraine's pen tapped on the desk.

'Probably not.' Chloe flicked through the report. 'Where is it – ah, here. There were traces of solvents on the inside of his nose consistent with breathing them in. Newman was alive when he went into the van.'

'Right. So first, we double-check those fingerprints.'

'I'm on it.' Chloe was already typing.

'Then, we go and see Lyndsey and get her story about Saturday night. That should be a nice surprise for her.' Lorraine caught Robyn's nod of approval and smiled.

Into the positive feeling from action came a nasty thought. Robyn realised if Becky was out and about in town, she could run into Julie and then face exactly the situation she'd tried to avoid. Hunkering down at her desk, she tapped out a text.

Becky, I ran into your mother in town earlier – she is here for the Loveless conference. She was not happy to see me again so I wanted to warn you. Hope you are finding things to do, not sure what time will be back. Love, Dad.

'Oh boy!' Chloe clapped her hands. 'This is our lucky day. You know you suggested going to see Lyndsey?' She swung the monitor round so Lorraine could see it. 'When we go, we can ask her why her fingerprints are the only ones on the door of Newman's van.'

'They were Lyndsey's?' Robyn made sure the text had gone.

'I swear they weren't in there when I searched before – I ran it again and just got a match.'

'They must have come from the rubbish you took from Bartholomew's flat, Guv.' Lorraine looked ready to go.

'Every now and again, you get a break.' Robyn smiled. 'The lab must have added them to the database after the forensic report was written. Let's go. And Chloe, we need you. After all, this is your idea.' Her phone buzzed.

Dad, I watched the whole clip from Saturday. Let's talk this evening. B.

She had to read it again to be sure. A surge of relief mixed with joy. On top of the doctor's message, everything seemed to be slotting into place.

'Ah, Guv?'

Robyn became aware of Chloe and Lorraine both waiting by the door looking back at her.

'If you're ready, Guv?' Lorraine opened the door. 'How do you want to play this?'

Robyn grabbed her bag. 'Well, first we've got to get Lyndsey on her own. If Bartholomew is in, we'll have to ask him to leave and, if he gets cocky, I've got no problem with taking him down to the station on an assault charge. If he's serious about health and fitness, twenty-four hours of our nutrition regime should have him prepared to say anything.' They walked into the corridor.

'I'll challenge him to a press-up competition.' Chloe laughed. 'At kick-boxing, the instructor makes us do a hundred just for the warm-up. He sounds like the type who won't be able to resist beating a girl.'

Robyn stopped. For the first time in days, her brain felt as if it was working, a story coming together in her mind.

'Aren't you coming, Guv?' Chloe took a step towards her.

'Change of plan – let's check a couple of things first.' Robyn smiled at Lorraine's raised eyebrow. 'If Bartholomew is in, that's a good thing because while Lorraine interviews Lyndsey about Newman, Chloe and I can talk to Bartholomew about the street attacks.'

'What – really?' Lorraine shot back down the corridor. 'OK, explain.'

'Come on.' Robyn led the way back into the office. 'We've been looking at the hotel attack as if it was an isolated incident. But what if it wasn't?' Digging around on her desk, Robyn found a picture of Shazia. 'What if the rape was actually the latest in the series of attacks? Someone said to me today, if a man is knocked back by a woman, the next time he'll strike twice as hard.'

'That's a big step though, from grabbing someone on the street to rape in a hotel room?' Lorraine frowned.

'He's done this before.' Certainty made Robyn speak faster. 'Each time somebody fought back, he's changed his approach. I found out today that the fourth victim, Meredith Fuller, broke his nose when she struggled and he was nearly caught. So, for the next one, he changes his plan and drags them into a car where he thinks he can operate out of sight. Then Dominika used pepper spray on him and he doesn't dare use the car anymore. So, he takes advantage of the hotel room.'

'It makes sense.' Lorraine put her bag down with a thump. 'Again, can we prove it's Bartholomew?'

Robyn spread the photos out on her desk, looking at images of Bartholomew in football kit, at the wedding and selfies showing off his muscles. 'Damn, none of these have dates on. We need to find out when he broke his nose.'

'His Facebook profile was a joy to look at.' Chloe slipped into her seat. 'About six photos a week of him in one daft pose or another. Let me see if we can get something there.' She scrolled down the page. 'He is so in love with himself – aha. There were only a couple of photos posted between the nineteenth and twenty-eighth of January and none of them showed his face. Right.' She dashed over to the printer and fidgeted while the sheets chugged out. 'And here are the photos posted on the eighteenth and the twenty-ninth.' Although the quality was poor, a new kink in Newman's nose was visible.

'And here's another thing.' At her desk, Lorraine pointed at her screen. 'He bought a car in February. A four-door Astra is registered in his name.'

Robyn stood up. 'Right. Now we go.' As they left the office, she was smiling.

30

The three of them walked across Flotilla block's car park, Lorraine leading.

'Last time I was here in Uniform, I had to deal with an argument over a poker game.' Chloe was trotting to keep up with Lorraine. 'They say online gambling is bad but at least you don't get stabbed over a stake.'

'There's the Astra.' Lorraine pointed to a faded green car parked diagonally across two spaces. 'We need to impound it, check for traces of pepper spray. If we can get that, we've got another link.'

The block's front door was propped open. 'Do you think the girl knows about what Bartholomew does?' Chloe stepped into the lift.

'I don't know and we shouldn't rely on getting anything out of her.' Robyn was planning the day: get the arrest over with, arrange an appointment with the doctor and then a better evening with Becky. 'Most of the victims can't give any description, so the car is our best hope for getting evidence of the other crimes.' The doors opened and they stepped into the lobby.

'Guv, just thinking about things.' Lorraine put a hand on Robyn's arm. 'Last time we were here, the way I saw this girl, she was scared, damaged even. You can talk to people – I reckon she'd feel more comfortable with you.' Lorraine looked around, no humour in her eyes. 'And before you get paranoid, I didn't mean because you're damaged. It's just you've got a lot more patience than me – I'd probably end up telling her to get a life.'

'OK.' Robyn decided to accept this at face value. 'If Bartholomew isn't there, can you two do some checking around, see if anyone heard anything on Saturday night?'

Outside Bartholomew's flat, Chloe held up her hand. 'Hang on.' She put her ear to the door. 'There's a radio on.' She knocked then listened again. 'Now it's been switched off.'

'That probably means Lyndsey is on her own.' Robyn kept her voice low. 'Bartholomew wouldn't care about people knowing whether he's in or not.'

'Where is he then?' After a few seconds, Chloe knocked again. 'Miss, are you there?'

'Who is it?' Robyn had to lean closer to catch the voice. 'Colin's not here.'

Behind her, she heard Lorraine and Chloe moving away. Robyn smiled, conscious of an eye at the peephole. 'It's Robyn Bailley. I need to ask a few more questions and it would be easier inside. May I come in?'

'What questions?' There was a muffled noise as if the girl was leaning against the door.

'Questions about Saturday night. A friend of Colin's died and we want to find out how.' On the edge of her hearing, she caught a sound from inside, lost as Lorraine banged on a neighbour's door. Robyn leaned closer. 'Miss, can you help us find out how Jake died? His girlfriend needs to know because she has to tell their baby son.' She held her breath, waiting to catch any response. 'Miss, could I come in, please?' The solidity against Robyn's body eased as the latch clicked and the door swung inwards. She stepped in, just far enough so the door could be shut. 'Thank you.'

The girl stood in the light, leaning back, her clavicles sharp lines under the baggy sweat top. The pose was like an imitation of a model in a fashion shoot though her hands were balled into fists. Behind her, the bathroom door was open: Robyn could see the stacked protein powders.

'Perhaps we could sit down?' Robyn took a step forward, willing the girl to relax.

The girl took an equal step back. Some of the multiple holes in her ears were scabbed.

'There's nothing to worry about.' Robyn smiled. 'I have some more questions and I think you can help me. This won't take long, Miss – I don't know your surname?'

'Just Lyndsey.' The girl dropped her eyes, a finger of her left hand picking at the skin around her thumb nail.

'Lyndsey, OK. Let's sit down.' Robyn moved towards the one chair. The girl blinked before she jerked away and slumped onto the weight-lifting bench, knocking over a can of liniment spray which clanked against a weight.

Robyn sat down. 'Thank you. I don't have many questions. How long have you been living here?'

Lyndsey's lips pressed together.

'Don't worry, I'm not from the benefits office.' 'I just need to check a couple of things and then I'll go. Were you here on Saturday night?'

Arms folded around herself, Lyndsey shook her head once.

'Were you out? It was a miserable night, wasn't it?' This meant another lie Bartholomew had told them. Robyn smiled again, even though the girl's head was down.

'I was working.'

'Can you tell me where?' There was no answer. 'Was anyone with you?'

'Cleaning. Just me.' For the first time, Lyndsey's eyes met Robyn's.

'Do you get lonely? Working on your own?' The young woman's defiance looked brittle: Robyn kept her tone soothing, thinking the girl was used to aggression so might be disarmed by sympathy. 'I hope you don't have to travel alone late, there have been some attacks on women recently. Did you know about them?'

Her lips pressed together, Lyndsey shook her head.

'What time did you get home?'

'Dunno.' The answer was automatic.

'We think Colin and a man called Jake may have had an argument on Saturday and, somehow, Jake ended up in the back of his van. Did you know?' Robyn was sure Lyndsey's breathing had speeded up. 'It's just, I know you know about it because we found your fingerprints on Jake's van.' She leant forward. 'Now I don't think for a second you would be able to carry a big bloke like Jake around. Maybe you looked into the van to see if he was all right?' The lines of blusher on the woman's cheeks glared out because the colour had drained from her face. 'Lyndsey?'

'He was asleep, so I made him a pillow.' The words came out in a whisper. 'I got off the bus and Colin was in the car park doing something in the van. He was in a really bad mood. When he'd gone, I looked and saw the man. His face was on the floor, so I made him a pillow so he'd be comfortable and found something to cover him.'

Robyn let a long breath go. 'Do you know what Colin and Jake had been fighting about?'

'I wasn't there.' Lyndsey pushed up her sleeves.

'Are you and Colin a couple?'

Lyndsey cocked her head on one side, arms folding again. When Robyn kept up the same easy smile, at last she shook her head.

'You're just flatmates?'

There was a sharp nod.

'So you know Colin pretty well then? I'm just trying to understand him so I know why he and his friend Jake had a fight.'

'I told you, I wasn't there. I didn't see him all day because he was at the wedding. Why don't you ask him?'

Robyn had what she needed. 'I will when he's here.'

'You fancy him?' Lyndsey's eyes widened. 'He wouldn't even look at you. What are you anyway?' Her shoulders went back and in the crook of her left arm, Robyn saw lumpen marks on the white skin.

Robyn's stomach twisted: she focused on keeping her face neutral. 'I'm a police officer, Lyndsey. Nothing else.' She stood up. 'Thank you. You've been very helpful. Please tell Colin we need to speak to him.'

In the corridor, Robyn pulled the door shut and took a deep breath. In the lobby, she could hear voices: Lorraine and Chloe were waiting by the lift.

'We've got something, Guv.' Chloe pressed the lift button. 'Most of the neighbours were either out or not saying anything but an old lady downstairs remembers a thud on the ceiling at about eleven fifteen on Saturday.'

'Good.' Robyn nodded. 'Lyndsey told she made Newman comfortable with the rags and the dust sheet after Bartholomew put him in the van.'

Behind her, the fire escape door banged shut.

Lorraine whistled. 'Does she realise what she did?'

'I don't believe so.' Robyn shook her head. 'In terms of charges, I think we would struggle to get Bartholomew on any more than assault whereas Lyndsey is potentially guilty of manslaughter.'

'Christ. How can the bastard keep getting away with things?' Lorraine stabbed at the lift button. 'He'll find some way to wriggle out of the attacks at this rate. Can we at least give his car a parking ticket?'

The lift bumped to a stop. The three of them straggled out to Lorraine's car.

'Now what, Guv?' From the back seat, Chloe sounded plaintive.

'We keep watch here for a bit.' Robyn tried to make this sound positive but in reality, she didn't have any other suggestions. He'll come back here.'

'There must be something else we can find.' Lorraine struck the steering wheel with the flat of her hand. 'Guess we can track the car on cameras now we know the number plate, see if it was parked near the attack sites.'

'And find where his mobile was. We can also check CCTV on his route home.' Chloe stretched out across the back seat. 'Leave it with me. And do you think we can track down the woman you met, Guv? Would DI Prentiss help us find her?'

The thought of asking Prentiss for help was not appealing. 'We can try. It's just people like her often take steps to make sure ...' Robyn paused as another thread in her mind made a connection. She looked between Lorraine and Chloe's blank faces. 'We've got him. Steps. We can nail him with steps.'

After turning to Chloe, Lorraine raised an eyebrow. 'OK, Guv, what are you talking about?'

'When we met him, he was wearing a fitness tracker. If he's got the data linked to an app, it will show where he was.' Robyn twisted in her seat. 'Think about it, we should be able to place him at the crime scenes on the days of the attacks. Those things also measure heartbeat – if his pulse goes up at the right time, we've got him.'

'Self-tracking criminals.' Lorraine laughed. 'They'll do us out of a job.'

'And there's another thing.' Robyn replayed the recent interview. 'I think I know what Dominika meant by the attacker smelling "intense". It's the sport liniment he uses.'

'Look!' Chloe was staring through the passenger-side window. Lyndsey ran out of the flats, a holdall slung across one shoulder, a bulging plastic bag in her hand. As she turned her head, a red streak was visible across her face.

'Christ, someone's attacked her. Looks like she's running for it.' Lorraine ripped off her seatbelt.

Robyn's thoughts were now catching up with her actions. 'Hang on. We need to think this through. Bartholomew must have been there all along. Christ, if he realises she's talked to us, she's in danger. Chloe, go after her, she's the type who's used to disappearing.'

Chloe was already out of the car when Bartholomew charged through the flat's front door and stood, chest heaving. He could easily catch up with Lyndsey, only halfway across the car park, moving in a clumsy half-run, half-walk. He set off in the opposite direction. Robyn started after him, her feet protesting, hearing Lorraine's breathing close behind. 'No, back, he's going for his car.'

Bartholomew had started the engine before Robyn could intercept him. The Astra revved hard and took off down the lane towards the car park's exit. Robyn sprinted after him, burnt rubber scorching her nose. Ahead, Chloe was helping Lyndsey to cross the road. From behind, Robyn heard Lorraine's car in the next aisle.

The Astra swerved right towards the road, crunching as it knocked the wing of a car at the end of the line. Lorraine didn't try for the exit but drove her car straight at the kerb, cutting straight across the pavement and bumping down, blocking the road. Robyn raced across behind her. Screeching, the Astra swung into the exit. Robyn made it to the opposite pavement where Lyndsey lay at Chloe's feet. Hooking her arms around the skinny body, Robyn lifted Lyndsey, bloodied hair blowing into her face. Chloe's mouth was open: Robyn couldn't hear her over the crunching of metal as the Astra rammed Lorraine's car out of the way. Robyn turned, clumsy with Lyndsey in her arms. Bartholomew was driving straight towards them. The wall behind her was five feet high. If she dropped Lyndsey, she could get over it.

31

The Astra mounted the pavement. Lorraine's car surged alongside trying to barge it out of the way. Glass went flying but the Astra was still coming, there was nothing else in its way. With the engine's screaming in her ears, Robyn bundled Lyndsey's body over the wall. There was no pain when the car struck her, she couldn't see anything apart from the green blur that filled her eyes. She felt her feet losing their solid contact with the ground as she was scooped up onto the bonnet, flung into the air and began falling, falling.

Acknowledgements

This is a second book and writing it was a different experience to the first one.

A very special thing was the reaction of my colleagues. They made the whole process very enjoyable by being encouraging, regularly asking about progress and saying nice things about my first book. Thank you everyone.

This book has been supported by a number of people who have been so generous with their time and personal stories, in particular Katy-Jon and Kate.

Huge thanks to PCs Nick Pulham and Matt Essam who took me on a ride-along police shift, involved me in what they were doing and answered my endless questions. They do an amazing job.

I'm very grateful to the people who donated to Emmaus UK for the chance to get their name into *She's Fallen*. The winners drawn were Crystel Marcos and Ed Jones. I also couldn't resist adding Henrietta (Hetty), as this was to commemorate an anonymous donor's mother and grandmother. I hope you are all happy with your characters and thank you again for your generosity.

Emmaus UK helps homeless people across the UK by providing them with a place to live and a job. Find out more at www.emmaus. org.uk.

About Alex Clare

After nearly twenty years of being a committed corporate person, Alex Clare was made redundant. She had always enjoyed writing, studying fiction part-time through the Open University and managing to complete a novel in her commuting time, though no one had ever read it. Now, with lots more time on her hands, there was the opportunity to take writing more seriously. She began to enter competitions and joined a writing group, which encouraged her to try out new genres and styles. After a period focusing on short stories, she wanted to try another novel. Inspiration came from watching Parliament debate the Equal Marriage Act in 2013. Astounded by the intensity of feeling generated, she created a fictional world to explore some of the issues and attitudes.

Twitter feed: @_alexandraclare